BLACK TIGER

ROBERT BRACE

BERKLEY BOOKS, NEW YORK

THE BERKLEY PUBLISHING GROUP
Published by the Penguin Group
Penguin Group (USA) Inc.
375 Hudson Street, New York, New York 10014, USA
Penguin Group (Canada), 10 Alcorn Avenue, Toronto, Ontario M4V 3B2, Canada
(a division of Pearson Penguin Canada Inc.)
Penguin Books Ltd., 80 Strand, London WC2R 0RL, England
Penguin Group Ireland, 25 St. Stephen's Green, Dublin 2, Ireland (a division of Penguin Books Ltd.)
Penguin Group (Australia), 250 Camberwell Road, Camberwell, Victoria 3124, Australia
(a division of Pearson Australia Group Pty. Ltd.)
Penguin Books India Pvt. Ltd., 11 Community Centre, Panchsheel Park, New Delhi—110 017, India
Penguin Books (NZ), Cnr. Airborne and Rosedale Roads, Albany, Auckland 1310, New Zealand
(a division of Pearson New Zealand Ltd.)
Penguin Books (South Africa) (Pty.) Ltd., 24 Sturdee Avenue, Rosebank, Johannesburg 2196,
South Africa

Penguin Books Ltd., Registered Offices: 80 Strand, London WC2R 0RL, England

BLACK TIGER

A Berkley Book / published by arrangement with the author

PRINTING HISTORY
Berkley edition / February 2005

ISBN: 0-425-20119-8

BERKLEY®
Berkley Books are published by The Berkley Publishing Group,
a division of Penguin Group (USA) Inc.,
375 Hudson Street, New York, New York 10014.
BERKLEY is a registered trademark of Penguin Group (USA) Inc.
The "B" design is a trademark belonging to Penguin Group (USA) Inc.

PRINTED IN THE UNITED STATES OF AMERICA

10 9 8 7 6 5 4 3 2 1

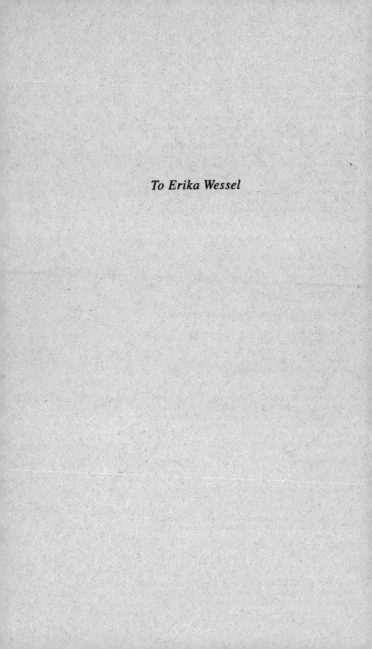

To Erika Wessel

Acknowledgments

The author wishes to acknowledge with gratitude the generous and professional help of his editor, Leona Nevler, and also Susan McCarty, of The Berkley Publishing Group; and his agent, Caitlin Blasdell, and also Liza Dawson, of Liza Dawson Associates, in bringing this novel to fruition. He also wishes to especially thank Erika Wessel.

ONE

MY life was saved by an Americano highball. I'd drunk one before going to bed, sitting on the terrace while the sun went down, watching the yellow vines turn green and then blue as the light of the long summer day gradually faded. It's a silent time, a quiet intermission between the afternoon cicadas and the evening crickets. I'd gone upstairs as the first amorous bullfrog began booming away, somewhere down by the Rappahannock.

In my marine days I could have drunk a keg of beer and not gone to the bathroom for a week. Not anymore. Sometime in the middle of the night I woke up, and checked the time. The bedside clock wasn't working. I felt around for my watch, an old friend who had to be wound up daily, just like me. I'd looked at that same luminous dial on a hundred sweaty nights like this, in Panama, in Haiti, in the Middle

East, even in the jungles of Southeast Asia. It was 1:00 A.M. I got out of bed and padded away to the bathroom.

Apart from me the house was empty, and had been that way for a long time. There was no need to shut the door. I hit the light switch, but nothing happened. It took me a moment—standing there in the dark dumbly flicking the thing up and down—before I realized why the clock wasn't working either. The power was out. But blackouts don't occur in the middle of the night, when usage is low.

That meant the power had been cut. The house wasn't empty after all.

There wasn't much to steal in my place: a little cash; no jewelry; none of the high-end electronics that thieves usually favor, apart from an expensive CD player whose frequently used power made it just as well that the nearest neighbor was over a mile away.

I tried to think if I owned anything else of value. There was a silver art deco cocktail shaker that an antiques dealer could probably hawk for good money, and a Persian rug that was worth a lot, if the thief knew his carpets. The cellar would fetch a good price at auction—the '94 Colgin was currently going for a grand a bottle, an outrageous price for any wine. But I suspected that as the intruder looked around downstairs he was probably already disappointed—a state of unhappiness that I intended to increase once I got my hands on the gun that I kept in the table by the bed. I turned to get it.

The bedroom was suddenly lit up by staccato muzzle flash, and filled with the waterfall roar of automatic gunfire. Someone, unseen from where I stood, was unloading a clip into my bed. Some sort of small assault weapon I guessed— one of those endless 9mm variations on the Uzi with which every hoodlum feels the need to adorn himself these days. Stupid weapons, really. Loud, like the people who use them.

Wildly inaccurate, heavy (because of the oversized clips), and wasteful—suitable only for those who have hearts too frail and hands too shaky for a steady and deliberate aim. In other words, a coward's gun.

Nevertheless, a better weapon than I currently had.

This is an unusual level of violence for a housebreaker— even in Virginia, where we tolerate a certain inclination toward shoot-outs as the price of the Second Amendment. Presumably once the idiot had emptied the clip, and the goose down had finally settled, he would realize that the bed had been unoccupied. He would start to look around, and soon notice that there was a bathroom. The time had come for me to leave.

The only other exit was the bathroom's window, which was already open, left that way to catch any evening breeze in the sweltering summer weather. I stepped onto the sill. It was on the second floor, and in the moonlight I could see below the stone-paved path that would be difficult to clear if I jumped. I looked up, hoping there might be an overhanging eave with which to haul myself up onto the roof. There was something better: a circular louver built into the wall directly above, hinged in the middle so that it swung about the horizontal axis, and intended to be left open in summer to vent the attic. (My house was built in the days before air-conditioning, or intruders carrying Uzis for that matter.)

I reached up and tapped the bottom of the louver, hoping that the thing still worked. It did, and a moment later I had lifted myself into the attic. I was still for a minute, catching my breath, listening for movement below. I could hear nothing, but that was probably just an aftereffect of all the noise from the Uzi. It was possible that whoever was downstairs might not search up here, but I didn't intend to count on it. I needed a weapon.

In addition to the pistol in the bedside drawer there were

two other guns in the house: a 30.06 high-velocity rifle and a 12-gauge bird gun, both hunting weapons, both locked in a gun cabinet in the study. That meant I had to get downstairs. Then I remembered something else. I had another weapon, one that I'd never used. And it was somewhere up here.

There was no light in the attic. Edison was still a boy when the house was built, and the original owners had apparently not thought to include the attic when adding electricity. I felt my way over to the bench by the stairs, and located the candle and matches. I soon had a light, and moved quietly over to a dusty old trunk in the corner.

I opened it. The smell of camphor mothballs filled the air.

Inside, on top of everything else, was a small wood-and-glass display case, a present from my mother. For the medals, she had told me at the time. At first I had thought it was some sort of bad joke, but then I realized just how little my own mother had known me, to have imagined that I would ever want to put the things on display. I put the box aside.

My discharge papers were underneath. Dishonorable.

Below that were the old uniforms, khakis and field grays, one set still bearing the insignia of captain, a rank that had been removed from me long ago. I ran a hand underneath the uniforms and soon found what I was looking for: a heavy mahogany box, which I pulled out and placed carefully on the floor. I used a few drops of wax to seal the candle in place, then, with both hands free, opened the case.

The interior was felt-lined, but so old that the felt had worn through in places. Lying in a space shaped to hold it was a large revolver, an 1893 Colt .45. It was original, not a replica, first owned by an officer who had fought in Cuba during the Spanish-American War. I fondly imagined some fresh-faced Midwesterner charging with Teddy up San Juan

Hill, treating the entire thing as some sort of wholesome boy's own adventure. We all start that way.

When it had become clear that I would be leaving the marines (although not before first enjoying an extended vacation, courtesy of the federal government, in beautiful Leavenworth, Kansas) my troops had presented it to me as a farewell gift. The card was still inside, bearing their signatures, and despite the urgency of the present situation I could not help taking a moment to examine it. If my number was about to come up, then this wasn't a bad last thing to see.

There had been nothing but signatures, because there had been nothing left to say. Most of the names I could remember easily, but I was annoyed to find that I could no longer put faces to some of them. There was even a name or two that I couldn't recall, although it had only been ten years ago. Perhaps they had been new, joining the unit after it happened.

The lieutenants' signatures—Wilson, Alvarez, Legare—were small and reluctant, tucked away in the corners, as if they had felt the danger of too overt an association with the gift. Easy Black—the young sergeant I had recommended for officer school—was the John Hancock of the group, having boldly placed his firm writing right in the middle of the card. Another sergeant's signature—Luke Trainor's—was conspicuously absent, but I was unlikely to ever forget his name. Even had he wanted to sign it, he would have been incapable of doing so at the time.

Enough nostalgia. I replaced the card and picked up the massive revolver. It must have weighed as much as a small mortar does today. I began loading. Fortunately the rounds were not original, having been supplied with the gift by troops too well trained not to know that a weapon without ammunition is not a weapon but a liability.

Six chambers, six rounds. No reloads. I hoped he was alone down there.

I quickly put on a pair of uniform trousers and a shirt, without insignia, but left the combat boots where they were—silence was more important than protection for the feet right now. I checked the weapon, spun the cylinder to test the action, pulled back the hammer that was big enough to have driven nails, and clicked off the safety. It was time to move out. I began going gently down the stairs.

I paused at the second floor, but could hear nothing. I kept moving, wanting to get to that gun cabinet for a better weapon, and made it down to the first floor. I had taken the back stairs, intended for servants in the days when people had servants. At the bottom was a small corridor, running transverse, with linen closets on the opposite side. One end gave onto a door leading outside (originally to a wash house, separate from the main building). The other end intersected with the hall, where it led between the storage space under the main staircase and the kitchen, at the rear of the house.

A wise man would have gone straight for that door leading outside. I went the other way.

I got to the hall, looked toward the entrance foyer, and caught a glimpse of shadow disappearing into the study. I feared for my shaker, in which I had mixed many a memorable cocktail. I tiptoed carefully down the hall, shifting weight slowly, trying to prevent the floorboards from squeaking.

Eventually I was outside the study, back to the wall, gun held in two hands, ready to move in. I listened for a moment, hoping for some sound that would help me locate his position within the room, but heard nothing. I took a deep breath and sprang inside.

He was standing, silhouetted by the moonlight from the window behind him, an easy shot. In the instant before he turned to face me I had him in profile, and was surprised to see that he was wearing a night vision device: basically a big set of electronic goggles with light enhancement or infrared capability. Kind of technical for an intruder, even in Virginia.

I fired. We were both knocked backward, him from the blast to the chest, me from the enormous recoil of the weapon. I was used to modern handguns of more modest caliber, 9-millimeter semiautomatics in which the recoil is used to reload and action the weapon for the next shot, not to knock over the shooter. I was glad that the only witness to this was no doubt now dead.

I got up and went to inspect the corpse.

When you shoot someone, they fall down. Not backward, just down. This is because the projectile doesn't push the body, it simply penetrates, rushing through tissue and bone, and keeps going out the other side, continuing to destroy things on the way until all of its kinetic energy is eventually dissipated. Little of that energy is transferred to the target itself. However, if the target is wearing something that prevents the projectile from passing through (like, say, body armor) then all of its kinetic energy is instantly transferred to the target. *That's* when someone flies backward.

If it hadn't been one o'clock in the morning, perhaps I would have realized that the intruder was wearing body armor. But years of training had taught me that any approach to a dead body should be made cautiously, under the assumption that the other guy is faking. My gun was already on him when the prostrate body suddenly came alive and began firing a fresh clip in my direction.

I pulled the trigger. He was wearing no body armor on his face. This time he was as dead as the proverbial doornail.

But there was still sound coming from the combination

of bone, blood, and brain matter currently oozing over my Persian rug. I looked closer, and in the faint light was able to see that, along with the night vision device, he had been wearing an earpiece, which had fallen out. There was sound coming through it.

It's not uncommon for intruders to wear an earpiece. They attach it to a scanner tuned to the local police frequency. They might not hear a silent alarm, or an awakened owner quietly dialing 911, but they'll hear the alert over the police radio easily enough, giving them time to evacuate before the arrival of the authorities.

I followed the wire down to a device strapped to the dead man's left arm. It was no scanner—it was a frequency-hopping transmitter/receiver unit, a military model that I recognized, in fact had used myself. This was not good. You do not need transmit capability to monitor police broadcasts. The radio meant that the guy currently ruining my carpet had not been alone. I presumed that his partner was a watcher, probably outside in the getaway vehicle.

I picked up the dead man's weapon, and received yet another surprise. In my marine days the standard automatic had been the good old M-16, which was, like most NATO carbines since the 7.62's replacement, 5.56mm in caliber. That was what I held now: some kind of 5.56mm Armalite variant that was not a coward's spray toy, but a serious high-velocity automatic weapon. And this was a special operations' version: short heavy barrel, big clip, retractable butt, drilled stock—suitable for tight work against heavy odds.

This, also, was not good. Advanced though Virginia's criminals are, they are not yet known to use equipment designed for special operations.

A stun grenade came rolling through the door. At least I assumed that it was a stun grenade, because surely they would not have used the other kind, with one of their own people down and no way of knowing if he was dead or alive. It came to rest by the body. My Persian rug was taking a real beating tonight.

I grabbed a leather seat cushion from the sofa and held it over my face while performing a running dive through the window, cushion leading the way. The window shattered. I landed in the rose bed outside. The grenade went off. Shards of wood and glass went flying through the air—it was a real grenade after all. I wouldn't like to be wounded in the jungle with these people backing me up.

While waiting for the debris to settle, I stopped to smell the roses. I cultivate vines for a living, roses for pleasure. They like May best, although now—June—is a good time, too. By August they would be done, which is just as well because the vines demand full attention in the weeks leading up to the harvest. I glanced up from the dirt in which my face was currently buried to see a few yellow petals of Chatsworth come floating down, blown off by the grenade blast, and beyond these some St. Mary, cream at the base, then flowing through pink to a deep crimson at the tip—a lovely flower.

I heard them begin the entry into the room behind me. Now was the time to move. I got up and ran for a stand of trees about fifty yards away.

I was almost there, apparently unseen and already slowing, when I hit the trip wire. It was a perimeter barrier, not meant to actually trip, just to alert. We used to set these up for defensive protection when bivouacked, usually with some antipersonnel claymores wired in along the most obvious insertion routes.

Until now there had been a number of possibilities as to what was going on in my house, in which killing me was only collateral to the primary mission. Not now. This wire had been established not to warn of people coming in, but of people going out. And that could only mean me. It seemed that some sort of tactical assault team, using advanced weaponry and equipment, had come to kill me. Obviously a mistake because I'm just a farmer, but that made no difference now. The pair in my house would not have been alone. There would be a command and communications post somewhere, probably with the vehicle or vehicles they had come in. No doubt they would be parked somewhere along the mile-long drive leading through the vineyards, far enough away from the main road to be out of sight, but not so close as to be seen from the house, and positioned to close the drive as an exit. Not that I would have tried a vehicle—they would have disabled them before cutting the power.

The presence of the perimeter wire meant that there was probably a second team somewhere, ready to respond if I made it out of the house. Had I been setting them up I would have positioned them by the northwest corner, in a gun emplacement that gave a field of fire over both the kitchen and side doors, and close enough so that they could quickly back up the lead team if necessary.

I was on the southeast side of the house, which meant that I was clear for the moment, but I had to get into the forest to make good an escape. Trees are the great equalizer, a military lesson that has been taught throughout history, from Robin Hood to Ho Chi Minh. That's why we did to the Iraqis in a few weeks what we couldn't do to the North Vietnamese in ten years: there are no trees in Iraq.

There was a vast stand of second-growth timber that stretched between me and a big turn in the Rappahannock, several miles to the east. Like Sherwood Forest it was not exactly jungle, but it was good enough. If only I could get to it before they got to me. I was separated from the

forest by twenty acres of cabernet sauvignon, some cabernet franc, and a little merlot. I started running.

Soon I heard a vehicle come over the crest behind me,
and caught the flash of jolting headlights through the vines.
They had found me, and by the presence of the vehicle I
guessed that the command post was joining the pursuit.

Great wines, like great art, are produced through struggle.
Fortunately it's not the winemaker that has to struggle, it's
the grapes. By planting the vines relatively close together,
and thus forcing the plants into competition, the resulting
crop will be high in quality (although low in quantity).
That's what I do: plant the vines close in order to maximize
the intensity of the grape. As a result, the paths between the
long rows of vines are too narrow for a vehicle. In other
words, they would have to follow me on foot.

I ran as if doing a 400: fast, because of the need to open
range between me and the sniper's rifle no doubt already
being set up, but not a sprint, which would have led to exhaustion before reaching the tree line. I risked a glance behind me, expecting to see a vehicle stopped at the edge of
the vineyard. Instead what I saw was a dirt bike, racing down
between the rows of vines.

Very bad.

The guy on the bike opened up with an automatic
weapon. It was a mistake. His chances of hitting anything
while firing one-handed on a motorbike bouncing down a
dirt path were minimal. He should have stopped and calmly
killed me. But instead he kept coming, wasting rounds,
mostly into my maturing grapes.

He came too close. At about thirty yards' range I stopped
running, turned, and took careful aim. He was hemmed in
by the vines, and could do nothing to evade. I fired once,

missed, and fired again. He came off the bike, which continued unridden for a moment before crashing to a stop. I turned and resumed running, finally making it into the forest. The rest of them were pursuing on foot, but I was well out of range.

I should have been safe now, and would have been so if not having earlier decided against taking my boots. What I should have done was tie the laces together and hang them around my neck until needed. On the grass of the lawn and on the dirt of the vineyard I had had no problem. But now, with all the detritus of the forest floor underneath feet made raw from running, every step was painful.

I could hear voices behind me. They were almost through the vines.

Going deeper into the forest would be a mistake now; they would hunt me down for sure. I had two options: climb a tree and hope that in the dark they would pass underneath without noticing, or make for the road and flag down a car.

Then I remembered the night vision device. They would find me in a tree.

I headed for the road.

I'm glad I couldn't see what I was stepping on that night. Some things moved, others were suspiciously soft. Suddenly I was looking into another face. It was an owl, a big one, with a great moonlit moonface, calmly regarding my stumbling progress from a low branch. He looked as amused as owls ever look, which isn't very amused at all. I felt the same way.

My left pant leg was torn and blood covered, presumably from diving through the window. It was as well they didn't have dogs because I was leaving a good trail. I could tell by the sound behind me that they were moving deeper into the forest, not across it like I was.

Soon I could see occasional headlights from vehicles on the road, and I prayed that there would still be traffic when I got there. There wasn't. By the time I struggled through the fence to the side of the asphalt there wasn't a car in sight. I waited, wondering how long it would take the pursuers to figure out that I'd changed direction after entering the forest.

Finally there was the sound of an approaching car, a loud one, followed by headlights coming down the straight. I stepped onto the road and waved my hands over my head, urging the driver to stop. He showed no sign of doing so. I pulled out the Colt and held it up, so the driver could not help seeing it. But instead of the sudden application of brakes I had hoped for, he changed down the transmission and hit the gas. The engine note deepened as the gas poured on. Whatever sort of car it was, it was obviously powerful. The lights remained unwaveringly on me. The driver apparently had no intention of swerving to miss.

I was getting tired of being everybody's target tonight.

I fired a round over the top of the car, high enough to demonstrate that the miss had been intentional, but near enough to make the point. Then I held up one hand like a traffic cop, and took careful aim at the car with the other.

The driver got the message. The car skidded to a halt, coming to rest a few feet in front of me.

It was a Porsche, an old one, air-cooled, squat fat hips hugging the flat six. As I walked around toward the driver's window the interior lit up with a match. The driver was female, a long-limbed dark-haired woman who would have gone well with the highball. She lit a cigarette and blew the smoke in my face.

"I believe the correct signal is a raised thumb," she said.

"I wanted to be sure I had your attention." I put the gun to her temple. If the gesture disturbed her, she didn't show it. "Name?" I asked.

"Valentina Mariposa."

"Address?"

"Currently in residence at the estate of Mr. Marius Preston."

"Occupation?"

"Lawyer."

"If I'd known that, I wouldn't have missed."

"Funny, you look like the kind of man who could use a good attorney right now."

"Keys."

She turned off the engine and gave them to me. I limped around to the passenger side, got in, and gave her back the keys.

"Drive," I said.

She restarted the engine, but instead of proceeding, she looked disapprovingly at my torn trousers.

"You're bleeding over my upholstery."

"Yes," I agreed. "I'm wounded."

"It's leather," she said, apparently unimpressed by the fact of my wound. I tried to shift my leg off the seat cushion, so as to bleed less inconveniently. Valentina sniffed disapprovingly.

"And you smell like my grandmother," she added.

"Sorry, mothballs."

If they hadn't already figured out that I had headed for the road, then the shot would have told them. While Valentina was delivering this commentary on my poor grooming, behind her a dark-clad figure emerged from the undergrowth.

"Could you lean back a little?" I asked.

Valentina leaned back a little. I raised the gun and dropped him with a single shot through her open window. She turned and watched as he fell to the ground.

"That was my last round," I said. "Do you think we could go now?"

She hit the gas and dropped the clutch. The Porsche took off. It was a real Porsche, not one of those emasculated four-wheel-drive versions they build for the American market, as if expressing in technology a German head-shaking bewilderment at our drivers in particular, and our culture in general. The car fishtailed away down the blacktop in a blazing display of over-axle oversteer, something that has all but disappeared in this age of dreary computer-controlled engine responses.

Valentina put the headlights on high beam. They illuminated a pair of figures setting up what might have been a .50-cal machine gun at the end of the straight. Without warning she put the car into a controlled slide. The tail flicked out and whipped the Porsche into a one-eighty, ending with the vehicle facing in the opposite direction but rolling backward, still moving toward the machine gun.

"There's a gun in my bag," Valentina announced.

I leaned across and politely said, "Excuse me," while grabbing the Gucci purse that lay by her leg on the other side of the stick shift. I emptied the contents at my feet. A number of interesting things fell out, including a pistol, a neat little .22 automatic whose brand I didn't have time to identify, the sort of gun James Bond might wear because it was small enough not to crease a dinner jacket.

Meanwhile Valentina worked the clutch and stick shift in fluid combination, bringing the car away from the gun emplacement in a billowing cloud of tire smoke that might have been a deliberate attempt to cover our retreat, but was probably just a heavy foot.

A pair of armed figures came out onto the asphalt a hundred yards ahead of us. Valentina wordlessly hit the button for the sun roof. Apparently we were going to keep going. Under the present circumstances a .22 was all but useless, but the noise and muzzle flash might put the other pair off their aim.

I actioned the weapon, stood up through the roof, and let go half a clip. I'm not sure if I hit anything, but Valentina did, collecting one victim with the low-slung hood. I ducked as he went hurtling over the top of the car.

"No silicon in this car," I said.

"I'm glad to see that you're a man who prefers things natural," she replied.

I wondered if she meant the Porsche.

The straight ended. We rounded the bend, and were soon past and clear. Valentina didn't slacken speed, which was by now well into three-digit territory. I presumed she was putting as much distance as possible between us and the others, in case they pursued, but it turned out that Valentina always drove this way.

"Where to?" she asked.

"Washington."

"V-A or D-C?"

"V-A."

Washington, Virginia, is a modest village at the foot of the Blue Ridge Mountains, and serves as both the Rappahannock county seat and the headquarters of the local police force. It is usually referred to as "Little" Washington to avoid confusion with D.C., which is only ninety minutes away by car, or forty-five in one driven by Valentina Mariposa.

I gave her a brief account of what had happened.

"You need an attorney," she announced when I'd finished. "I charge $300 an hour."

"$300 *an hour*?" Surely she meant a day.

"An hour," she confirmed. "Plus extraordinary expenses," she added.

All I needed was to file a police report. That couldn't take more than an hour or so. And I figured that after shooting a bunch of people, having a lawyer with you when explaining it to the authorities was probably a good idea.

"Okay," I said.

"Don't forget the expenses part," she warned. "I've got a feeling they're going to be a lot in your case."

TWO

SOON we were approaching Little Washington. Valentina slowed as we entered the village. After a while I was able to unclench my knuckles.

We drove by large houses and past the inn at the main crossroads. Eventually we pulled in to the police station. A pair of cruisers were parked outside, which may have been the entire vehicular assets of the county police. We got out and went inside. I left the gun in the car. It's never a good idea to walk into a police station with a loaded weapon.

The front desk was unoccupied. There was a young cop with a brush cut in back of the room, sitting with his feet up on a second chair, eyes closed, head lolling in front of a television set whose programming had turned to static long ago. It was obviously past his bedtime.

We walked up to the front desk. Valentina pointed at a

magazine lying open, cover up, across the counter. I reached over and turned it around. The title was *Locked & Loaded*, a magazine for gun enthusiasts. Good—they were going to need all the weaponry they could get.

A toilet flushed somewhere in the building, soon followed by a second police officer coming through the side door. He was an older man, gone to fat, wearing a short-sleeved shirt with sergeant's stripes, and moving with the slow tread and bored demeanor of someone waiting out the pension. His arms were tattooed; ex-Navy perhaps.

He stopped when he saw us. From the look on his face it seemed that he didn't like people reaching across the front desk. And he didn't like people touching his gun magazines. We weren't going to hit it off.

He glanced at Brush Cut, rolled his eyes, and turned back to face us.

"What can I do for you folks?" he asked, in a voice deliberately too loud. Brush Cut woke up with a start, spent a few seconds in blinking confusion, then sheepishly got up and stepped over to his boss's side.

This pair wouldn't last a minute.

"My name is Mariposa," Valentina announced in an authoritative voice. "I'm a lawyer, and this is my client. We're here to report an assault."

"Anybody hurt?" Sergeant Tattoo asked. Undoubtedly he hoped that the answer would be no, which would relieve him of the obligation to deal with it.

"One confirmed dead," I said. "Could be as many as four."

Brush Cut's eyes opened about as far as they could. Tattoo shook his head—he knew from bitter experience that violent death was an administrative burden.

"You don't know exactly how many?" he asked.

"I didn't stop to check them," I explained.

"You mean *you* killed them?"

"Yes," I admitted.

Brush Cut unclipped his holster strap and moved around the counter, between us and the door. Subtle.

"My client acted purely in self-defense," Valentina added, "using the minimum force necessary to protect his own life."

Pretty good for a lawyer who as yet didn't know much more than they did.

"A team of paramilitaries attacked my house tonight," I explained. "I escaped and came straight here."

"After first contacting your lawyer," Sergeant Tattoo added.

He didn't like lawyers, but then who does?

"No, she was driving the car I flagged down. She just happens to be a lawyer."

"I guess we'll go check out the house," he said.

I cleared my throat before continuing.

"They were armed with automatic assault rifles, body armor, grenades, night vision devices, and frequency-hopping communications gear," I explained. "There's probably ten or twelve of them."

The sergeant said nothing more about checking out the house. I had hoped this brief listing of assets might prompt him to summon help. But instead of reaching for the telephone, Sergeant Tattoo reached for that good old standby of police procedure, the statement form.

He placed it on the counter, picked up a ballpoint pen, and read the first box aloud.

"Name?" he asked.

The assault team had probably already completed the extraction, and would now be long gone. There was no point in trying to explain faster than Sergeant Tattoo could absorb. I suppressed a sigh of resignation, and told him my name.

"Lysander Dalton."

"Lysander?"

"Spartan admiral," I explained. I shrugged my shoulders. "It could have been worse."

"Address?"

I gave him my address, telephone number, Social Security number, and date of birth. With any luck, we would get through this by Labor Day.

"Occupation?"

"Vintner."

"What's a vintner?"

"Winemaker. I grow grapes and make wine."

"In Virginia?"

"Thomas Jefferson was convinced that great wine could be made in Virginia."

The sergeant ponderously filled in the blank. He didn't much care about Thomas Jefferson's thoughts on the issue, one way or the other. He completed filling out the form, then spun it around and put the pen next to it on the counter.

"Sign here," he said.

"My client hasn't made a statement yet," Valentina objected.

"Lady, save the defense lawyer stuff for the judge," the sergeant said irritably. He looked back at me. "Sign here."

Valentina calmly picked up the pen, dropped it on the floor, and crushed it with the sole of her shoe as if extinguishing a cigarette.

"As a matter of fact," Valentina said, entirely unruffled, "I practice testamentary law, not criminal law. Although out here in Hicksville you probably don't know what testamentary law is."

The sergeant leaned over the counter and looked down at

the floor, at the plastic shards and spreading ink blot that had until recently been his pen. He gaze rose to Valentina's, who calmly returned it.

"Testicle law, huh?" the sergeant said. "Well I guess that's something you'd be pretty good at, since you obviously got quite a pair of your own." He snickered.

Behind us, Brush Cut snickered too. I sensed that this was a mistake, and I couldn't help feeling sorry for them.

Valentina pivoted on one of her high heels, and delivered the other in a swift leg extension into Brush Cut's groin. Even I flinched. The wind went out of him like a pricked balloon. He doubled over, eyes watering. Valentina grabbed the .38 Police Special from his holster before he knew what was happening. She opened the cylinder as casually as a Sunday shooter, checked the load, and closed it with a flick of the wrist.

"Hey," he croaked, the last word he ever said.

Valentina put the gun to his temple and calmly said, "Don't move."

But Brush Cut made a grab for her gun arm, his second major mistake of the evening. Valentina pulled the trigger without hesitation. The back of his head bloomed out into a blossoming spray behind him.

Meanwhile Sergeant Tattoo had been struggling to get his own gun out of the holster. As Valentina switched her aim to him, he finally pulled the weapon clear. Before he had a chance to raise it into the firing position, Valentina put a pair of slugs in a tight grouping into his chest. He stood transfixed an instant, as if unable to believe that he had been shot. Valentina fired a third slug into his head, clearing up any lingering doubts. A great spurt of blood gushed from the exit wound of this last round, and Sergeant Tattoo's body collapsed to the floor.

I looked at Valentina in amazement as the gunshot echoed away.

"Counselor," I said admiringly, "you're quite an advocate."

"Now you know why you're paying $300 an hour." She nodded toward the dead sergeant. "Get his gun."

Valentina began searching Brush Cut's pockets. I carefully picked my way past the remnants of Sergeant Tattoo's head. I was still barefoot, and tried to avoid stepping on the squishy bits.

"I think you violated this guy's civil rights," I said.

She didn't reply, but I saw a smile. Most women I knew would have been losing their sense of humor around now. I retrieved Sergeant Tattoo's handgun and checked the load. Two rounds had been fired, recently.

"Enthusiasm's good," I said. "But I think that a successful career in jurisprudence will require a better relationship with the police, don't you?"

"They're not police," she said

"Not anymore," I agreed.

"Not before, either."

She walked into the adjoining room, from which the sergeant had first emerged. I followed her. There were two bodies on the floor—the real police officers—dressed in underwear. Both had been bound hand and foot, and both had been executed with a single round through the back of the head.

"How did you know?" I asked.

"The kid's uniform was too big. I've seen cops grow out of their old uniforms. Never seen one shrink."

"He could have been dieting."

"They didn't call EMT, although you're bleeding all over the linoleum. They didn't call a duty detective, although that would be standard procedure for any report of a violent death. And they didn't call the state troopers, which they should have done as soon as you told them the story."

"And that business with the statement?"

"My guess is that's why they didn't kill us right away: they wanted you to sign a blank form first. Setting you up for something, probably for these two in here."

"You don't miss much."

"I don't miss anything," she corrected.

"Actually, you *did* miss one thing—"

She cut me off. "If you mean the fact that the sergeant was left-handed, but wore his weapon on the wrong side, then no, I didn't miss that, either. It's why I took the kid first, of course."

There isn't much you can say to something like that.

"Come on," she said. "We better get out of here before their friends show up."

We returned to the car and were soon out of Little Washington. As Valentina tore through the countryside I tried to think through what had happened.

I'd known one of the real cops. Not well, just a nodding acquaintance. I have no farmhands, preferring to do it alone, but the one time I needed help was during a harvest. Usually I wait until the forecast is for several days of fine weather, giving me time to complete it myself. But one year an unexpected thunderstorm threatened hail, with the crop only half in. Hail can ruin grapes. The local radio station put out a call letting anyone know that if they wanted to get their hands dirty, they could come to my place. Among the people who'd shown up to lend a hand was the cop, in a cruiser, in uniform. He'd rolled up his sleeves and started picking.

There had been people in my life I'd known better, and who'd been killed worse. But they had been soldiers, and it comes with the territory. This guy was just a good-natured country boy. We'd talked afterward, over a beer. He'd told me he was married. Had a toddler, too, I think.

I knew it was no good dwelling on it. "Move on," they'd taught us at special ops school. You would want your team to if it was you lying facedown. But I wished I could remember his name.

I looked around outside.

The road was simple two-lane country blacktop, but Valentina drove as if it was German autobahn, accelerating hard along the straights, followed at every approaching corner by a slashing down in gears and the whine of the high-revving engine. There were probably sparks coming off the brakes.

"I don't think we're actually being followed at the moment," I said after a while.

"So?"

"I don't think it's necessary to drive so fast."

"I'm not driving fast," she explained. "I'm driving normally."

"Most people wouldn't consider this normal."

"Most people have driver's licenses."

"You don't have a license?"

"Lost it," she said.

"As in misplaced?"

"As in taken away for repeated speeding violations," she replied.

"Isn't driving without a license risky for a lawyer?"

"Lawyers get disbarred for felonies," she explained. "I'm strictly a misdemeanor girl."

THREE

I said no more to Valentina Mariposa for the remainder of the journey, wanting nothing to distract her attention from the road. We continued to race through the countryside for another ten minutes or so, until finally slowing and turning off the main road into what was presumably the Preston estate.

This part of Virginia is horse country: white-painted fences surrounding rolling green fields, and grand manor houses with acres of pristine pasture between them, unsullied by lesser dwellings, as if northern Virginia was feudal but without the serfs, a land in which only barons remain. Some estates were real working farms, many were for display purposes only. The Preston estate looked to be one of the latter. As we went up a long drive lined with beech trees (paved, in contrast to my modest dirt) I could see no water troughs in the paddocks, nor the hoof-tramped bare earth around the gates that you would expect in a real working stud. I guessed that the grasses in these fields were for decoration, not nutrition.

We approached the house, a huge two-story Palladian structure, faced in brown limestone. The drive swung around in front, forming a loop with a fountain in the middle. Steps led up to a columned portico. It was exactly the sort of place owned by those for whom the transmission of assets to succeeding generations requires the services of a testamentary lawyer.

Valentina skidded to a stop and turned off the headlights. The big house was dark, not even a front light was left on. The butler needed reprimanding.

"Will your client object to his lawyer showing up with an uninvited guest?" I asked.

"Mr. Preston is in Washington tonight for a political function. He's staying overnight at the Hay-Adams, and won't be back until tomorrow afternoon."

"Any staff?"

"Plenty, but they all live off the estate. We've got the place to ourselves."

She shut down the engine and got out of the car. I followed her onto the portico. The front door was solid and painted black. There was an elliptical fanlight above it. Valentina had keys to the multiple locks—burglar-proof Chubbs. If I ever got out of this and back to my place, I was going to put the same locks onto all of my doors.

We went inside. Valentina turned on the lights. The entrance hall was tiled in a black-and-white checkerboard pattern. There was a staircase at the end, with slender spindle banisters. The walls were painted in a soft cream. On one side was a hat stand, the coat closet, and a console supporting a vase full of flowers.

On the opposite side was a key code panel for a burglar alarm. Beside this was a video screen. It was blank. Wherever the camera was, it apparently wasn't turned on. Valentina went straight to the panel, quickly pressed a series of keys, and the blinking red light turned to steady green. She hit the reset, and it returned to blinking red.

I was thinking that Marius Preston kept an unusually secure house. But then I realized the truth was probably that I had kept an unusually insecure one. I was foolish: I'd bought a farm to be away from people, and had wrongly assumed that therefore people would stay away from me.

Valentina continued down the hall and disappeared through a doorway. I followed her through a large sitting room of awkward formality, and then beyond that into another room much more comfortably furnished—the library. Valentina went straight to the sideboard, on top of which sat a silver tray loaded with bottles and decanters.

"Scotch?" she asked. This was a woman who had her priorities straight.

"And soda, please."

She bent to open the bar refrigerator. The dress lifted. Her legs were very long.

I tried to think of something else, so I examined the room while she mixed the drinks. The library occupied the corner of the house. The two interior walls were lined with books. There were French doors at the side, giving onto a lawn and gardens beyond. The doors were locked. I could see a wire leading under the floorboards; the doors had microswitches attached to the alarm system.

Valentina finished mixing the drinks. She took a seat on the sofa. I sat in a comfortable armchair by the side.

"You were pretty good back there at the police station,"

I said. "Not many women are so comfortable with weapons."

"I grew up in East L.A.," she said. "That stuff tonight was Little League."

I looked down at the gash in my trousers.

"We should do something about this wound."

"Do what you like," she said. "Just don't bleed on Mr. Preston's furniture."

"Are you related to Mother Teresa, by any chance?"

Valentina ignored this remark, instead retrieving a briefcase from beside a small secretaire. The briefcase was slender and expensive, no doubt made from the tanned hides of many a $300-an-hour client. She took out a yellow legal pad and an elegant fountain pen.

"Lysander Dalton," she said, writing my name at the top of the pad. "You strike me as more the Alcibiades type."

She was more accurate than she could guess. Alcibiades, too, had done his time in some Athenian Leavenworth.

"Lysander's a mouthful," I said. "Most people call me Lee."

"Lee?"

"Yes."

"Okay," she said, looking doubtful. "If you insist."

"What should I call you?"

"You mean besides 'Ms. Mariposa'?"

"Yes."

Valentina thought about it for a moment before replying. "I don't care. Just don't call me 'Tina,' " she warned. "Ever."

Valentina Mariposa was apparently not a fan of the diminutive.

"Address and Social Security number?" she demanded, much as Sergeant Tattoo had an hour before. At least Valentina didn't stick her tongue out when writing them down.

While repeating the details, I got to my feet and dropped my trousers. Valentina glanced up with a sharply appraising eye before returning her attention to the legal pad.

"I'm unimpressed," she said dismissively.

"But these are my best boxers."

I took the antimacassar from the back of the chair and limped over to the sideboard, where I soaked it in whiskey.

"Tell me everything that happened tonight," she said, "from the beginning."

I got back to the chair and retold the story while dabbing at the wound with the alcohol. It was an ugly cut, but there didn't seem to be anything embedded in it. I tried not to flinch as I applied the cloth. When the wound was clean I took a second antimacassar from the couch, folded it into a makeshift field dressing, and stuck it to my leg with Scotch tape from a dispenser on the secretaire. It wasn't great, but it was better than anything Florence Nightingale here had volunteered to do.

"I'm adding those doily things to your bill," Valentina warned. She made a note on her legal pad.

I returned to my chair and finished the account of the evening's events up until flagging down her car. When it was over we sat for a few moments in silence, drinking the whiskey.

"Why you?" Valentina eventually asked.

"Wrong address."

"I'm serious."

"So am I," I said.

"You really think those people simply went to the wrong house?"

"Yes."

"That doesn't seem likely."

"I'm just a farmer. There's no reason for any of this to happen to me. But a lot of the people who have estates around here don't exactly make their living by tilling the earth."

"What do you mean?"

"Those intruders were equipped for far more resistance than I could ever have offered."

"And yet here you are," she said.

"Pure luck. They expected to encounter serious trouble. The sort of trouble that accompanies Mafia dons or drug lords. My guess is that it was some sort of organized crime hit that simply got the wrong target."

"Do you have any enemies?"

"A few," I admitted. "But as far as I know none of them have tactical assault units on call."

"So you think it's just a mistake?"

"Has to be. There's no other explanation."

She took an organizer from the briefcase, paper rather than electronic, held shut with a large rubber band, and with various scraps of paper and notes poking out. She was not a digital girl. As with the old-fashioned Porsche, I got the feeling that Valentina Mariposa preferred life unfiltered and unfined.

"I'm going to call Jim Bethnal, the partner who heads our criminal law department," she said. "I'll put the matter in his hands."

"Okay."

"He charges $500 an hour, plus extraordinary expenses."

"That figures."

"If I tell him you're my friend, maybe he'll drop it to $450."

"Lucky me."

"Don't forget the plus expenses part."

"I haven't."

She took a small cellular phone from her briefcase, and began dialing a number from the organizer.

"What are you doing?" I asked.

"I'm calling Jim Bethnal."

"Before you press *send,* can I ask you something?"

"What?"

"How did that pair you shot get to the police station before us?"

Valentina was annoyed by the question, which she obviously thought frivolous. Eventually she shrugged a how-am-I-supposed-to-know shrug.

"They drove faster, I suppose."

"Faster than you?"

She must have realized the unlikelihood of this. "Okay, I don't know," she admitted. "How do you think they did it?"

"I think they were already there."

"Where?"

"In Little Washington."

"But how could they have been?"

"Before they performed the insertion tonight, these people went to the trouble to cut the power to my house."

"So?"

"I presume they would have cut the telephone wire, too."

"Okay."

"It wouldn't make sense to cut the phone wire, but ignore cellular."

"You can't cut a cellular call."

"No, but you can monitor it. They would have had a scanner sorting through any cellular traffic, which wouldn't be very heavy here in rural Virginia during the early hours of the morning. If I'd called the police, they already had a team in place to prevent them responding before getting their own people out."

"That's going to a lot of trouble," she said doubtfully.

"It is," I agreed. "But can you think of another way to

explain how that pair got to Little Washington before we did?" She thought about it before replying.

"No," she eventually admitted, "I can't."

"Neither can I."

Valentina looked at the phone in her hand. "Do you think they're still monitoring it?"

"Wouldn't you?"

She considered this for a moment, then put away the cellular phone.

"I'll use the house phone in the study," she said. Valentina stood and walked from the room. It was a good walk.

I went to the sideboard and topped up the glass. The Scotch was an expensive single malt; Mr. Preston had obviously done well for himself. I wondered how he'd made his money, and looked through the bookshelves for a clue.

There was none that I could tell. Most of the books were fiction, running from leather-bound classics to paperback romances. The nonfiction was heavy with illustrated volumes of Americana: Ansel Adams photographs, a Route 66 picture book, aerial shots of the Grand Tetons, and such like. There were several atlases and dictionaries. The only thing the library revealed about Mr. Preston was that he was multilingual: many of the books were in foreign languages. I recognized German and Russian, and several in a graceful flowing script that was presumably Arabic.

I looked up from the shelves. Valentina had returned, silently, and was leaning against the doorjamb, casually observing me.

"Well?" I said.

"He's taking care of everything."

"He'll contact the police?"

"No, one of his subordinates will. Jim's going to call him, then drive down here. Jim won't tell him where we are, so that when the police ask he'll be able to honestly answer that he doesn't know. Meanwhile Jim will be in his car, incommunicado as far as they're concerned, but I've got his cell phone number if we need it. Jim will contact the police directly when he gets here—that way there's no possibility of them questioning you without him being present."

Jim Bethnal was a thorough guy—and for $500 an hour he should be, too. "How long will he take?"

"From Bethesda? At least two hours."

"We should get some sleep," I said.

But whatever Valentina was ready for, it wasn't sleep. She casually pulled up her dress, raised one long leg, and placed her foot on the top of the secretaire. Then she reached into the briefcase. From her posture I would have guessed she was taking out stockings, but instead her hand emerged with some sort of black leather device with buckles.

"What's that?" I asked.

"A thigh holster," she replied. "If we run into your visitors again, I don't want to have to find my purse to get a gun." Valentina strapped the thing to her left leg.

"Doesn't that chafe?"

She smiled and put the .22 into the holster. "Let's take a walk outside," she said.

With a six-inch gash in my leg I wasn't really much for walking right now, but whatever was on Valentina's mind, it obviously wasn't my health.

We went outside. The night was clear and clean and still moonlit. The air was warm, but fresher now that the day's heat had radiated away.

The grounds to Marius Preston's estate were as impressive

as the house. We strolled in companionable silence through a formal French garden—all symmetry and order—then beyond that along a serpentine path running under chestnut and oak trees into a flower-filled English bower. There was a trellis arch covered with varieties of climbing roses that had Edwardian girl's names like Clare and Hermione. The air was heavy with their scent.

I realized what a good idea it was to have come outside and walk quietly around the grounds like this—it was a calming act, something to put a distance between us and the events of the night. But I had underestimated Valentina's intentions.

She took us across the lawn toward something that in the dark at first looked like a wall, but which as we got closer I realized was a hedge maze. Valentina led me inside.

The hedges were eight or ten feet high, set close, blocking out the moonlight. I could barely see Valentina ahead of me. We hit a dead end. She turned before I realized what had happened, and I accidentally walked into her. Suddenly we were face to face, and very close. I could see her smile.

"Are you good at puzzles, Lysander Dalton?"

"I don't know," I admitted.

"If I'm going to help you, you're going to have to help me."

"I've told you everything I know."

"Are you sure?"

"What else is there?"

"There has to be a reason those men came to your house," she said. "There's a reason for everything."

"Is there a reason we're in the middle of a hedge maze at three A.M., whispering like conspirators?"

"Yes, there is."

"What is it?"

In reply she kissed me. It was a long, slow kiss, and when it was over she took a small step backward, reached behind her, and unzipped her dress. It slipped off her shoulders and fell to the ground. Underneath she was wearing a black bra, thong, and of course the thigh holster, still with the handgun inside.

The truth was that I could have used some sleep, but under the circumstances, I was manfully prepared to do without. In any case, it wouldn't be wise to say no to a woman with a gun strapped to her thigh.

We ended up in the center of the maze, where, spread-eagled upon a large marble bench, Valentina metamorphosed into a sacrificial virgin, although no sacrificial virgin ever made as much noise. Finally she lay back, sheathed in sweat, virgin no longer, wearing nothing but a smile and the .22 automatic. I was right: the holster did chafe, and I now bore the marks to prove it.

We must have dozed off. When I woke up Valentina was still asleep. I decided to go back to the house and check the time before waking her. I got up and wandered quietly around the maze for five minutes or so, trying but failing to find Valentina's dress and my trousers on the way. Finally I arrived at the exit, and immediately froze.

A figure was standing twenty feet away, back to me and staring at the house. He wore night vision goggles and carried an assault rifle in the ready position. Combat trained, by his posture. He took a few steps forward. Like me, he was limping—perhaps that's why he was on secondary instead of the entry team. I held my breath and carefully backed up into the maze.

I quietly tiptoed back to the center, forcing myself to

memorize the way: *first right, third left, second left then immediately right,* and so on. Valentina was still asleep. I gently shook her awake.

"Valentina," I whispered, "don't make a sound."

She stretched like a cat and smiled, apparently believing this was part of a new game. I put my lips next to her ear, which she took for nuzzling until she understood what I was saying.

"The team that came to my house tonight are here. My guess is they think we're inside. They don't know we're in here, so it's crucial that you don't make a sound. Do you understand?"

I looked her in the face. A nod of comprehension, but no trace of fear. She was not a woman easily frightened. I put my mouth back to her ear.

"When they discover there's no one in the house they'll search the grounds. We have to get out of here before they do. First we exit the maze. The guy I saw was close to the entrance, but facing away, toward the house. We have to quietly sneak behind him around the corner of the maze. Understand?" Another nod. "After that, we'll cross the lawn and head for the trees. They'll have a perimeter wire set up, so it's important that you follow behind me. Match my footsteps as best you can. When we come to the wire, I'll stop and point it out. Make sure you step over it." Another nod. "I'll take the gun. If they spot us, we split up. You run as fast as you can for the trees. Once you get in there keep going and don't stop."

"And you?" she whispered.

"I'll be fine, because I have the gun." It was nonsense, of course. A man wearing only boxers with a half-empty .22 is no match for body armor and assault rifles, but I could buy her some time. "Carry your shoes," I added. "I know they're high heels, but you'll be grateful for them in the woods."

I took the gun from her holster. I dared not risk the noise of actioning the slide. Valentina dressed in her underwear and picked up her shoes.

"Ready?" I whispered. She nodded. I began the exit, reversing the directions I had memorized when coming back in.

At the entrance the same man was still there, still facing the house. He was so close that I could faintly hear transmissions on his radio. We had two things going for us: the goggles restricted his peripheral vision, and the earpiece made it less likely that he would hear us.

I gave a hand signal for Valentina to proceed, then pointed the gun at the man. It was not cocked, of course, but the sight of it would hopefully cause him to take evasive action rather than shoot, should he happen to pick this moment to look around.

He didn't, and as soon as Valentina had disappeared around the corner of the maze I followed. The nearest trees were well away, not only past the lawn but past a meadow beyond that. Fortunately the moon had not set, and it was easy to cross the lawn while looking for the perimeter wire. There was none, and we got to the fence unhampered. They must have decided that there wasn't time to set one up.

We climbed over the fence and, free now of the worry of wires, scampered across the meadow to the safety of the trees beyond. We stopped to catch our breath. Valentina put her shoes on.

"Do we find a road and flag down a car?" she asked, still whispering although we were well clear now.

"Dressed in underwear?"

"They'd stop for me."

"And when I showed up?"

"Then what do we do instead?"

"We keep going for a while, then rest until it's light," I said. "After that we look for a house, get some clothes, and call your partner."

She nodded in agreement. We had a plan.

FOUR

I let Valentina take the lead so that she set the pace. We had gone for two hours or so, Valentina tottering precariously on high heels, me with sore feet but admiring what I could see of the view ahead.

The sky began to lighten. We suddenly came out of the wilderness onto a back road. It was empty, apart from a lonely gas station a hundred yards farther down. A gas station would have a phone. We headed for it.

It was a real gas station, not a convenience store with pumps out front and a clerk encased in bulletproof glass, but an old-fashioned place with two big bays for mechanical work. The closest thing to a convenience store was an ancient Coke machine sitting out front of the office. The place was closed and, according to the sign listing opening hours, would remain so all day this Sunday, but there was a pay phone attached to an exterior wall. Valentina headed for it while I surveyed the station.

Several cars sat rusting on blocks by the side, patients that had not survived the operation. One was an old Plymouth Roadrunner SuperBird, recognizable by the enormous rear wing. Another was an Oldsmobile 442, complete with Hearst shifter. Muscle cars—artifacts of an era long gone now, built before America had lost the last blush of its youthful vigor, back when we still liked things big and fast.

The hood of the Olds was undone. I lifted it and looked inside. There was a loose pipe bracket, which I unscrewed and straightened out.

The windows in the office were wood-framed. I slid the bracket between the window and the frame, and soon had the latch undone. I opened it and crawled inside.

There wasn't much in the office, and no cash in the till, but next door in the workshop I found what I'd been looking for: coveralls and work boots. The closer of the two mechanic's bays was empty, but there was a vehicle in the far one, another SuperBird. I looked it over. Unlike its sibling outside this car was in pristine condition. The other had probably been cannibalized for parts.

I took a pair each of the boots and coveralls, and went back outside.

Valentina had hung up, and was leaning against the wall by the phone, looking at the ground, lost in thought.

"Clothes," I announced. I held up the coveralls. "We have 'Bob's Auto' in navy—very chic—or a Texaco star on your basic black, which of course goes with anything. Take your pick."

"They found the real police officers," she said, "but not the other two."

That was unsurprising. The assault team had arrived in

Little Washington, found us already gone, and taken the bodies of their own people.

"Did they go to my house yet?"

"Yes."

"What's wrong?"

"That's where they found the real police officers."

"What?"

"The bodies of the real police officers were at your place."

There was a bench seat. I sat, and thought about what she was saying.

"Did they find anything at the police station indicating they had been shot there?"

"Nothing. Apparently the desk log shows an anonymous complaint called in against you. The first police officer was dispatched to investigate. Fifteen minutes later, an urgent call for backup, to which the other one responded."

I was starting to get the picture now.

"And both cruisers were found at my place?"

"Correct."

"Weapons?"

"Only a .38 Police Special. Two chambers fired."

"The sergeant's gun," I said. "The one with my finger-prints all over it. And the one whose ballistics will match the rounds that killed the real officers."

"I assume so."

"Do the police have a theory?"

"They've already asked for the warrant."

They certainly hadn't wasted any time.

"Did you tell them where we were?"

"Of course not."

"What did your partner tell you to do?"

"Convince you to surrender. Turn yourself in before it gets out of hand."

"Naturally."

"It's good advice."

"It's suicide."

"Don't be ridiculous."

"They have the death penalty in this state. Shooting two cops: I wouldn't stand a chance."

"Aren't you forgetting something?"

"What?"

"You have a witness, remember?"

"And aren't *you* forgetting something?"

The question puzzled her. She wasn't a woman often accused of forgetting anything.

"What?"

"Since the police know you're with me, they'll go to the Preston estate."

"So?"

"Where they will find certain evidence."

She was still puzzled.

"What evid—" But she stopped in mid-sentence, having apparently figured it out. "Of course. We are lovers. And, therefore, I'm a tainted witness."

"Exactly."

"Damn."

"I wouldn't change a thing," I said. No need be ungallant, no matter what the circumstances.

"It doesn't matter," Valentina said. "We're both credible, sex or no sex. Upstanding members of the community and all that. It's not as if we have criminal histories."

I gave her a look which she instantly understood. She rolled her eyes and said, "Oh, no."

"Afraid so."

"Federal or state?"

"Federal."

"Tell me it wasn't for a violent crime."

I didn't answer. After a while she answered for me.

"Stupid question," she said. "Of course it was a violent crime."

It occurred to me that this comment was a little unfair, considering that last night she herself had calmly shot two men to death. I decided against pointing this out, and instead passed her the Bob's Autos. I began putting on the Texacos.

"There's a car inside," I said. "I'll hot-wire it." She put on the coveralls. Never have mechanic's garments looked so good. "Give me as much time as you feel comfortable doing," I continued.

"What are you talking about?"

"Before you call them."

"Call who?"

"The police, I guess."

"But I'm coming with you."

"Don't be ridiculous."

"I'm your lawyer."

"And if you want to stay a lawyer, you'll call back and tell them where I am."

"If I want to stay a lawyer, that's precisely what I won't do. That would constitute a serious breach of attorney-client privilege, enough to get me disbarred."

"But you can't come with me."

"Of course I can. Short of aiding in the commission of a crime, I'm bound to represent your interests to the best of my ability. That's what you're paying me for, and I intend to see that you get your full $300-an-hour's worth."

It seemed that she was serious. I shrugged my shoulders and went back into the garage, wondering if there was any ethical conundrum beyond the rationalizing powers of a lawyer.

* * *

I wasn't sure how to hot-wire an automobile. Fortunately the SuperBird was too old to be fitted with a steering lock, so I guessed that all I needed to do was experiment until finding the right combination of wires.

I switched on the radio, then buried myself under the dashboard and fooled with the ignition wiring until the radio made noise, proving that at least the battery was charged. Aerosmith, "Walk This Way"—the sort of stuff you might expect to come from the radio of a Plymouth SuperBird.

"I have something for you," Valentina sang out.

"What?"

"Come and see for yourself."

I dug my way out from underneath the dashboard.

Valentina was standing on the hood. She was wearing the coveralls, but high heels instead of the boots, obviously unconcerned about the effect these might have on the bodywork. Her hips were moving in time with the music from the radio. She reached to the top of the coveralls, and began unbuttoning.

Well, it had been quite a night.

I sat up and watched the show taking place on the other side of the windshield. When the last of the studs was undone, Valentina let the coveralls fall from her shoulders, much as the dress had earlier this evening Besides the underwear and thigh holster, there was something glittery in her belly button.

I suddenly realized two things. Firstly, Valentina had found a key to the car. Secondly, she had a pierced belly button—something that the combination of soft moonlight and absence of body jewelry had prevented me noticing earlier. Now the key ring was apparently performing the function of a navel ring.

I got out of the car. She sat on the hood and smiled as I hobbled around to the front of the vehicle.

"You're a very resourceful woman," I said.

"I try to be helpful."

"Where was it?"

She nodded toward the office. A hook board was fixed to the wall by the door leading into it, presumably where the keys of cars under repair were kept.

I held out my hand for the key, but she made no move to unfasten the ring.

"Are you going to give it to me?" I asked.

The smile grew wider.

Valentina leaned back across the car, one leg dangling over the fender, the other hooked around the combination of ram-air scoop and four-barrel Holley carburetor protruding through the hood.

"Why don't you come and get it?" she replied.

Eventually we and our sweat-stained Plymouth were on the road. I closed both the garage door and office window, hoping to leave no obvious sign of forced entry. With any luck, no one would notice that the car was missing until the place opened up for business on Monday morning.

The SuperBird was not exactly suited to a subtle escape. The engine sounded like an F-14 with a smoker's cough, a deep, uneven rumble that could have caused rock slides in the nearby Blue Ridge Mountains. The burnt orange paint gleamed, and the big rear wing stood high over the roofline, a beacon inviting police cars to come and take a look. I kept the car carefully within posted speed limits.

"Where are we going?" Valentina asked.

"New York City."

"What's the plan?"

"I haven't got one yet."

"Then why New York?"

"Remember the sergeant?"

"What sergeant?"

Now *that's* what I call short-term memory loss. "The one whose head you left spread over the police station," I reminded her.

"What about him?"

"He had a lot of tattoos."

"I remember."

"While I was prying his fingers off the gun, I got a look at the tattoo on the back of his hand. It was some sort of death's head with wings."

"So?"

"Over the top it said 'N-Y-C.' Underneath it had the number '81.' "

"That's it?" She seemed unimpressed.

"Yes."

"And this tattoo is your entire reason for going to New York?"

"That, plus the fact that it's well away from here, and it's an easy place to get lost in."

"No one gets lost anymore," she said, "not in the digital age. They'll find you soon enough. The best thing you can do is turn yourself in before they do."

"I intend to."

"When?"

"When I find out who those people at my house were."

"Through a tattoo?"

"It's my only lead."

"Okay," she said. "I just hope the Plaza isn't booked."

"Plaza?"

"Yes."

"As in 'Plaza Hotel'?"

"Yes."

This was obviously not someone familiar with the exigencies of being on the lam.

"I don't think the Plaza's a good idea," I said cautiously.

"But I *always* stay there," she insisted. I thought I could detect a slight pout. "It's next door to Bergdorf's," she added, apparently in the belief that such fortunate geography clinched the argument.

"Valentina, I'm sorry to disappoint you, but we've got no money."

She was silent for minute. I couldn't figure out whether or not this meant that she was taking the news well. Eventually she put her feet up on the dashboard, and reached a hand down through the front of her coveralls. I still couldn't figure out whether or not this meant that she was taking the news well.

"I used to be a Girl Scout," she said after a while.

I found this hard to believe. "I can't wait to try your cookies," I replied.

"Our motto was 'Be Prepared.' "

"So I've heard."

"And that's what I am: prepared."

I wondered exactly what it was she was prepared for. Her hand emerged from the coveralls. She was holding something, which she held toward me. It was a credit card.

"American Express," she said. "Never leave home without it."

"Where did that come from?"

"Inside the lining of the holster."

"How come?"

"I keep it for emergencies."

"Nice idea," I said. "But we can't use it. They'll be checking your credit cards."

"Who said it's mine?"

She held it in front of me. As credit cards go, it smelled good. I read the account name.

"Who's Gillian Devereux?"

"My mother," she announced. "After she divorced my father, she reverted to her maiden name. Last year she died. Since I'm a trusts and wills lawyer, I wound up the estate myself, but when I came upon this card I decided to keep the account open. You never know when a credit card in another name might be useful. No one knows about it, except me."

"You deserve a merit badge."

"What I deserve is a room at the Plaza."

"Agreed."

"And the cost of which I'm adding to your bill."

I'm always too quick to agree with a beautiful woman. "I guess you wouldn't settle for a quaint little place I know."

"Describe this 'quaint little place.'"

"Toll Booth Motor Lodge, just by the Jersey entrance to the Holland Tunnel." No reaction. "Vibrating beds, fifteen minutes for a quarter." She seemed unimpressed. "Okay, the Plaza it is then."

I concentrated on driving while beside me Valentina smiled the knowing smile of a woman for whom no outcome is ever seriously in doubt.

We made New York by early afternoon. Actually we made Fort Lee, New Jersey, as we had no cash to pay the toll for a bridge or tunnel crossing of the Hudson. I wiped the interior and hood for fingerprints, then left the windows down and keys in the ignition. Hopefully the SuperBird would be stolen—restolen—before the police found it. We walked across the George Washington Bridge, the only free way to enter the city from New Jersey.

On the other side we found a subway station, jumped the turnstiles to the A-line downtown, and finally presented ourselves at the reception desk of the Plaza Hotel. The desk manager was determinedly polite, but could not prevent his eyebrows rising at our approach. The Plaza doesn't get many guests arriving in mechanic's coveralls.

"Do you have any rooms available for tonight?" I asked.

"I'm sorry, our rooms are fully booked this evening." Translation: we weren't welcome. Good, it meant that we could now search for a midtown branch of the Toll Booth Motor Inn. "But," he continued, "we do have several *suites* available."

I hesitated just a moment too long.

"We'll take one," Valentina said. "Whichever one's the best."

The desk manager smiled warmly. Valentina smiled warmly. Two out of the three of us were pleased.

We were shown to the suite. It was suitably vast, and had been furnished with all the tasteful restraint for which the hotel's restorer, Donald Trump, is so renowned. Our room must have been decorated by Louis Quinze on LSD. I sat on an uncomfortable chair and reached for the eighteenth-century telephone, intending to order room service.

"I'm going to Bergdorf's," Valentina announced.

"Okay."

She stood with hands on hips, obviously expecting something.

"Their men's store is right across Fifth Avenue," she said.

"Okay."

She didn't move.

"They close early on Sundays," she added. I hung up. Food, it seemed, would have to wait.

Once outside, the first stop was an ATM machine and a thousand-dollar withdrawal, the maximum allowed, and half of which Valentina handed to me.

"Thank you," I said politely.

"It's an emergency loan from Tate, Tate & Buchanan," she said.

"Thank you, Tate, Tate & Buchanan."

"The firm charges interest for unsecured emergency loans to clients: Fed Funds plus two hundred and fifty basis points, accruing on a daily basis. It'll be added to your bill." At the rate she was charging, I suspected that the firm would soon be Tate, Tate, Buchanan & Mariposa.

The next stop was Bergdorf Goodman's men's store, where Valentina signed an open American Express voucher before retiring to the women's store on the other side of Fifth Avenue. An hour or so later, having been shuffled between the labyrinth of departments, I returned to the hotel, now appropriately outfitted. Valentina took considerably longer.

While she was not here to witness my whimpering, I did what I had known I was going to have to do for a while. I took the two little gin bottles from the minibar, some towels from the bathroom, the sewing kit from a drawer, and a packet of matches from one of the ashtrays. I drank one of the bottles dry, and spent the few minutes while the anesthetic took effect double-threading the needle. I dropped my trousers, removed the dressing, wiped away the blood with one of the damp towels, and washed the wound in the remaining gin. After bending the needle into a curve, and using a match flame to sterilize it, I went to work. I hope the neighbors didn't mind the noise.

When it was finished, I had six stitches. They weren't pretty, but no one would have accused me of being pretty to begin with anyway.

I was asleep when Valentina finally returned. She came through the door with a bellhop in tow, tottering under a skyscraper of Bergdorf boxes. She was wearing a beige silk skirt and jacket, with something soft and not quite opaque underneath, and high-heeled sandals of matching color. There was still a little smear of carburetor grease by her left knee.

The bellhop stacked the boxes on a luggage rack, accepted a tip, and left. I stared at the pile in disbelief.

"I'm having a bath," Valentina announced. "Have you made a dinner reservation yet?"

"No," I admitted. "I've been giving myself stitches."

She looked at the wound.

"*Green* thread?" she asked. "Why on earth did you use green?"

"To match the gangrene," I replied. If I'd had any expectations of sympathy, Valentina had set me straight. She began disrobing en route to the bathroom.

"Aureole, at eight," she instructed. "We'll have cocktails in the Oak Bar at seven, and walk from there." She closed the bathroom door without waiting for a reply, a princess taking the execution of her commands for granted.

It was late when we got back to the hotel. I was looking forward to sleep, having had little in the last twenty-four hours, but when I came out of the bathroom it was obvious that sleep would not be happening anytime soon. Valentina was standing by the open windows. Apart from a pair of high-heeled shoes she was completely naked, without even the thigh holster, which for her was very naked indeed.

"Come and admire the view," she said.

"Can't be better than the view from here."

She smiled and gestured for me to join her.

Our suite was on the top floor of the hotel, and our window emerged from the mansard roof onto a tiny balcony. We were on the Plaza's northern side, which gives onto Central Park. The lights of Manhattan twinkled before us, disappearing in perspective up Fifth Avenue. The paths through the park were lamp-lit, and away to our left we could see the fairy-tale constellation that was Tavern on the Green.

"Very nice," I said.

Valentina handed me a woven rope, tasseled at the ends, which I recognized as being the cord that had until recently held back the curtains.

"This is for you," she said. She stepped onto the balcony and draped herself over the railing.

I took a deep breath and joined her, trying to recall how to tie a clove hitch.

FIVE

THE next morning over rolls and coffee I checked the Yellow Pages under "Tattooing." There was a page of listings, scattered throughout Manhattan, but with a concentration of addresses in the East Village. That seemed the area to try first.

After withdrawing another wad of cash, Valentina and I took a cab down to Saint Mark's Place. She was dressed for the occasion as if having shopped in anticipation of it: tight black leather miniskirt, cropped top that failed to reach her belly button, and platform shoes which added several inches to her height. We got out at the corner of Second Avenue, list in hand, and began searching for the first tattoo parlor.

The East Village is the lair of the New York demimonde, and there were plenty in evidence that morning: retro punks and heroin vegans, the homeless and the hopeless, teenage runaways and the just plain lost—vague, jittery people with night eyes and moon tans, uncertain in the harsh light of day, passing time until CBGB's opened.

We came to a tattoo parlor. I had been expecting the usual squalid hovel occupied by a proprietor of doubtful hygiene with ink-stained hands and hepatitis B. Instead, the first place we came to was called Espresso and Tattoo. It turned out to be a combination tattoo parlor and coffee bar—clean and airy, a quiet refuge for enjoying a leisurely cappuccino while touching up the bodywork.

We went inside. There was a coffee counter on the left, with stools and newspapers in a rack. The floor was polished hardwood. Several round cafe tables occupied the center of the room. On the far side a plush barber's chair sat in front of a mirrored wall. It was currently unoccupied. There was no partition for privacy. Here, tattoo was a public art.

There were a few people at the counter. A blackboard on the wall listed the coffees, which had names like "Cool Breeze Off a Summer Lake." I read the description. It sounded like iced coffee to me.

A man approached us, late twenties, well groomed, more at home in a hair salon than a tattoo parlor. He smiled when he eyed Valentina, who radiated hip, but he looked at my blazer and chinos with disapproval. Blazers aren't big in the East Village.

"Ink or drink?" he asked. Despite the lack of visible tattoos, he had the proprietorial air of an owner.

"Ink," I said. "I'm trying to locate a particular tattoo design."

"Can you draw it?"

"I can try."

He fetched a sketch pad and pencil. We sat at one of the cafe tables. Some had binders sitting on them, filled with tattoo designs, intended for browsing while drinking the coffee. I tried to draw the design that I had seen on the back of the sergeant's hand. It wasn't very good.

"It has N-Y-C across the top," I explained. "Like this."

"And a number underneath?"

I hadn't drawn that yet.

"Yes," I admitted.

"Is the number eighty-one?"

"Yes."

"I know that design," he said, stating the obvious. "But I won't do it," he added.

"I don't want the thing done," I said. "I only want to know what it is."

He sat back and regarded me through suspicious eyes.

"The public library is at Fifth and Forty-second," he said. "You can get information for free there."

I pulled out a twenty-dollar bill.

"You insult me," he said.

"Okay, how much?" I asked.

"It's not a question of money," he stated. "I'm an artist."

"So exactly what is it a question of?"

Valentina interrupted.

"He wants to do a tattoo," she explained.

He smiled widely. "It's nice to see that there's someone besides me in this room with a little delicacy in their soul," he said. Of all the tattoo artists in the world, I had to get one with a delicate soul. He picked up a binder and pressed it toward me.

"All the designs are mine," he said. "All original."

"I don't want a tattoo," I said.

"Of course you do," he insisted.

He opened the binder and urged me to examine them.

Valentina glanced at the book. "Hey, some of these are pretty good," she said. She took the book herself and began flicking through the pages. "I wouldn't mind getting one."

"Wonderful." He clapped his hands in delight.

"But it would have to be somewhere that wouldn't show in public," she warned.

"Of course," he said confidentially. "The tushy?"

Valentina shook her head. "I wear thong bikinis."

"Just above the breast, perhaps?"

She thought about it for a moment, then nodded in agreement. Since they were apparently soon to be in intimate contact, he introduced himself and offered his hand. "Ramon Seger," he said. "*Artiste* of the body."

"Valentina Mariposa," she replied.

They shook hands warmly.

"Come to the comfy chair," Ramon said. "Take your time and go through the book till you find the right design. Would you like some coffee?"

"Arabian double mocha with a dash of cinnamon extract," she said, without glancing at the board. He smiled approvingly before turning to me.

"And for you?"

"Regular coffee."

He looked like a *fromagière* who's been asked for a can of Cheez Whiz. "*Regular* coffee?"

"Yes, regular coffee."

Ramon shook his head in bewilderment. "I'll see what I can do." He went to the coffee counter and gave instructions to the person serving there. I got the impression that Ramon didn't think much of my soul's delicacy.

"What about this one?" Valentina asked.

I stood beside the chair and looked over her shoulder. She pointed to a design. It was a series of Chinese characters. "How many Mandarin speakers do you plan on showing this to?" I asked.

Valentina rolled her eyes. She didn't think much of my soul's delicacy either.

"It's calligraphy," she explained. "The beauty is in the characters themselves."

"I see," I said. I didn't see, but then I have an indelicate soul.

"Read the translation."

I dutifully read the translation. *"Vanquish the endless longings of love."*

"Kind of erotic, isn't it?" Valentina said.

Sure, but was it the sort of thing you wanted permanently inscribed on your body? I thought it best to simply agree.

Ramon rejoined us, cups in hand.

"Tu Fu," he said. I hoped there wasn't any in my coffee. "Famous Chinese poet of the T'ang dynasty," he continued. "There's a painting of him in the Met, sitting in his thatched cottage by the Washing Flower Stream."

"That settles it," Valentina said. "Paint me, Ramon."

She stood and walked to the big barber's chair, removing her top on the way. Ramon accompanied her.

I took a newspaper and retired to a table. My regular coffee was pretty good. I suspected that it was really "High Plains Drifter," which according to the board came with a hint of chicory.

"Oh, my," I heard Ramon exclaim. Valentina was now sitting in the big chair. Her short skirt had ridden up, and her thigh holster was plainly visible. She ignored him and continued to thumb through the designs.

Ramon swung the chair to face the room, perhaps to get the best light. This tattoo was to be done without a needle. Instead, the dye would be applied directly to the skin with a calligraphy brush. Ramon ceremoniously unrolled a reed mat on a table with all the dignity of a samurai about to commit hara-kiri. He placed a lacquered box by the side, which was opened with due gravity. The inks and brushes were inside. He selected one of the latter, inspected it for stray bristles, and opened an inkwell. The calligraphy itself was soon complete. None of the people who came and went during this operation showed the least surprise at seeing all this with their morning coffee.

At Ramon's urging Valentina remained in the chair, allowing the ink to fully dry, while we completed the formalities of the transaction. I handed over a fistful of cash. Calligraphy does not come cheap.

"Now tell me about the tattoo," I said.

"Where did you see it?" he asked.

"On the back of a man's hand."

"What sort of man?"

"A dead man."

Ramon nodded, as if this was unsurprising. "Right hand or left?"

"Right."

"That's unusual. Was he left-handed?"

"As a matter of fact he was," I admitted. "How did you know?"

"He tattooed himself. That's the easiest place to do it."

"You're telling me this guy was a tattoo artist?"

"No, only an amateur. They do it in prison. Sharpen a paper clip, use ink from a ballpoint, something like that."

Not at Leavenworth. I guessed my prison had been too upmarket for that. Perhaps Leavenworth Federal is the Plaza of penitentiaries—the only place to be incarcerated, really.

"You're telling me the tattoo signifies a particular prison?"

"No, it signifies membership in a particular club. But it's often done in prison. The club initiation sometimes involves doing time." His voice was barely above a whisper, and his eyes were lowered. He was unhappy talking about this.

"What club?"

He paused before answering, unwilling to do so, as if it was bound to come back and haunt him. "The Hells Angels," he admitted.

"As in motorbikes?"

"Yes."

"And the number eighty-one?"

"New York City chapter."

"Do you know where they're located?"

"Everyone around here does. They're down on Third Street, near Avenue A."

"Thanks." I turned to get Valentina, but Ramon stopped me.

"Mister," he said, "let me give you some free advice. Whatever it is, forget about it. Just walk away."

"That's good advice," I said. "Thanks, Ramon."

Valentina resumed her clothing, and we headed down to Third Street. I have a bad habit of ignoring good advice.

SIX

WE found the Hells Angels' clubhouse on Third Street. The front door was painted with the same winged death's-head that I had seen on the back of Sergeant Tattoo's hand. Below this were the words "New York City, Chapter 81."

A handful of motorbikes stood outside, parked rear to curb. All of them were Harley-Davidsons. Anyone could park there, but I guessed that the Hells Angels rarely had problems with other people taking their space. I knocked on the door and waited. Eventually a small viewing window opened. A big, ugly pockmarked face appeared.

"Yeah?"

"I want to speak to the guy in charge," I said.

Pock Face took a swig from a beer can, considering the request. "Get lost," he finally said. The window closed.

I knocked on the door again. After a moment Pock Face reappeared.

"I want to speak to the guy in charge," I repeated. "If not, I'll drive my three-ton sport utility through every one of these bikes on the way out. You've got sixty seconds."

Pock Face was too taken aback to immediately react. He was not used to being on the receiving end of threats. I looked at the watch I didn't have.

"Fifty-five," I said. The window closed.

Half a minute later, the door opened. The man who stood there made up in girth for what he lacked in height. He had long wiry hair, turning to gray, and a huge grizzled beard, gray except near his mouth, where it had been stained nicotine yellow. His face had the arid landscape that comes from a lifetime of heavy drinking.

He glanced at Valentina, but paid most of his attention to me, like an undertaker silently taking measurements.

"You the suicide?" he asked.

"You in charge?" I replied. He nodded. "I need to talk to you."

The Bearded One stood still a moment, a king considering whether or not to hear the plea for mercy before going ahead with the execution. Eventually he stepped back in silent invitation. I was to be granted an audience.

We stepped into the clubhouse. I would have preferred that Valentina stay outside, but knew her well enough by now to realize that there would be no point in asking her to do so. The clubhouse was dimly lit, which was a mercy as it disguised the filth. The room stank of stale beer and cigarette smoke. Full ashtrays and empty bourbon bottles competed for table space. Posters adorned the walls: fading pictures of motorbikes by themselves, or motorbikes with naked women. The haircuts on these latter were those fluffy styles favored at about the same time that *Charlie's Angels* was on television. The music, loud heavy metal, was from the same era. It was coming from, of all things, a record player. It seemed that Chapter 81 of the Hells Angels had never gotten out of the 1970s. I wondered if they had any idea how quaint they were.

The middle of the room was dominated by two pool tables. A fat biker was supine on one of them, either dead or asleep. The other showed evidence of a game in progress. Pock Face and another biker, this one with a ponytail, held pool cues. Maybe they had been playing, or maybe the cues happened to be the most convenient weapons.

Ponytail and Pock Face took up positions either side of The Bearded One. Pock Face finished his beer, slammed the empty can flat on his forehead, and then folded it single-handed. Very impressive, if you're an orangutan.

The interview was delayed by the arrival of another person from a back room. This biker was female, good-looking but rough, younger than the others, although no girl. She wore dark eye shadow and a cigarette at the corner of her mouth. Her hair was cut short and the ends were burnished to a glittering bronze. It may have been intended as a statement of individuality, or might simply have been the worst dye job in history. She wore biker's boots, tight cut-off jeans, and a leather vest that concealed little of the anatomy. I counted eight pieces of body piercing decoration, variously adorning the ears, nose, eyebrows, and belly button.

She stepped between us and The Bearded One, then glanced dismissively at me before focusing her full attention on Valentina. They appraised each other for a moment in silence. The Biker Chick reached out a hand and rubbed it slowly down Valentina's hip.

"Nice," she said, although whether this referred to the leather skirt or what was beneath it was not clear.

If this gesture was meant to unnerve Valentina, it didn't work. She reached out her own hand, casually undid the tie on the Biker Chick's leather vest, and opened it to reveal one of her breasts. It, too, was pierced. Valentina fingered the nipple ring.

"I've got one at home just like this," she said.

Biker Chick didn't respond. Valentina moved her hand upward, fingers lightly going from breast to throat to chin. She slowly ran her fingertips over the other's mouth before coming to a stop at the cigarette. Valentina gently removed this from her mouth, and then took it to her own, where she inhaled deeply before speaking.

"Would you like to see my new tattoo?" she asked.

The Biker Chick smiled, acknowledging that she had been out-seduced, and nodded to a nearby couch, to which the two of them retired.

The Bearded One and his attendants, who had watched this proceeding with wry amusement, returned their attention to me.

"She's too much for you," The Bearded One said.

"You got that right," I admitted.

"So," he said, "any last requests?"

"I want to know about a man who has one of these tattoos." I pointed to the club tattoo on his own arm. "Same number, eighty-one. He had it on the back of his right hand, and he was left-handed. Six foot or so, the wrong side of two hundred pounds, about fifty years old." I could see by his expression that he had already guessed who I was talking about, but I continued with the description. "When I saw him he had a regular haircut and no facial hair, but that may have been recent. You know him?"

"Who wants to know?"

"I do."

"And who the hell are you?"

"I'm the guy who killed him." Not strictly true, but it would have been ungracious to admit that Valentina had done it. They were silent for a moment.

"Around here, we're kind of Old Testament," The Bearded One eventually said. "We're eye-for-an-eye people."

"I need to know who the guy was."

"And what I need," he said, "is for you to explain why I shouldn't break you into little pieces." He smiled, enjoying the exercise of power.

At this stage I was supposed to play scared and adopt an apologetic tone, at which point, having demonstrated submission, he would deign to tell me enough to get rid of me. There would be no violence and he could retire, status intact. The script was there between us, all I had to do was follow it. The trouble was that being frightened by such a grotesque slug is simply beyond my meager thespian talents.

"What you need," I explained, "is a six-month supply of diet pills, and a mighty powerful breath freshener."

The Bearded One's smile faded. He had no choice now, but I could tell that he wished he hadn't gotten himself into this position. Without taking his eyes from mine, he stretched an arm behind his body. Ponytail placed a pool cue in his hand.

There was a dusty trophy—marble base with a metal motorbike above—on the table next to me. I had been intending to use it to knock The Bearded One senseless when suddenly the thing exploded.

All four of us turned toward the couch, from where the shot had been fired.

Valentina sat perfectly relaxed, legs crossed, smiling as if slightly amused by our antics. Her left arm was draped around the Biker Chick's shoulders, cigarette held casually between long fingers, a curl of blue smoke rising from the tip. Her right arm was extended in the firing position. That hand held the .22 automatic, and there was blue smoke there, too, coming from the barrel.

The Biker Chick removed her hands from Valentina in order to clap in appreciation.

"Nice shot," she said.

The Bearded One laughed exaggeratedly, and assumed a smile of benevolent toleration.

"Well, little girl, I guess you just saved this guy's ass."

"No, fat boy," Valentina replied, "I just saved yours."

The Bearded One didn't reply. I got the feeling that he wasn't long for the leadership in this particular troop of monkeys. Ponytail had a lean and hungry look: my money was on him to be the Cassius of the group.

Valentina removed her arm from around the Biker Chick, put the cigarette in her mouth, and went to a two-handed grip. She kept the gun on The Bearded One as she rose from the sofa and moved to join me. I opened the door, and we both backed out.

"Nice meeting you," I said. I waved good-bye and closed the door.

We walked swiftly down the street. When we turned into the avenue, Valentina stopped and put the gun back in the holster, a maneuver which in any other city would have caused pandemonium, but in the East Village was worth nothing more than a curious glance in passing.

"Your interview technique could use a little work," Valentina said.

"I didn't see you discovering much, apart from the delights of Sappho."

" 'Solicitude and empathy are the key ingredients to the

successful deposition of a hostile witness,' " she quoted.
"Techniques of Legal Examination 101."

"If you say so."

"By the way, the guy's name was Yip Yip Martin."

"What guy?"

"The guy *I* killed, and for whom *you* are now apparently
taking credit."

"How did you find that out?"

Valentina took a last drag on the cigarette and stubbed it
out with her shoe before replying.

"The girl told me."

"How come?"

Valentina shrugged her shoulders. "Guess she liked the
tattoo."

The telephone directory in our room at the hotel listed hundreds of Martins but, predictably, only one of them was
named Yip Yip. The address was in Tribeca.

It was dusk by the time we found it, an old building on
the edge of the meat-packing district, paint peeling from the
brick, fire escape scarring the facade, the type of place that
probably began life as a semi-respectable boardinghouse,
and deteriorated from there. Its current incarnation was
as itinerant apartments—for the building, the last step before abandonment, and for the occupants, the last step
before homelessness.

The cab pulled quickly away, unwilling to risk picking
up a fare here. Trash cans littered the sidewalk. One,
knocked over, was having its contents explored by a pair of
rats who took no notice of us.

"Charming," Valentina said.

"Don't say I never take you anywhere nice."

I went up the steps to the front door. There was a rack of

mailboxes and, above that, an ancient intercom. The name
Martin was scrawled in the slot next to 4C. I pressed the
buzzer. It sounded, but there was no reply.

A basement door swung open underneath the stoop, followed by a head peering up at us. The face was that of an
old man, covered with several days' growth of gray whis-
kers. He had obviously given up the task of regular shaving.

"Can I help you?"

The super, I guessed, or maybe the landlord, checking
on people coming and going.

"Do you know Yip Yip Martin?"

"You debt collectors?" he asked.

"No."

"Just as well," he said. He closed the door and began to
slowly climb the stairs. "You'd be wasting your time. Ain't
seen 4C in weeks."

"He's behind on the rent?"

"Three months."

"When did you last see him?"

He struggled the last few steps to join us by the front
door. From the smell I guessed he had given up regular
bathing as well.

"Well, now," he said, still panting from the ascent, "ain't
you curious?"

I handed him a twenty. At least we weren't required to
get a tattoo.

"Two weeks ago," he said. He folded the bill carefully
and tucked it into his shirt pocket. "Threatened to get an
eviction notice if he didn't hand over the rent."

"Did he?"

"No. He said he was coming into a lot of money. Told
me he'd pay up by the end of the month."

"You believed him?"

"Yeah, stupid, ain't I?" He looked idly at the rats

exploring the trash can. "But he had an air about him, you know? Confident like. Don't often get that around here. So, yeah, I believed him."

"Did he tell you how he expected to get this money?"

"No, sir, and I sure as heck didn't inquire."

"Did he have any unusual visitors recently?" Valentina asked.

"No, only Olga."

"Who's Olga?"

"Friend of his. Girlfriend, I guess you'd say."

"Any idea where we can find her, or what her last name is?"

He shook his head.

"Did he work?"

"Sometimes. Down at the Factory."

"The Factory?"

"Nightclub over on Vestry," he explained. "At least they call it a nightclub. Vice squad probably got their own name for it."

He spat on the steps, hacked a bit, then spat again. I wasn't sure whether he was expressing an opinion about the Factory, or simply clearing his throat.

"What did he do there?"

"Beat people up."

I assumed this meant he was a bouncer. There seemed nothing more to ask, so I thanked him and we went down to the sidewalk. The old man accompanied us. "If you see Yip Yip, tell him if he hasn't paid by the end of the month I'm pawning all his stuff."

"If I find him," I said, "I'll be sure to let him know."

But the old man wasn't listening. His attention was focused on the knocked-over trash can. He softly stepped up to it and then suddenly flipped it, not right way up, but inverted. The rats were trapped inside.

"They'll fight," he explained, grinning at the thought. "I'll come by in the morning, and see which one survived." He shuffled away back down to his basement.

Charming old man.

SEVEN

THE Factory was a dark, windowless ex-meat-packing warehouse near West Street, converted to use as a night-club. The doors were padlocked. There were no windows, nor any sign of activity. Discarded newspapers and advertising leaflets blew along the sidewalk. A series of posters was glued in a haphazard line along the wall, as if it was the exterior of a city construction site. They were all identical, all advertising a "Mid-Summer Blast" at the club. There was a list of DJs and dates, including today, but no times. The Factory obviously didn't get going until late at night, although the area was so deserted that I wondered if it ever opened.

We walked up to Soho, found a place that served good food and better margaritas, and passed the next few hours companionably. When we returned to the Factory, the place was hardly recognizable.

We could hear it before we saw it, the frenzied buzz of an eager crowd, and below that the deep bass of dance music booming through the night. The atmosphere had gone from forlorn to frantic in a few hours. Limos outside the front doors were unloading those privileged enough to get in without waiting. The remainder formed a line of anxious humanity that stretched along the sidewalk and around the corner, eager and expectant, apparently willing to wait hours for the chance of entry.

There were two Neanderthals in black jeans and T-shirts on the front door, who between them had a pair of eyebrows. A third man was wearing a suit—a very shiny suit—and was obviously in charge of the entrance. He had on a combination headset and boom mike, on which he was constantly talking. It was his job to admit the beautiful, and sneer at the rest.

His sharp gaze fell upon me as we approached. A split second of evaluation, which no doubt would have quickly dissolved into a sneer if Valentina had not been with me. He took one look at her then nodded to a Neanderthal, who opened the door as we walked up the steps.

"Welcome to the Factory," he said smoothly.

"Thanks."

In fact all I had wanted to do was talk to him about Yip Yip Martin, but since we were to be granted the rare privilege of unobstructed entry, it seemed a shame not to see the place. We went inside.

There was a small vestibule with a coat check, and a desk where the cover charge was collected. I paid, then we went through the next set of doors into the club itself.

The first thing that hit me was the wave of noise. It was more than just sound, the music here was relentless, an intense tangible presence that seemed to physically suck the air out of your lungs. It was raw and relentless, that harsh urban techno music that thrives south of Fourteenth Street.

The decor was industrial chic. Metal walkways hung on chains from the ceiling, or stood fixed by gantries to the wall, more at home above the turbines of a power station or the vats of a chemical plant than in a nightclub. Smoke came billowing from a huge ventilation duct, gradually settling in a steady haze over the massive dance floor. One wall was a giant patchwork of television monitors, operating in synch, displaying a rapidly changing sequence of thirty-foot-high images: clips from music videos, cartoons, sex movies, television advertisements, old black-and-white newsreels; and, in an amusing pun, scenes from Fred Astaire and Ginger Rogers films. Lights pulsed and laser beams flowed in waves over the dancing crowd, a sea of murky vagueness whose details were occasionally revealed by the transfiguring burst of a strobe light. Few were wearing street clothes. Many women were topless, several all but naked. I suddenly understood the presence of the coat check, which had seemed odd to me in the middle of summer. People checked not their coats but their clothing—and inhibitions.

Apart from the technical effects, it might have been a Dionysian festival in the fading days of Rome, with the Goths at the gates and all constraint gone.

On the far wall across the vast space was a neon sign: "Bar." We threaded through the dance floor toward it, then took seats and surveyed the scene while waiting for a bartender. My eyes had become accustomed to the lighting, and I was able to see things more clearly. The dance floor itself was a pulsing mass of spandex and flesh. The scaffolds seemed to be reserved for those who had more or less completely succumbed to the Bacchanalia.

The bar was large and circular, and above it was a platform, backed by twenty-foot-high mirrors, on which a dozen or more women were dancing. These women were particularly attractive, and I soon realized why: access to this prime dancing spot was, like access to the club itself, strictly controlled. The stairs leading up to it were roped off, and a pair of men standing guard there apparently had the arduous task of selecting from among the many women thronging around the base, eager to be allowed up.

One of the bartenders approached. He was a step up from Neanderthal, presumably to the point of remembering a drink order, but from the steroidal bulk it was apparent that his primary mission was still intimidation.

He raised an eyebrow, his way of asking what we wanted, not a bad procedure in the noise of the Factory.

"Two martinis," I said.

He grabbed a shaker, scooped the ice, poured in a river of gin without measuring it, and then tapped the side of a vermouth bottle with the closed shaker before mixing and pouring. This was my kind of bartender. He added olives and slid the two glasses in front of us.

"Fifteen dollars."

I gave him a fifty.

He returned in a moment with the change, which he slid across the bar to me. I slid it back.

"Hey, thanks," he said. His face creased with a genuine smile.

"Yip Yip Martin," I said.

The smile disappeared.

"I got no idea where he is, man."

"I want to know about him. Who his friends were. What he was into."

He shook his head and pushed the change back in my direction.

"Enjoy your drink."

He disappeared down to the other end of the bar. Valentina gave me one of those looks.

"Okay," I admitted, "my solicitude and empathy need a little work."

We picked up our glasses and toasted silently before sipping. The martini was very good.

"Perhaps I should do the talking next time," Valentina said.

I was about to agree when I noticed two men in dark suits edging through the crowd. Fully evolved, and no sheen on the fabric. One surveying, the other with eyes unerringly on me. Jackets buttoned, each holding a hand flat at the top button, ready to slide inside the jacket quickly if the need arose.

I turned to Valentina. "I think my interview technique wasn't so bad after all."

She followed my eyes and caught the company. Her hand began to disappear into the leather skirt.

"No," I said, "let this one ride for a while."

She nodded and resumed her grip on the martini glass. I kept both my hands visible, so that there would be no errors of judgment. We come in peace.

The two men came to the bar either side of us. One fair and balding, the other dark and sharp. Dark and Sharp was by me. He bent close.

"Mr. Leonetti sends his compliments, and asks if you would be kind enough to join him for a drink."

"Fine," I said.

I got off the bar stool. So did Valentina, but Dark and Sharp quickly held up a hand.

"Mr. Leonetti regrets that he is not suitably prepared to receive a lady, and asks that your companion remain here. Mr. Leonetti gives his personal guarantee that she will be able to do so in complete safety."

He nodded over our shoulders. We looked behind us. The bartender had returned and was now standing, arms folded, on the other side of the counter, apparently intending to remain so during my absence.

I looked at Valentina. She shrugged her shoulders matter-of-factly. All the steroids in the world were no match for her, she seemed to say. I had to agree.

I turned to Dark and Sharp. "Let's go."

We eased through the crowd toward the wall. The other man acted as point, leading us by twenty feet, surveying the whole time. Dark and Sharp stayed with me, left hand gently at my elbow, as if to guide me, although the grip would quickly have tightened were I to have gone in any direction other than the one indicated.

We arrived at a heavy door with a key code panel by the side. Fair and Balding was now standing back to the wall, continually scanning the crowd, while my guide released me and stood in front of the panel to enter the code. The door unlocked and we went inside.

The noise from the other side was all but silenced when the door closed. I wondered what was in here, that they needed such a solid door. There was a dimly lit metal staircase leading up, which we took. At the top was another door, and another key code panel. We went through the same routine, except this time Fair and Balding kept his eyes fixed firmly on me.

We entered a room through a magnetometer. Fair and Balding went first. Whatever he was carrying under the jacket instantly set off the alarm. He went to a control panel on the other side, silenced the metal detector, then reset it. Dark and Sharp urged me forward.

I passed through. Nothing.

A woman entered the room through a far door. She was dressed in a business suit, wore glasses in fashionable frames, had her hair pulled back, and was holding a clipboard. She was as sleek as a cat.

She turned to the other two. "Thank you, Mr. Smith, Mr. Jones." The accent was precise and clipped, Back Bay perhaps. She must have been suckled at Smith and raised at Radcliffe. I wondered how a girl like her ended up in a place like this, and would have asked if the question wasn't so hackneyed.

Messrs. Smith and Jones nodded and left via the same door through which she had come. When it was closed behind them she turned her blue-eyed gaze to me.

"My name is Miss Honeysuckle," she said. Of course it was.

"Pleased to meet you," I replied.

"I am Mr. Leonetti's executive secretary." She offered a hand, which I took. Her grip was cool and firm.

"Lysander Dalton," I said, hoping to induce a first name in response. But she was having none of that.

"Mr. Leonetti regrets that he is forced, by considerations stemming from the actions of certain overzealous prosecutors, to have all visitors checked for wires." There are no more criminals in America, only overzealous prosecutors. "Mr. Leonetti hopes that you will not object to me doing so now."

"I can't think of anything I'd enjoy more," I said.

Miss Honeysuckle smiled tightly and placed the clipboard on a table.

"Please take off your jacket, shoes, and belt."

I did so and handed them to her. She took them to what I had thought was a photocopier on the far wall. In fact it was a small X-ray machine. Miss Honeysuckle put the articles inside one by one, studying the images carefully before deciding that they were wireless. She returned to me.

"And now for the body search," she said.

"My favorite part," I replied.

"Please face the wall, Mr. Dalton." I faced the wall.

"Feet eighteen inches apart." I did as ordered.

"Hands against the wall." I did that, too.

She slowly ran her hands over my back, feeling through the shirt for anything but flesh beneath. Then she ran her hands down my chest, pressing her own firm body against mine as she did so. She undid a couple of buttons and slid a hand inside the shirt. Then she pulled the shirt tails out and ran her hand up underneath the T-shirt. Miss Honeysuckle was pressing very firmly now, and I thought I could detect a faster rate of breathing, although that was probably just me.

Then she went lower. At first she restricted herself to patting down the trouser legs, but then she unzipped and unbuttoned. The search continued. Miss Honeysuckle was a woman of much thoroughness and little discretion.

Eventually the search ended, as all good things must. I resumed my clothing as calmly as I was able. When I was dressed, Miss Honeysuckle led the way through the far door.

The room we entered was large—part office, part lounge, part security station, part observation tower, part bridge of the starship *Enterprise*. It was circular, or almost so. Two-thirds of the wall was glass: the inside of the gigantic mirrored panels above the bar that we had seen from outside, and which made the office an excellent vantage point from which to observe the women dancing on the platform outside, as well as providing a sweeping view of the club beyond. Obviously the mirrors were one-way.

I could hear the music, but noticed that it was not coming directly from the other side, but instead from speakers discreetly placed above the glass. I guessed they could be turned down, and that the room could be made a cocoon of silence against all the noise outside.

At the rear of the room, where the glass paneling ended, the walls were lined with four big flat-screen monitors.

One of these showed the same rapidly changing images displayed on the wall of television screens in the main dance room. The others were apparently connected to the security cameras. There must have been more than three of these, because the screens slowly sequenced through them. There were obviously several at the entrance, a number over the dance floor, and at least one at the bar, where I saw Valentina calmly drinking her drink, and the bartender still standing behind her. Even the bathrooms were videotaped.

At the extreme rear of the room was a small bar that looked to be well equipped. Messrs. Smith and Jones had taken up positions on either side of it, standing backs to the wall, awaiting orders like the obedient pets that they were.

The center of the room was dominated by a huge desk of postmodern design, a great slab of shiny chromed metal that, perhaps while still molten, had been curled back on itself and down to the floor to form the base. Maybe it had been purchased by a decorator intent on maintaining the industrial theme.

Sitting on the desk were a telephone, a control panel, and a pretty girl dressed in a patent leather bustier whose shine competed with the chrome.

Behind the desk sat a man in his mid-forties who was, I presumed, Mr. Leonetti. He was smiling. Mr. Leonetti was a happy man, and I couldn't blame him.

He rose and came around the desk. "Thank you for accepting my invitation, Mr. Dalton."

He already knew my name, which meant that the room next door was wired. Considering the thoroughness of the body search, I hoped that it wasn't videotaped as well. We shook hands.

"You have a very nice place, Mr. Leonetti."

He looked around, as if seeing it for the first time himself, then nodded. "I get by." He clapped his hands. "Now, you've met my associates Mr. Smith and Mr. Jones." We nodded. "And of course my executive assistant, Miss Honeysuckle. My apologies for the necessity of the wire search."

"It was very instructive," I replied. "I had no idea they could be so well hidden."

Miss Honeysuckle, who had been sashaying away toward the bar, looked over her shoulder and smiled. Leonetti turned to the leather-clad creature on his desk. "And this is Cindy," he said. "Cindy is my valet."

Besides the bustier, Cindy (the valet) wore a thong, fishnet stockings, and stiletto-heeled shoes. I nodded in greeting, but she was staring at my feet and missed it. She looked to be about sixteen years old.

A voice came from a speaker on the desk.

"Yes or no, Mr. Leonetti?"

Leonetti returned to his desk and hit a button on the control panel. One of the flat screens went to a view of the front entrance. Shiny Suit was in the foreground, looking up at the camera, obviously having been the source of the question. A famous rap artist was getting out of a limo behind him, retinue in tow.

"No," Leonetti said.

Shiny Suit nodded and signaled his troops. Leonetti turned off the sound, but we continued to watch the monitor. There was a brief scene, tempers flared, but the rap artist and his attendants soon backed down. They returned to the limo and drove away.

"He's been indicted on gun charges," Leonetti explained. "I don't associate with criminals."

Perhaps, notwithstanding the wire search, he always spoke as if a transcript of whatever he said would end up in court.

"Can I get you a drink?" he asked.

"Martini."

Leonetti held up fingers for two. Miss Honeysuckle began mixing.

"Please take a seat," Leonetti said.

I sat on one of a pair of leather sofas which were arranged in a broad arc either side of the desk, perhaps so that everybody could see the view through the one-way mirrors. And a fine view it was. The platform was still crowded with good-looking women—some danced facing the crowd beyond, but several, attracted by the prospect of watching themselves perform, faced the mirrors and, consequently, us.

Miss Honeysuckle brought three drinks on a silver tray. She placed one next to me on a metal end table, whose design matched that of the desk, served the second to Leonetti, then took the third for herself before sitting on the arm of the other sofa.

Leonetti held his glass aloft.

"Good health," he said. I wondered if there was an implied threat to the toast.

We drank. The martini was good, but not as good as the one downstairs. Cindy's eyes had never left my feet during this time. Now she leaned across the desk and whispered into Leonetti's ear. He smiled like an indulgent parent, then turned to me.

"Cindy asks if she may polish your shoes, Mr. Dalton."

"My shoes?"

He shrugged his shoulders. "What can I say? She's into leather."

"Should I take them off?"

"No, not at all. Just sit there and indulge her."

He nodded permission to Cindy, who jumped off the desk and scampered back to the bar, returning a moment later with a shoe-shine box. She knelt in front of me, opened the box, and took out the brushes.

Leonetti cleared his throat.

"Now, Mr. Dalton," he began, "I understand that you are making inquiries concerning a former employee of mine."

"Former?"

"Perhaps I should say part-time. Yip Yip Martin is not on the regular payroll. He's only employed on an as-needed basis."

Cindy covered my shoes in wax and began brushing.

"Your concern for his welfare does you credit, Mr. Leonetti."

Leonetti smiled. "Very well," he said. "The situation is this: I myself have no particular interest in the whereabouts of Mr. Martin. However, I have a friend who does."

"A friend?"

"Perhaps I should say an acquaintance."

"Can I ask why?"

"My acquaintance has an interest in various sporting events. I understand that Mr. Martin expressed certain views to my acquaintance concerning a particular sporting event, with special emphasis on the result. Mr. Martin expressed his view very forcefully. As it turned out, Mr. Martin's view was in error. My acquaintance wishes to discuss this with him. Unfortunately, Mr. Martin seems to have disappeared."

Cindy put down the brushes and started buffing with a polishing cloth. It occurred to me that, given her obvious fetish, she would actually make a pretty good valet.

"How forcefully did Martin express this view?" I asked.

Leonetti held up ten fingers, then opened and closed them five times. So Yip Yip Martin was fifty grand into a bookie. He was lucky Valentina had killed him.

"Bad luck for your acquaintance, Mr. Leonetti. The last time I saw Yip Yip Martin, his head was doing a Jackson Pollock all over the floor."

Leonetti shrugged his shoulders. "My acquaintance will approve of the end, but will be displeased that he himself was not the means. Might I ask who performed this service?"

"I did."

"I see. And where might my acquaintance view the remains?"

"That's the problem. There's no body."

Leonetti smiled a smile of polite disbelief. "Surely Yip Yip is not a credible candidate for resurrection?"

Cindy now began to spit shine my shoes. She did this by slowly licking the toes, then rubbing in a dab of polish. I found it hard to concentrate.

"Yip Yip Martin was involved with a group of people who attacked my house. They're the ones who disposed of the body. I'm trying to find out who they are."

"And exactly who are you, Mr. Dalton?"

"An innocent bystander."

"I find that a little hard to believe."

"Would I be here for any other reason?"

"I can think of one or two."

"Such as?"

"Such as this: Yip Yip Martin had suddenly acquired—how shall we put it?—great expectations. He would unlikely have expressed his view to my acquaintance so forcefully otherwise."

"Agreed."

"Perhaps you found out about these great expectations. And perhaps you decided to realize these great expectations for yourself."

"I see."

"Now, Mr. Dalton, personally I have no view on this matter one way or the other. But my acquaintance would be most gratified if I could pass on your sincere acknowledgment of his prior claim, were you to suddenly realize the late Mr. Martin's expectations."

Cindy was doing a good job. My shoes were ready for the parade ground.

"Sincere acknowledgment made."

"Thank you."

"But tell your friend not to hold his breath," I added. "Yip Yip Martin was one of life's losers, and any expectations he had were unlikely to be realistic."

"Too true."

"What can you tell me about him, Mr. Leonetti?"

"As you say, not a man marked for success. Muscle, but not enough brain to use it wisely. Interstate trucker by trade, but too unreliable to hold down a regular job. He was on the dispatchers' lists, but they would only call him if there was no one else available. Between the occasional trucking assignment and intermittent employment here, he subsisted."

"Criminal history?"

"I assume so, but I never inquired."

"And the Hell's Angels?"

"Used to be a member, but I understand that Yip Yip was forced to sell his bike some time ago, which more or less rendered him an ex-Angel, at least until he acquired another."

"How did he get the name Yip Yip?"

"As a young man he was in Vietnam. According to him, 'yip' was the last sound a VC made when you shot him. Apparently he decided to call himself Yip, one for every enemy soldier he killed."

"He killed two?"

"No, he said that his full name was Yip Yip Yip Yip Yip Yip . . . etc. His little joke."

No one was laughing.

"If Martin was ever in the army," I said, "it was probably in the quartermaster corps. The nearest he would have got to killing anyone would have been food poisoning."

Leonetti smiled. "I agree with you," he said. "Although, for the record, he claimed to have been in the marines, not the army."

A coincidence; at least I assumed it was.

Leonetti wasn't telling me much that was useful. I looked out the windows, trying to think of another question. One particularly large-breasted woman, dressed in a patent leather cat suit, was shimmying in front of the mirrors while slowly unzipping.

"Good view, isn't it?" Leonetti said, as if reading my mind. "I never get tired of sitting here and watching."

"Beats television."

"I call that the panorama platform."

"Aptly named."

"I was hoping that your friend might dance there tonight. She's a good dancer."

He smiled, registering my surprise at the remark.

"Yes, Mr. Dalton, I have a very good memory for people. Especially women who look like your partner." He spoke as if he had caught me trying to trick him. "I know as well as you do that she has been to my club several times, well before Yip Yip disappeared. Which, of course, means that you are something other than the innocent bystander you claim to be." He held up a hand to forestall any protest. "As I say, Mr. Dalton, it means nothing to me. The truth is that I wish you and your beautiful partner every success. I just don't want you to forget my acquaintance's prior claim. Are we clear?"

"Perfectly."

He nodded, satisfied. I took a slug of the gin, and wondered exactly who Valentina Mariposa was.

The same voice as before came over the loudspeaker, but more strident this time.

"We got trouble, Mr. Leonetti."

Leonetti hit a button on the console and turned to face a monitor.

Shiny Suit was looking anxiously across the street. A handful of men were approaching. Their walk was determined, and they weren't dressed for dancing. One of them had a gimpy stride that looked familiar. I had to admit that Shiny Suit had a good eye for trouble.

The guns came out before a word was spoken.

"I'm sending the shooters," Leonetti said. "Talk them down."

I could see Shiny Suit nod in acknowledgment. Leonetti clicked his fingers, and Messrs. Smith and Jones raced out of the office. Shiny Suit stood in front of the door, opened his hands, and began a "Hey, fellas," routine, trying to keep the intruders at bay until the armor arrived. But they walked right through him.

"Do you have a back way out of here, Mr. Leonetti?" I asked.

He pointed toward a door behind the bar, which I had already guessed served this purpose. That was when the gunfire started. Screaming followed. Whether Messrs. Smith and Jones had entered the fray, or the intruders were simply killing anyone in their way, I never found out.

Cindy the valet scooted away. She didn't like gunfire, she liked shoes.

I picked up the metal coffee table and hurled it through a glass panel, hoping that the stuff wasn't bulletproof. Not only was it not bulletproof, it wasn't even tempered, and shattered into a shower of tiny fragments on impact.

I heard a brief protest from Leonetti behind me, but he was too frantically working the console to do anything more. The voice net was a confusion of shouting, and the fog of battle had settled in.

I stepped onto the panorama platform. The music hadn't stopped, and most people were still dancing, as yet unaware that anything unusual was happening. This included the large-breasted woman in the cat suit, who was now fully unzipped, and who winked at me when I stepped onto the deck. I winked back. A man should always have time for courtesy to a lady.

There was more gunfire, and I could see a wave of panic in the crowd by the front door as the intruders pressed forward. They were dropping smoke canisters behind them, blinding anyone who might follow. I stepped onto the outside of the platform, hooked my legs into the rail, and lowered myself so that I hung upside down above the bar.

Valentina was below me. She was leaning back against the bar, martini glass held casually in her left hand, the other concealed behind her body. I was pretty sure the .22 would be in that hand, cocked and safety off.

"Valentina," I shouted. She looked around, obviously having heard her name, but unable to tell where the voice had come from. "Up here."

She looked up and saw me. Her right hand emerged holding the weapon, as I had guessed.

Valentina reholstered the automatic and leapt onto the bar. At this point the bartender, who had been distracted by the commotion, suddenly realized what was happening. He grabbed one of her ankles. I knew this was a mistake as soon as he did it. Before I could warn him to let go, Valentina delivered a crushing kick to his face with her other foot. By the time it was fixed, he would have provided some orthodontist's child with a college tuition.

Valentina jumped up and grabbed my arms. We held each other trapeze style. I could feel the stitches in my leg begin to open. I began to sway, side to side, in ever increasing arcs. Those people nearby who had not already taken cover because of the gunfire did so now to avoid the swinging heels.

"This time," I said, at the beginning of a swing. She nodded.

I put all my effort into it. At the last moment we released. She had good momentum, and was able to grab the rail with a hand and hook a leg over as well. We both struggled onto the platform.

The shooting had stopped for the moment, but the panic below was complete, and the screaming had reached a level to compete with the music. Valentina retrieved the gun from her holster.

"Head shots only," I warned. "They'll have body armor."

"Got it."

"This way."

I led her through the remains of the glass panel into the office. Leonetti was gone, perhaps having chosen the better part of valor. Only Miss Honeysuckle remained, now sitting at the desk, calmly directing the operations of the troops, a Benedict Arnold refusing to submit, although her Horatio Gates had fled to his tent.

She and Valentina eyed each other appraisingly..

Miss Honeysuckle scribbled something on the back of a business card, then stood. She walked over and handed it to me.

"My number," Miss Honeysuckle explained. She looked at Valentina, then back to me. "For when you've grown beyond guns and leather," she added.

"You should try contacts," Valentina said. "Unless of course you *are* a librarian."

If hackles were bullets we'd have all been dead by now. I hustled Valentina to the back of the room and through the exit before the fur flew. The door was one of those emergency exit-style doors, unlocked from the inside but unopenable from without. It gave onto a small landing, enclosed in a shaft inside the building, with a narrow metal staircase leading down, which we took. There was only one light, a dim bulb hanging from bare wires, and whose illumination became ever weaker the further we descended.

And descend we did, well beyond street level. The staircase ended in a basement. It was unlit, apart from very faint street lighting coming through thick glass tiles embedded into the sidewalk above us.

The basement had once been used for wholesale meat storage. Metal rails lined the ceiling, and from these hung huge meat hooks. I was glad we couldn't see clearly, because it seemed to me that one of the meat hooks was currently occupied. This was just the sort of place the mob would use for business discussions, and I was afraid that the thing on the meat hook might have been someone who had failed an interview.

"Don't touch anything," I whispered. The last thing we needed was to add our fingerprints to another murder—we had enough murders of our own.

I stopped under one of the skylights. There was a shadow moving back and forth overhead. We could see nothing of the person, but we could see the tread well enough. Boots, with a heavy, thick tread pattern, like combat boots. I guessed this guy was assigned to cover the rear.

We continued through the cellar, which led under the street above and connected with the cellar of the building on the other side. It, too, had once been a meat-packing warehouse, obviously now long abandoned. An overhead pipe slowly dripped water onto the floor. In the middle of the room stood a gigantic vertical band saw which would once have cut down whole carcasses into bloody shoulders and loins, but now sat rusting and silent. We made our way around it and found a set of precarious iron stairs. These led up to a pair of steel doors, flush with the sidewalk, giving onto a side street. I mounted the stairs and slowly opened one of the doors, trying to make as little noise as possible.

We emerged onto the street above, which was empty. I went to the corner of the building and risked a glance around. I could hear the noise of people leaving the night-club, and in the distance police sirens, but could see no sign of the guard at the rear of the building. Then suddenly there was a faint whirring noise above us.

A shadow, thirty feet above street level, went zooming away through the air.

"What is it?" Valentina asked.

"A guy wire," I said.

"How can you tell?"

"I've used the same thing. It's a standard special forces' technique, when you need a quiet but rapid extraction."

Another shadow went racing along the wire.

"Where's it lead to?"

"I can't see," I said. "They'll have a vehicle there, outside the perimeter the police will set up. There's probably an alternate extraction route, too, in case something goes wrong with this one."

"These people are fast," she said.

I nodded, although it wasn't setting up the wire that impressed me—that could be done in minutes—it was the speed of the planning. Whoever was in charge of the team had a very sharp operational mind. I hadn't done this stuff in ten years. If my luck ran out, I would be no match for the person running this show. And the first thing they teach you in special ops school is that your luck always runs out.

"Where to now?" Valentina whispered.

"Back to Yip Yip's place."

"Why?"

"I want to ask the old man a question."

She shrugged her shoulders in acquiescence. We moved out, keeping close to the wall. I was anxious to keep out of sight of the wire above us, but I made certain that my back was never to Valentina.

EIGHT

VALENTINA and I arrived back outside Yip Yip Martin's tenement. The trash can was still inverted, but there was no sound coming from the creatures inside. We went down the stairs to the basement from which the old man had emerged earlier that evening.

I knocked on the door and waited. Nothing.

I knocked again, louder this time. The door came ajar from the force of the knock. I looked down and saw that the lock had been broken away from the doorjamb.

I silently put my hand out, and soon felt Valentina's gun placed in it. The metal was warm; it had had a snug resting spot. I actioned the slide, thumbed off the safety, gestured for Valentina to stay where she was, and began the insertion.

Insertions into buildings give me the willies. I could never be a cop. I'd done them for real perhaps a dozen times, better armed and better armored, and I always felt that every one would be my last. It's different when you're not enclosed by walls, in the jungle edging through the undergrowth toward an enemy camp; or in the desert, crawling up on a tank revetment under a cloudless, starlit sky. I liked that work fine. But buildings are too close, too dark, too easy to booby-trap. Usually I just lit them with a laser and called in an air strike to take care of the rest.

But not this time. I entered the front hall while trying to remember the technique. Keep low: traps are often at chest or face level. Head always looking forward, peripheral for everything else. Slowly, slowly, except past doorways.

I came to a doorway. Best to leap through them, if you can. I leapt.

I caught a sudden movement and went into a body roll. I fired one slug for evasion, steadied, then three more into the target.

No more movement. I tried to catch my breath, and wondered if I was going to heave. I tried to keep it down—the troops get discouraged when their officers throw up. I felt around on the floor, found a shoe, and threw it to the far wall. If there was anyone left alive down there to react, they didn't do so. I waited. Still nothing.

Eventually someone was going to have to turn a light on, and I guessed it was going to be me. I crawled to the doorway and felt around for the light switch. I turned it on, gun pointed in the direction of that one flash of movement I'd seen. I soon saw what had caused it. It was a cat—*was* being the correct tense.

It had been on the counter by the sink. Now it was kind of all over the place. I heard Valentina come into the building and step down the hall. She stopped at the doorway behind me and made a noise of disgust.

"What a mess," she said. I had to agree. I turned, intending to mumble an apology for having needlessly wasted the tabby. But she wasn't looking at the cat. I followed her eyes.

It was the old man. He was spread-eagled on the bed, tied securely by hands and feet to each of the corners. His throat was slit, and there was a pool of blood around the wound.

But that had come last. Most of the work had been done with a pair of meat skewers, probably from his own kitchen. One had been driven under each kneecap, between the patella and the joint, where just a little movement in the shaft causes a great deal of pain. It's a good technique—in fact I'd seen it used before, a favorite method of the guerrillas we had fought on what had turned out to be my last mission. The guerrillas had been using child mutilation as a means of convincing villagers to rally to the cause. One particular village hid their children. Sharpened bamboo shoots under the parents' kneecaps had been the guerrillas' method of persuading them to reveal where they were.

I wasn't feeling very nostalgic. The wet towel they'd used to muffle the screams was beside the bed.

"I guess you won't be asking him your question after all," Valentina said.

But in fact he'd already answered it. The interval between the time we had entered the Factory and the time the assault team had come in after us was insufficient for the operation to have been set up, no matter how good the commander. That meant they hadn't been tipped off from someone inside the nightclub itself. They had to have known earlier that we would go to the Factory. And there had been only two people besides me who knew we were going to the Factory: the old man, and Valentina.

So my question to the old man would have been "Did you tell anyone we were going to the Factory?" And the answer, laid out here on the bed, was an emphatic *yes*. He would have told them anything and everything they wanted to know.

I was pleased with the answer. If it had been no, I'm not sure what I would have done with Valentina.

Now would have been a good time to ask her who she was, but I decided against it. With no information of my own, I would be forced to accept any story she told me. And I also got the feeling that I was safer not letting her know that Leonetti had recognized her. Instead, I would try to find out about her myself, and use the knowledge when the time was right.

I searched the place. There wasn't much to search, just the one main room with a small bathroom leading off it. In the hall I found a keyboard with the spares to all the apartments. We took the key to 4C and headed upstairs.

Yip Yip Martin's apartment was even smaller than the landlord's. It was at the rear, with a single dirty window giving onto the building on the other side, about three feet away. Even on the sunniest of days it must have been a wretchedly dismal place in which to live.

The bed was a strip of foam rubber lying on the wooden floor. An old sofa upholstered in frayed fabric was the lone seat in the place. There were no table and chairs. A sink in the corner with an ancient grease-caked gas ring beside it apparently constituted the kitchen. There were no dishes in the sink, just pizza boxes and Chinese take-out packages— Yip Yip had apparently eaten his meals straight from the container.

The small refrigerator held nothing but beer and a lone milk carton whose contents had turned solid days ago.

There was no television or radio or stereo, perhaps because Yip Yip had apparently been an avid reader. The apartment was full of magazines, including *Locked & Loaded*, the magazine we had seen him reading in Little Washington. He had also subscribed to a number of biker magazines, of which *Bitchin' Babes & Bikes* was my favorite, although *Hogs & Hooters* was similarly erudite. A fading centerfold from an old edition of the former was the sole decoration on the wall. Finally there were the technical publications of his trade: *Interstate Trucker Monthly* looked to be the professional bible; *Rigs & Jugs* was less sober.

Everything personal was missing. There were no papers, no letters, no photographs—nothing that could have helped us. Even someone as innocuous as Yip Yip leaves a trail, unless someone else erases it.

Now I understood why they had been here tonight. With Yip Yip dead, they were ensuring that there was nothing left linking him to them. The landlord was an unexpected bonus. Somehow he had gotten himself in their way. Maybe he had asked them, as he had us, what we were doing there. Maybe he had even mentioned us, hoping to trade the information for cash. Instead, he had been signing his own death warrant.

At least the rats would have been pleased. We left the apartment.

It wasn't until we were out of the building and heading down the sidewalk that I thought of something, something important. I raced back to the landlord's basement. There were no small keys on the keyboard, but in one of the drawers there was a screwdriver which would do just as well. I went back up the stoop, and used the screwdriver to break the lock on 4C's mailbox.

My good luck was holding. The mailbox was jammed full, no doubt a result of Yip Yip's extended absence. The other people had not thought to check it. It was a mistake—not much of a mistake, but I needed to take advantage of every break I got. With this little treasure under my arm we walked up to the Village and found a late-night coffee shop. We ordered, then examined Yip Yip Martin's mail.

There were some mail-order catalogues, but few for a

modern American mailbox. I guessed that Yip Yip didn't make it onto many retailers' target lists. The latest *Hogs & Hooters* was in, as was *Interstate Trucker Monthly,* featuring hot tips for avoiding weigh stations along the I-95 corridor. Most of the letters were bills and the like. His teamsters union membership was past due, but the other bills—Con Ed, Verizon, a trucking firm account—showed no unpaid balances brought forward. There was even a credit card statement, evidence of how, in their usurious frenzy to get their Shylockian claws into as many people as possible, America's banks had become the world's least discriminating lenders.

Only one piece of mail was personal. It was a card, a birthday card, whose front picture featured an overdressed woman with cat's-eye glasses frantically playing a slot machine. The caption inside was "Hope you hit the jackpot on your birthday." Below this, in a childish ballpoint scrawl, were just two words: *Love, Olga.*

The sentiment tied in with the rest of the evidence: as Leonetti had made clear, Yip Yip Martin had been a man with great expectations. And whatever it was, his girlfriend had wanted to wish him luck with it on his birthday. Instead his birthday present had turned out to be a trio of .38 slugs, fired by a woman who just happened to frequent the club at which he was a bouncer. Fired by the woman sitting across the table from me.

The envelope was more revealing. Olga had stuck a return address sticker on the top left-hand corner. Her last name was Gudren. I could see by the little symbol on the sticker that it was from a charity, one that includes sheets of the stickers with their solicitation letters, hoping that the recipient will feel obliged to give in return.

The postmark was dated a week earlier. I studied the other postmarks, and they confirmed what the landlord had already told us: Martin had not been home for two weeks. I wondered if Olga was an easy mark, to have made it onto the charity's mailing list. Her address was in Chelsea, just above the Village. Valentina and I decided to go and find out for ourselves. We paid the bill and left.

Olga's neighborhood was even less salubrious than her boyfriend's. Her building was on the far West Side, jammed between a cab company and an auto repair shop near Eleventh Avenue. The cab company, which presumably never closed, was not the only enterprise still active at this late hour. The sidewalks were patrolled by several women wearing more makeup than clothing, and they needed all the makeup they could get.

We entered the building. Olga's apartment was, like Yip Yip's, a fourth-floor walk-up. I knocked on the door. There was no response. I knocked again, louder this time, but with the same result. I tried the door handle, with more hope than expectation, for there were two locks on the door.

It opened. My luck was still holding.

Once again I reached behind me, and felt the gun placed in my hand. We were getting used to this routine. I checked the weapon, went to a two-handed grip, kicked the door fully open, and sprang inside.

Olga Gudren was in. At least I assumed it was Olga, hanging from the end of a rope, strung from an overhead sprinkler pipe.

"You can come in," I said.

Valentina entered, shut the door behind her, and stood beside me. She said nothing; there was nothing to say. The body gently swayed in the air. We stared at it in silence, avoiding the overturned chair underneath. It was not rope she had hanged herself with, it was telephone cable, doubled up for strength. I could see where it had been ripped away from the wall. Under the weight of the body it had gradually torn through the throat, finally coming to a halt against the hard cartilage of the larynx.

"Your friends have had a busy night," Valentina eventually said.

"No," I said, "not this one."

"How can you tell?"

But she sniffed before I could reply, and discovered the answer herself. Above the stale odor of cigarettes and cheap perfume, there was the faint semisweet smell of meat that has been left out of the refrigerator a little too long. Olga had hanged herself days ago.

"I don't get it," she said.

"Neither do I," I admitted. "Let's look around."

There wasn't much in the apartment. On one side was a narrow camp bed with dirty sheets. There was a bowl of prophylactics on the bedside table, and a tube of lubricating gel. At least Olga hadn't had a long commute to work.

The most interesting thing was on the wall: a poster which was identical to the centerfold that had adorned Yip Yip Martin's apartment. Below this, occupying pride of place on top of a dresser, was a picture frame. It contained a fifteen-year-old copy of *Bitchin' Babes & Bikes,* from which the centerfold had apparently come, and the cover of which featured a photo of the same woman.

I opened the frame and thumbed through the magazine. The pages were yellow with age. There were more pictures of the woman, one draped awkwardly across the motorbike seat; another leaning over the handlebars, large sagging breasts swinging underneath. The only thing that redeemed the layout from complete hideousness was the woman's smile. She had been an enthusiastic model—like a little girl, she had been delighted to be the center of attention.

This had apparently been Olga Gudren's moment in the

sun, and it was obvious that she had enjoyed her Warholian fifteen minutes. The framed magazine was an altar to the memory. Perhaps it was her way of recalling a distant but happy past, a time when she had still believed herself to be beautiful.

There was a photograph wedged into the side of the mirror. It showed Olga and Yip Yip posing on a big Harley, and another man beside them on his own bike, all three smiling for the camera. The third man wore an eye patch. I took the photograph and put it in my pocket.

Laid out on top of the dresser, beside the frame, were a dozen or so small animals made from cut crystal. There was a puppy, a penguin, a smiling teddy bear. Olga must have collected them. It occurred to me that this apartment would have been a sad enough place without the body.

I'd had my fill of violence ten years ago. By then I had learned that all people are violent—the timid most of all, if given the chance. So when you've had your fill, the only cure is solitude, and that's what I'd chosen when leaving Leavenworth. Even before, while still in prison, I'd been left alone: other prisoners keep clear of someone who's in for nearly beating another man to death. Even murderers— there's a world of difference between shooting someone, and using nothing but your bare hands.

I yearned to be back in Virginia now, in my own home, among my own fields, away from all of this. I yearned to be left alone. If only it were possible.

I looked again at the naked body swinging from the rope. Flabby gray-white skin, except at the ankles and feet where the blood had pooled, blackening the flesh. The face was unrecognizable as that of the girl in the centerfold— grossly distorted now, with the eyes almost bulging out of their sockets—but as I looked closer I realized that the face had probably become unrecognizable long before.

I continued searching the apartment, and soon found the confirmation I had expected. The hypodermic was in a drawer below the frame. There was also a spoon and a candle, plus several foil packets.

I went back for a closer look at Olga, and eventually discovered what I took for needle marks, but on the ankle, of all places. Perhaps she liked to go sleeveless.

Up until then I was willing to assume that Olga Gudren had hanged herself. But the presence of the foil packets was a mistake, perhaps an error of judgment made by someone too engrossed in the theatrics of the setup to have realized the obvious: no drug addict commits suicide when there is a supply at hand.

And now I understood why the door had been unlocked. It would have looked suspicious had the corpse been found without her keys, otherwise how could she have entered the apartment? So they'd had to leave them behind.

"You were right," I said. "Olga was murdered, but they wanted to make it look like suicide." I explained about the heroin and keys.

"What does it mean?" Valentina asked.

"It means they would have killed Yip Yip themselves, if you hadn't done it for them."

"How do you figure that?"

"Because they killed his girlfriend. And why do that?"

"Same reason they killed the landlord: to stop her talking to you."

"No. Olga has been dead several days."

"Maybe just a day."

"I know how long it takes a body to rot. Even in the humidity of a jungle, it takes several days to get like this."

"You're saying they killed her before going after you?"

"Yes."

"But why?"

"Because Yip Yip was never going to live. They were always going to kill him, once his part was over. And they must have assumed that he had told his girlfriend what they were up to, so they took the precaution of killing her, too, in case she got talkative."

There was nothing more to see. We left the apartment and walked in silence back toward Midtown. The first light was beginning to appear in the eastern sky, above the distant skyscrapers. At the time we had found it, I had thought the discovery of Olga's address fortunate, but the lead had turned out to be a dead end. Literally dead, in this case. I had that sick feeling of a man who knows that his luck has finally run out.

NINE

WE had room service deliver breakfast the next morning. Continental—neither of us had much of an appetite. I ordered a large pot of coffee, something with which to wash away the taste of the previous evening. Neither of us said much.

Valentina disappeared into the bathroom. I examined Yip Yip Martin's mail again, starting with the credit card account. All the entries were from gas stations, identified as Mobil, Amoco, Exxon, and so on, along with their locations. All were dated from before he had disappeared, presumably a record of refueling during a recent trucking job, probably his last.

I looked at the amounts. Those big eighteen-wheelers use a lot of fuel.

I studied the trucking firm account next. The company was called Jim's Truck Rentals. According to the logo it was "The Independent Trucker's Favorite Place to Rent a Rig." They were located in Lodi, New Jersey. The dates matched the credit card statement.

I heard the shower start. It was the sound I had been waiting for. I put Yip Yip's mail aside and went to the telephone. The first call I made was to the operator in the 202 area code—Washington, D.C. I asked for the number to the law firm of Tate, Tate & Buchanan. A moment of silence, then the operator came back on the line to ask me for an address, from which I assumed she couldn't locate the number. In other words, the firm was fictional.

"I don't have an address," I said. "Just Washington, D.C."

Another moment of silence, then an automated voice came on the line with a number. So there was a Tate, Tate & Buchanan after all. Valentina hadn't lied about that much, but it didn't mean that she really worked for them.

I dialed the number. A receptionist answered. "Tate, Tate & Buchanan," she said, in a broad west Texas drawl. She was a long way from home.

"Valentina Mariposa, please."

"One moment."

I was left on hold. A minute later, the receptionist came back on the line.

"I'm sorry, she's not in today. Would you like to leave a message?"

"No, thanks, that's fine."

So there was not only a real Tate, Tate & Buchanan, there was even a real Valentina Mariposa. It didn't necessarily mean that she was the same Valentina Mariposa as was currently in the shower.

I hung up, then dialed the operator in the 540 area code, my own. I asked the automated voice for the number to Marius Preston, in Rappahannock County. I had no address but doubted there would be more than one Marius Preston. The automated voice soon gave me the number.

I hung up, then dialed.

The maid answered. "The Preston residence," she said.

I said nothing.

"The Preston residence," she repeated. "May I help you?"

Still I said nothing.

The maid tried one last time but, getting no response, simply hung up.

I sat there for a few minutes, Louis Quinze receiver still in hand, and tried to figure the odds of both a receptionist in a Washington law firm (in the 202 area code) and a maid in a Virginian estate (in the 540 area code) having precisely the same voice, right down to that same flat west Texas drawl.

The more I found out about Valentina Mariposa, the less I knew. I needed facts, something solid to use as an anchor. The American Express card was a fact. I noted down the number and expiration date on one of the Plaza's notepads.

The gun was a fact, too. I checked out the thigh holster, looking to see if there was a manufacturer's name, but I could find none. Custom made, no doubt. I would like to have been the person taking the measurements.

I picked up the gun and examined it closely for the first time. It was a Beretta, .22-caliber as I had guessed. The short barrel could be opened like a shotgun, allowing rounds to be placed directly into the breach, which meant that the weapon could be loaded without having to pull back the slide against the heavy return spring: a woman's weapon. Of course it also meant that the weapon could be loaded noiselessly: an assassin's weapon. I noted down the serial number, for what it was worth.

I heard the bathroom door open, and quickly replaced the weapon.

Valentina came out. She was wearing only a towel. She saw me staring at her, and smiled.

"Can I help you?" she asked.

"Yes, you can," I said.

"And how may I do that, sir?"

"Reveal thyself, madam."

She curtsied in compliance, and dropped the towel. It wasn't exactly what I'd meant, but I wasn't going to argue.

It was after ten by the time I got to the shower. When I came out, Valentina was gone. She returned to the suite while I was dressing, shopping bags in hand, but this time among the Bergdorf bags there was one from Barnes & Noble. She had bought a road atlas of the United States.

"Are we going somewhere?" I asked.

She sat in an armchair.

"Did you have a close look at Yip Yip's credit card statement?" she asked.

"Yes."

"What conclusion did you reach?"

"All of the charges were for gas. Or, to be precise, diesel fuel."

"Anything else?"

"Presumably from his last trucking job," I continued. "He could have used the latest copy of *Interstate Trucker Monthly,* the one with the article for avoiding I-95 weigh stations. All the refueling stops were located in the Northeast Corridor."

"And anything else?"

I tried to think.

"Those big rigs get lousy mileage?" was the best I could manage.

But this answer seemed to please her. "Exactly," she said, in the voice of a teacher relieved that the dull kid was finally starting to get it. "That's precisely the conclusion I came to myself." She opened the road atlas and took out a calculator from the shopping bag. "Let's figure out how lousy, shall we?"

"Okay."

"First, we'll plot all the refueling locations on this map. Start from the top."

I did so, picking up the credit card statement and reading off the first entry, a Phillips 66 in Connecticut. Half an hour later we had charted all the entries, and were able to deduce the route Yip Yip had taken on his last trucking job. He had gone north on I-95 all the way to Boston, then west on the Massachusetts Turnpike before turning south on I-91 as far as Hartford, thence west again on I-84 until it connected with the New York State Thruway, which he had apparently taken back down to the city. Presumably he had finally dropped the truck back in Lodi.

We didn't really need the calculator, for there were far more stops than such a trip could have required. Some of the gas stations were less than ten miles apart, yet each refueling had been for hundreds of dollars' worth of diesel.

Valentina continued with the calculations nevertheless. We added up all the credit card charges, and divided the sum by our best guess at what diesel costs per gallon, arriving at a total amount of diesel purchased on the trip. Next we had to figure out how many of those gallons had actually been used. I read out mileages from the map while Valentina entered them into the calculator. Yip Yip's last trip had been 560 miles in length, including the pick-up and drop-off in Lodi.

We needed to get an idea of what a big rig's fuel consumption was like. I looked through the copy of *Interstate Trucker Monthly* and found a detailed road test of the latest Freightliner, which included fuel consumption under various load conditions. Even assuming a big load, it seemed unlikely that Yip Yip would have gotten less than four miles to the gallon. So, at most, he would have consumed around 140 gallons. From the credit card statements, we calculated that he had purchased nearly a thousand. What happened to the other eight hundred or so gallons?

"Any ideas?" Valentina asked.

"The fuel had to go somewhere. He didn't just pump it over the ground."

"A bad fuel leak?"

"He would have gotten it fixed," I said.

I picked up the account from the trucking firm. Besides the tractor—a Peterbilt—Yip Yip had rented a trailer, identified only by a serial number.

I picked up the phone and dialed the trucking firm. It would have been good if Valentina could have listened in, but the unit had no speakerphone capability. You forget how primitive things were back in Louis XV's time.

An operator answered on the first ring, a real human one. Jim's Truck Rentals was an old-fashioned business.

"I have a question about an account," I said.

"Do you have the invoice?"

"Yes."

"Can I have the account number?" the operator said. "Top left-hand corner."

I read it out loud, and could hear her tapping on a keyboard as I spoke.

"Mr. Martin?" she asked.

"Yes," I lied.

"Okay, how can I help you?"

"I want to check the type of trailer you have on the invoice."

"What's the invoice number?"

I gave her that, too. More tapping.

"I show that as a stainless steel, single-chamber, five-thousand-gallon diesel tanker."

"Good, that's what I have, too" I said. "I just wanted to check."

"Thank you for calling Jim's Truck Rentals," she replied, her voice betraying relief that there wasn't a problem. "Is there anything else I can help you with today, Mr. Martin?"

"No, that's it."

"And is your current rig satisfactory?"

"Current rig?"

"Yes, Mr. Martin," she confirmed, an edge of concern returning to her voice. I could tell she regretted having asked. "The computer shows you as having one of our Mack CH602s, plus a twin-bogie flatbed trailer, rigged for containers."

I had no idea what "twin-bogie" was, apart from something bad in golf. I wasn't going to raise her suspicions by asking.

"Yes, that's right," I said. "The rig's just fine. Thanks for your help."

"And thank you for calling Jim's Truck Rentals," she said again. I hung up, and told Valentina what the woman had told me.

"I'd like to find that truck," she said when I'd finished.

"Me, too," I agreed.

She was silent for a while before speaking again.

"I have no clue what to do from here," she said. "Do you have any ideas?"

"Just one," I said.

"What is it?"

In reply, I pulled out the photograph I had taken from Olga's mirror, and passed it to Valentina.

"Well?"

"It shows three people," I said.

"Olga, Yip Yip and some third person."

"Yes."

"So how does this help us?"

"I know the third person," I admitted.

She was obviously surprised, and I could see her wondering why I hadn't told her this before. It was a long story, and it seemed that the time had come to tell it.

Everyone knows that the marine corps is strong on discipline. And everyone knows that the marine corps takes a very dim view of striking a superior officer. What is less well known is that the marine corps takes an equally dim view of striking an *inferior* officer. That's what I did. I was subsequently court-martialed and dishonorably discharged, but not before spending six months in Leavenworth, an all-expenses-paid guest of Uncle Sam.

The inferior officer I hit was the third person in the photograph. His name was Luke Trainor. He was the sergeant in my company's Charlie platoon.

Luke Trainor was what the general public imagine when they think of the special forces. He was a big man, well over six feet tall, with arms brought to bulk through heavy bench presses and, judging from the bulging veins which give away their use, artificial steroids. His manner fitted the type: a loud-talking bragger, barely concealing the bully beneath.

The general public's conception is wrong. What we look for in a special forces' recruit is physical endurance and mental toughness, two qualities that are rarely found in either loudmouths or bodybuilders. The truth is that Arnold Schwarzenegger probably wouldn't make it through the first week of special forces' training. That's no knock on Arnie; few people would make it through a week of special forces' training.

Nevertheless Trainor had, and I was stuck with him. I assigned him to Charlie platoon because my most experienced troops were there. The newer guys tended to be awed by Trainor's size and bravado. The seasoned guys weren't fooled at all.

We were sent on a mission to the Philippines. The second largest of the Philippine islands is Mindanao. There had been a rebel movement operating on this island for two generations. During the bad old days of the Marcos regime, when half the country's gross domestic product had been spent buying shoes for Imelda, the rebels had gained widespread support. But since the fall of the dictator and the advent of democracy, people no longer needed to fight for their rights with guns. Now they had the ballot box instead. Over the years the rebels' support had evaporated.

But these particular rebels were Islamic fundamentalists. If the peasantry no longer welcomed them, they didn't much care, because Allah was still on their side. They were happy to coerce support that would not have been given freely, and the coercing had become very violent indeed— so violent that the government in Manila had lost control, and didn't know what to do about it. Finally they placed a 911 call to Washington. A week later we were rolling down the strip in a C-130, about to drop into Mindanao on a sweep mission whose details would never be acknowledged by the Pentagon. Officially, we were simply "military advisors." It's a term that covers a thousand sins.

It didn't take long to do the job—soldiers who slaughter unarmed civilians are not soldiers but cowards. When it was over, I took the company out of the jungle and down to a village on a bay. We bivouacked on the beach. I intended to give my people a few days unofficial R & R before calling in a MAC flight to take us out.

The villagers were more than happy to have us there. To

them it seemed that we were heavenly saviors—almost literally, as we had dropped out the sky itself. I thought it was a good idea to let the troops enjoy a little hero worship, because a public pat on the back for a job well done would never be given back home.

And so it was, one night. I was in my tent, finishing the report, when one of the troops hurried in.

"There's a delegation of villagers here, sir. I think you'd better come."

I put on my cap and went down to the front gate of the compound we'd wired off. There was indeed a delegation, obviously distressed, also angry. They were chattering in Tagalog, and I couldn't understand what they were saying. The women were crying.

I thought we had killed all the rebels in my sector, but from their behavior I guessed it was not the case, and that they had come to report another attack. My first thought was relief that I hadn't yet called for air transport, because it looked like we would be going back into the jungle. But then an old man came forward. He spoke a little English.

Yes, there had been an attack, he said. But not rebels. The attack had come from us.

A girl was solemnly brought forward. She couldn't have been older than twelve. She had been badly beaten. Her faced was so puffed on one side that her eye was not visible. Blood trickled from her mouth and ears. Some of her hair had been physically torn from her scalp. She held one arm at an awkward angle, obviously broken. She must have been in great pain, but she was the only female not crying. Apparently she was too shocked for tears.

I sent one of the guards for the medic then asked what had happened. According to the old man, one of my men had raped her.

I only had one question: Who?

The big one, the old man had said, the big one who wears the three stripes. I was suddenly very relieved.

The villagers of Mindanao are poor, and we had been briefed that they would try to extract money if they found an opportunity. I had never imagined that they would go so far as to badly beat one of their own children. But they'd made a mistake in picking Trainor, because I happened to know that Trainor was duty NCO that day. He was not allowed out of the compound. I turned to the other guard.

"Go and get Sergeant Trainor," I said. I intended to show him to the villagers, proving that he was here, and so innocent. But the soldier didn't move.

"Go and get Sergeant Trainor," I repeated.

He looked at the ground, and stayed where he was.

"Sir . . ." he said. He tried to say something more, but whatever it was got stuck in his throat. He was a young kid, had only been with us a few months. We were silent a moment.

"What is it?" I asked. But apparently he couldn't speak. "Look at me, soldier."

He looked up. He was very upset. You don't often see special forces soldiers upset, no matter how young they are. Something was eating this kid away.

"Well?"

He took a deep breath. "He's not here, sir."

"Where is he?"

"In the village." He took another deep breath, looked at the girl, then spat out what was on his mind. "He did it, sir."

"If you're on duty, how could you know that, unless you've been off base, too? Have you?"

"No, sir."

"Then how?"

A final deep breath. "It's not the first time," he said. I had no response to that. "He boasts about it, sir." And beneath this I could detect an unspoken rebuke: you're our commanding officer; you should have known. It's your business to know.

I told all this to Valentina. We were silent for a while. Eventually she asked me what happened next.

"I don't know," I admitted.

"How can you not know?"

"What I mean is I have no personal recollection. In fact I never really did get all the details straight. Apparently I walked down to the village. There was only one bar. Trainor was there with some of the younger soldiers, talking loudly. The Filipinos who served them cowered in the corner. The only part I remember is walking into that room. Trainor looked up and saw me. He smiled and said, 'Well, there go my stripes.' But he was going to lose a lot more than just stripes."

"And?"

"It wasn't until I read the medical reports submitted as evidence for the court-martial that I knew exactly what I'd done. I blinded him in one eye—gouged it right out, in fact. Compound fracture of the jaw. It was a year before he ate solid food again. Several cracked ribs, one of which pierced a lung. His hands were very bad. They said I'd deliberately stamped on them, to break as many bones as possible. I guess I wanted to make sure he wouldn't be handling any twelve-year-old girls again. Eventually they pulled me off him. One of the lieutenants called in a medevac for Trainor. And that's about it, I guess."

"What happened?"

"I was court-martialed."

I was court-martialed in Quantico, Virginia, which ended my career in the same place it had started: the USMC

Officer Candidate School is in Quantico. I could remember in between hearings looking at the school from the brig, and thinking that if the man who had been a cadet there had met me today, he would have found a stranger.

"What happened to Trainor?" Valentina asked.

"He survived."

"I mean was he court-martialed? Did he go to prison?"

"No."

"No?"

"The marines never took any action against him. Not even for being AWOL."

"What are you talking about? How can that be?"

I took a deep breath, and explained it as calmly as I could. "If I'd kept my temper that day, if I'd just charged Trainor and initiated an inquiry, then the process would have had him. They'd have flown people in, interviewed witnesses, had a formal medical examination for the girl, built a case and put him away. But from their point of view all they had was a mission which had fallen apart and whose commander had turned rogue. Their first priority was to get everyone out, which is what they did. At the time they didn't even know whether Trainor would survive. By the time they started an investigation the girl wasn't talking, or at least her family wasn't letting her. Even when they did, what was the use? He'd been nearly beaten to death by his commanding officer. On top of that, since we were supposed to be 'military advisors,' the mission itself was technically illegal. They wouldn't have been unhappy for an excuse to just let it alone."

I was angry again. I was always angry when I remembered it. Angry at the marines, but angrier at myself for being the basic reason Trainor had gotten away with it. I'd reached the point now where sometimes whole weeks would go by when I wouldn't think about it. But that was rare.

"They should have given you a medal," Valentina said, "not put you in prison."

"The marines don't work that way. You don't strike junior officers."

"The circumstances were mitigating. They should have at least suspended the sentence."

"That's what my counsel said."

"Why didn't they?"

"During the trial I gave no testimony. When it came time for sentencing, the judge-advocate told me to stand. He asked me if I regretted what I'd done. I said that yes, I regretted it very much. He nodded sympathetically, but I never know when to shut up. I said I regretted that I hadn't killed the bastard, but hoped to get an opportunity to correct that mistake in the future. That put an end to any suspended sentence."

Valentina laughed. It was a good laugh, and I laughed, too.

"And I thought I was the one with a bad temper," Valentina said. "Your parents should have named you Achilles, not Lysander."

She picked up the picture and studied it in silence for a few moments.

"Still think this whole thing is a case of mistaken identity?"

"No," I admitted. "Not anymore."

"So what now?"

"We find Luke Trainor."

"How?"

"Look him up in the phone book."

"What phone book?"

"Look at the picture again," I said.

She did so. It took her a minute to find it. The license

plates on the motorbikes were small, but legible. The bike on which Olga and Yip Yip sat had New York plates. The other one's were different.

"The ocean state?" she asked, reading the motto.

"Rhode Island," I said. "Can't be many area codes in Rhode Island. If he's listed, we'll get an address soon enough."

She nodded, then looked from the photo to me. "And when we find him?"

"We question him."

"And then?"

"And then," I said, "I correct the mistake."

She nodded. It was the answer she had been expecting.

TEN

RHODE Island is not an island but an approximate rectangle of land about fifty miles long and thirty miles broad, wedged in between Connecticut and Massachusetts. It is the smallest state, and has a total population less than even minor cities like Portland or Cincinnati. It has a single area code, 401, and in that area code there was listed only one L. Trainor, with an address in Newport.

I called the number, intending to hang up if Trainor answered, or to ask for "Luke" if someone else did. Instead I got an answering machine. I recognized the voice on the tape immediately. It was unchanged, as far as I could tell, in the ten years since I had last heard it, bemoaning the impending loss of his stripes. Trainor's jaw must have healed just fine.

We took a late-morning Amtrak train from Grand Central up to Providence. Newport is thirty miles away from

Providence, and when we arrived at the train station, Valentina wanted to simply take a cab. But I feared that a cabdriver might remember such a fat fare. We decided to take a bus instead, and spent the hour before its departure searching for a gun store. We found one, and I bought a box of .22 ammunition, preferring my reunion with Luke Trainor to be performed with a full magazine—and with one in the chamber for good measure.

We arrived at Newport in the afternoon. The robber barons of America's Gilded Age had chosen this town for their summer escape, the location of their so-called "cottages," and it was easy to see why. Newport is situated on a pretty peninsula surrounded on three sides by water, which provides not only plenty of space for the rich to display their latest yachts, but was also the best way to keep cool in the pre-air-conditioning summers of the nineteenth century. So it was today, the sky perfectly cloudless, and a summer sun which would have been oppressive if not for the fresh breeze blowing in off Narragansett Bay, just sufficient to keep the heat from becoming uncomfortable.

But the robber barons were long gone, and Newport had embalmed itself with their memory in order to become a sort of Gilded Age theme park. The cottages were the main attraction, where the envious could gape and drool in organized tours. Downtown, flocks of tourists twittered and clucked through stores that sold questionable antiques, or "nautical" items that had never been near any ship. At least the fishing boats were genuine, lining the wharves and already unloading the day's catch.

There was a tourist center. We took one of the maps and located Ochre Point Avenue, the address that the operator had given me. It was on the far side of town, by the Atlantic-facing eastern shore. We began walking.

Seagulls soared above us. We came to the top of a hill

and spotted the Atlantic for the first time. There were a dozen or so sails in the distance, all converging on a distant buoy; obviously an offshore yacht race. We were clear of the tourists now, and the breeze was fresher up here, cleaner, sweeping away my foul mood. I liked the feel of the sun on my face, the wind in my clothes, the fact that Valentina was beside me. It was almost a pity to spoil the day by shooting someone.

We arrived at the address. I had expected a hovel, something akin to Yip Yip's place in New York. Instead, we found ourselves facing the best address in Newport. It was the Breakers, a famous mansion that is the most opulent of all the summer cottages.

I checked the piece of paper on which I had written the address. There was no mistake: it was the same street number. Valentina and I looked at each other, then burst out laughing. I realized that there would be no shooting today.

There was a sign giving tour times.

"Since we're here," I said, nodding at the sign.

Valentina put her arm through mine. "Show me how the other half lives, Lysander Dalton."

We bought two tickets and joined the next guided tour.

The house was a Vanderbilt mansion. Our tour guide was Traci. She was about eighteen. Traci dutifully took a score or so of us through the house, urging us to marvel at the ornate decoration. The Commodore, having begun with nothing and ended up America's richest man, had decided to acquire the best heritage that money could buy: the palaces of Europe had been stripped to furnish the Breakers. In the dining room Traci carefully enumerated the astronomical cost of the banquets that had been held there, and in which the menus had obviously been selected not for their food but for their expense. She pointed out an old sepia photograph of Vanderbilt and his fellow plutocrats, fat men on fat chairs, sitting around the massive dining table that was still in the room. They had garlanded themselves with laurel wreaths for the occasion, apparently in the belief that their checkbooks had turned them into Caesars. The undiscriminating Traci saw not the least hint of vulgarity in this excess, and betrayed no irony when describing the various wretched indulgences that were scattered throughout the rest of the house.

By the end of the tour I was in a sour mood again. I was pretty sure that the architect of Monticello would have found little to admire in this house. I wished I could find Trainor, for I was now in a suitable mood to shoot someone. It was while thinking about the photograph of him with Olga and Yip Yip that I suddenly realized that the honey-colored stone in the background of that picture was familiar. The Breakers was made from honey-colored stone.

"Traci," I said, when we had been invited to ask any questions before concluding the tour, "how do you protect all these valuable things?"

Traci assured me that this was a very good question. There was a state-of-the-art security system, she said. And besides, they had a caretaker who lived there permanently.

"In the house?" I asked.

"Oh, no," she said, horrified by the thought. "He lives in the old groundskeeper's cottage."

The tour ended on the porch overlooking the lawn, with the ocean beyond. We were invited to walk around the grounds as much as we liked. Valentina and I strolled down to the cliff's edge. We sat on a stone wall, legs dangling over the side. The Atlantic breakers that had given the house its name rolled in below.

"You think Trainor's the caretaker?" Valentina asked.

"It's a better bet than the phone company having somehow gotten the wrong address," I said. I handed her the photograph. "Besides, doesn't that background look familiar?"

Valentina looked at the house then back to the picture before nodding. She returned the photograph, reached under her dress, and took out the .22.

"I guess you'll need this."

I took it, ejected the magazine, and removed the slide, partially dismantling the weapon. The gas cylinder, which takes blast pressure from a fired round to reload and recock, was below the barrel. I turned the thumbscrew, increasing the pressure.

"Sacrificing range for reliability?" Valentina asked. She knew her weapon better than most gun owners did.

"Yes," I admitted. "It'll be close work. The most important thing is that the gun doesn't jam."

I replaced the slide, pulled the action to the rear, and thumbed a round into the breech before allowing the ejector port to close. I slid the magazine back home and put the weapon in my pocket. A full clip and one in the spout: eight rounds, which should be more than enough.

"Let's find the groundskeeper's cottage," I said.

We strolled around the gardens, trying to look tourist-like. There were some rose beds which I would have taken the time to examine more closely if I wasn't preoccupied. Most of the male sightseers were more interested in the sight of Valentina.

What I took to be the caretaker's cottage was in the corner of the estate, surrounded by trees to hide it from view of the main house, and with an eight-foot-high brick wall to keep out the tourists. This was pierced with a double gate, large enough to drive a small vehicle through, and faced in green sheet metal on which the words "Private, No Admittance" were painted in white.

I looked for a video camera or other security apparatus, but could see none. The state-of-the-art security system was apparently reserved for the house itself.

I grabbed the top of the wall, wedged the edge of my shoes between the bricks, and managed to get myself up on top. I turned and helped Valentina come up beside me. No one noticed us as far as I could tell. We dropped quietly onto the other side.

It was a small L-shaped courtyard, with the cottage as the interior two sides, the brick wall we had just scaled as the exterior two, and the big stone wall that surrounded the entire estate sealing the ends of the L. It was a pleasant spot, a private little leaf-covered domain cut off from the outside world. A single lounge chair lay in a sunny corner, and under the overhanging branches of a massive elm there was a small, round cast-iron table, again with a single chair. One thing was clear: Trainor did not receive many visitors.

There was no sign of the motorbike, although I could see the oil stain and tire marks where it was normally parked.

I took out the weapon and thumbed off the safety.

"Can you whistle?" I asked quietly.

"No," Valentina replied.

"No?"

"Not a note."

"What about birdcalls?"

"Do I look like an Indian scout?"

"Okay then, you suggest something."

She considered for a moment. "I'm an excellent yo-deler," she claimed.

"Yodeler?"

"One year when I was in school we put on *The Sound of Music*. I did all the yodeling." That made for an interesting mental picture.

"Okay," I said. "You stand watch. If you hear a motor-bike coming, yodel."

"No problem."

"But do it subtly."

"Okay," she said.

I approached the cottage. It was brick, same as the wall, with small windows and a single door giving onto the court-yard. The two windows at the front and one at the side were all curtained, and I could see nothing inside. I listened at the door, and heard no sound from within. I knocked. No response. I knocked again, waited a minute, then went to a window and used the butt of the gun to smash one of the panes. I reached in, unlatched the frame, and was soon inside the cottage.

Luke Trainor had learned at least one thing from the marines: neatness. His cottage was as orderly as a barracks on inspection day. There were just three rooms: the living room I had entered, which from the single bed on the side obviously also served as bedroom; and a small bathroom and narrow kitchen, both leading off the main room.

I surveyed the place cautiously, for Trainor knew well how to disguise a booby trap. But there was nothing like that, indeed no more security than the lock on the front door. There were no windows or doors giving directly onto the street. Perhaps he assumed that the walled grounds pro-vided security enough, and that if anyone did intrude onto the estate their target would likely be the mansion itself, not his modest cottage.

In fact the security had not even extended to locking up the weaponry. I found a shotgun in the corner by the bed. It was a pump-action Remington 20-gauge, a model that had already been manufactured to be lightweight, but whose heft had been further reduced after purchase. The barrel was sawn off just short of the stock; the butt was completely gone, replaced by a pistol grip. Trainor had turned a hunting gun into a concealed weapon.

I unloaded the five rounds, tested the action, reloaded, and went outside.

Valentina was standing beside the gate, where she would have been hidden had it suddenly swung open.

"I found a shotgun," I said. "You should take the .22."

She dropped the gardening shears she had equipped herself with, and accepted her own weapon.

"What now?"

"I'm going to go through the place. Mind staying on watch?"

"No, I'll get some sun." She walked toward the lounge chair, unzipping her dress as she did so. Apparently Valentina didn't like tan lines. I returned to the cottage while I could still concentrate.

I began with the desk that stood under one of the front windows. In the top drawer I found a large clip holding Trainor's pay stubs. The most recent one was a double pay packet. In addition to the usual amount he had received two weeks' vacation pay, which accounted for his absence. Trainor didn't earn much, but I guessed that the cottage came rent free, and so he didn't need to. Utilities were probably included as well, as I could find no gas or electricity bills. There was just one phone bill, the most recent, with nothing but local calls. But there were a lot of local calls, and from the presence of the computer on the desk I guessed that Trainor spent a lot of time on the Internet.

I hooked up the modem, switched on the computer, found the Internet icon, and tried to log on, intending to examine Trainor's e-mail. But the opening graphics demanded a password, and after trying a dozen or so obvious examples without success I gave up and shut down the program.

Another drawer contained floppy discs. I put the first of them into the disc drive and examined the contents. None of the file names meant anything to me, but they were all preceded by an Internet Explorer symbol, indicating that they were files downloaded from the web. I double-clicked on the first file and waited.

The disc drive buzzed and the hard drive whirred. The screen briefly went blank before an Internet navigation program slowly loaded. The disc drive buzzed some more, and finally an image emerged on the screen, an image that by now I was getting to know well.

It was Olga's centerfold, the familiar drooping breasts and big smile, draped across the same motorbike. I opened the rest of the files. They were all photographs of Olga, all part of the same set, but including pictures that I could not recall from *Bitchin' Babes & Bikes'* original layout. Apparently the physical restrictions of the magazine didn't apply to cyberspace, and the Internet had given new life to the fifteen-year-old photographs. Perhaps the magazine, wanting to generate extra cash from old material, had sold them to an Internet publisher.

The pictures further confirmed what the photograph on Olga's mirror had already suggested: Trainor had been friends with Olga and Yip Yip. Presumably they had met through a mutual interest in motorbikes, although perhaps it was through a mutual interest in Olga.

I put the second disc into the drive. This, too, had Internet downloads, just three files. I opened all three. They were from a single website, which offered a location and direction service—you enter the address, they produce the maps.

The first map showed the mid-Atlantic states from New York as far south as Richmond. A red target graticule was over northern Virginia, and the website's suggested route was highlighted in neon yellow. This showed I-95 from New

York down to Washington, then the Beltway around to I-66.

The second map was more detailed, to refine the route nearer the end of the journey. It covered northern Virginia and western Maryland, with Washington, D.C., at the right-hand edge. This one had highways in addition to the inter-states, and Interstate-66 from the Beltway to U.S.-211 was highlighted.

The third map was the most detailed of all. It showed Rappahannock County, and any route big enough to warrant a number, even a county number. The highlighted route ended at the red target graticule that apparently indicated the precise location of the researched address.

The target graticule was right over my house.

Strange to be a target, having spent so many years pur-suing targets myself. And strange to think of Trainor hav-ing sat here looking at these same images, nurturing a hatred ten years old, slowly plotting his revenge.

So Trainor knew how to hold a grudge. That was okay; I knew how to hold one, too. But where had all the firepower come from? Why had he needed it? And why now, ten years later? It didn't make sense.

I went to the third disc. More pictures this time, but sev-eral orders of magnitude above Olga's. The woman in these photographs was genuinely beautiful, and obviously a model, as some of the photographs were covers from well-known fashion magazines. She had chestnut hair, matching eyes, and full lips that formed a permanent pout. I went through the photographs one-by-one, hoping for some clue as to her identity—although on second thought it was unlikely to be helpful, as presumably Trainor was simply an anonymous fan. At least that was what I thought for the first dozen or so images. But then I came to photo-graphs that were no longer covers.

The first was a shot of the same model in a wedding

dress, although the wedding dress was the sort of outrageous haute couture creation more often seen on a runway than at a real wedding. She was holding a bouquet of roses, which I recognized as pink Celestes and crimson Avernos. Heaven and Hell: not exactly bridal. The setting was a huge penthouse with very high ceilings, a loft perhaps, postmodern in decor and, from the presence of the Chrysler Building's distinctive spire through a window in the background, obviously located in New York.

Subsequent photographs showed the model standing as erect and immobile as a mannequin, while the dress was ever increasingly torn from her body by a plethora of male and female hands. Underneath, she wore a patterned silk corset, lilac, with garters that held up seamed stockings of the same color, and a matching G-string. We were still in the world of high fashion, however tenuously, but that pretense ended with the subsequent photographs. In some she was bound and gagged, in others chained to the wall. There were more people than simply the model and photographer, for the room had mirrored walls, and in several of the photographs you could see reflected an audience of twenty or more people, young and affluent, the men dressed formally in dinner suits, the women in evening gowns, sitting in straight-backed chairs, and as quietly attentive to the proceedings as if attending a chamber recital.

The photographs were not explicitly hard-core, but there been no attempt at restrained modesty either. In one shot the model, handcuffed to a chromium frame, was being candidly entered by a dildo. In another she was being fondled by two female hands entering the shot from either side, obviously different women, each arm covered by an elbow-length satin glove, one pink, the other crimson, matching the roses.

Audience participation? The bridesmaids perhaps?

I inserted the fourth disc. There were few pictures here. Mostly they were downloads of texts from extreme right-wing political websites. There were the usual diatribes against immigrants, foreigners, blacks, abortionists, the United Nations, and that mysterious entity known as the "New World Order." Several of them were characterized with religious overtones, often with awkward biblical quotes intended to back up the bigotry. It was the sort of stuff that appeals to the weak-minded, especially to those weak-minded whose achievements fall short of their egos, and who are desperate for someone to blame.

It occurred to me that many people would regard the third disc as the pornographic one, but as I continued to wade through the virulent nonsense on the screen it seemed to me that it was this fourth disc which was best qualified for the title.

Trainor was a fool. He lived in the best address in Newport, had a steady income backed up with a lifetime pension from the marines; his job would not have been unpleasant, and was certainly undemanding. He had never been the overly ambitious type, and for all his faults I had not numbered bigotry among them. What could he want that these people offered?

I removed the disc and pocketed it with the other three before turning the computer off and continuing to search the desk.

In the next drawer I found a bulging manila envelope marked "Marines." Trainor's service papers were inside. They confirmed what I already knew: he had never been charged, with rape or anything else. There was a package of VA material, mainly health associated. Trainor had been given a glass eye after I had removed the original with my thumb that day, although judging from the photograph of him with Yip Yip and Olga, he obviously still wore an eye patch from time to time, probably from vanity. Strangely they had not given Trainor a medical discharge. He had been allowed to stay on, even to stay on with special forces, but with one eye it was as an instructor only, no longer a participant in real world operations. His discharge from the service had been at the end of his twenty—honorable, complete with pension. From the bulk of the medical paperwork I got the impression that Trainor had never fully recovered from that night in the Philippines. Good. I bet the young girl had never fully recovered, either.

The only thing in the bottom drawer was a box of 20-gauge ammunition. I opened it and filled my pockets.

That was it for the desk, apart from the telephone. An old-fashioned answering machine, the kind that uses big cassette tapes, was plugged into the base. There was a red light, blinking twice: two messages. I pressed *Play*.

The first one was disappointing, with no message at all, just someone having apparently dialed the wrong number, but who listened to the tape and waited for the tone before hanging up. The second was a brusque male voice who did not identify himself. The message was short, just an address in the Bowery accompanied by a terse instruction to be there at midnight next Friday. The answering machine was too old to have come with a date stamp feature. There was no way of knowing when the message was left, and so no way of knowing which Friday "next Friday" might have been.

The tone of the message was businesslike, but business meetings do not take place at midnight. Not legitimate ones anyway. I wondered if Trainor was supplementing his pension and caretaker's salary with something a little less than aboveboard.

Today was Tuesday. Perhaps the Friday in question was this coming Friday. I noted down the address.

On the wall above the desk was a calendar, compliments of a motorbike spare parts shop, and predictably featuring tattooed women draped over large Harleys. A black felt marker line had been drawn through a block of two weeks, marked "vacation," and corresponding to the vacation dates from Trainor's pay stubs. He had scrawled a reminder note to himself on the day before: "cancel newspaper."

On the mantelpiece was a framed photograph of Trainor in dress uniform, taken against a portrait studio background, the sort that gets published in the obituaries. Beside that was a display case filled with medals, like the one my mother had given me.

There was a second framed photo. This one showed Trainor and Easy Black, and someone else whose back was turned to the camera. It was an unposed shot. They were inside a big mess tent, sitting on bench seats either side of a table. Both were wearing dress blues, or had been. Whatever the event was that had required dress uniform—a parade most likely—it was over. Their jackets were off and they were wearing just T-shirts and their dress trousers, one-and-a-half-inch red stripes down the side. Easy Black had a beer in hand, Trainor's was on the table. Both were laughing. Easy was looking at Trainor, same old wide smile on his face. Trainor had his head back, obviously having enjoyed whatever he'd just heard. Two soldiers kicking back after a dress parade. I tried to recall the occasion, looking for some clue in the background, but it was just an anonymous mess tent, and it could have been anywhere.

Trainor was not particularly photogenic, but it was a good shot nevertheless, the sort the recruiters would like to use in their advertising material. The caption would be something like "Make friends for life."

Of all the things in the room, this disturbed me the most. I'm not sure why, perhaps it was the very ordinariness of the thing, the seemingly good-natured kidding around of two guys after the work gets done. But one of the guys was a pedophile and a rapist.

The rest of the cottage yielded little. I found Trainor's old uniforms at the back of the closet, sergeant's stripes and special forces' insignia still attached. There were empty coat hangers there, too, confirming that Trainor had gone away for his vacation. Like Yip Yip's apartment, Trainor's refrigerator contained mostly beer, but unlike his there was nothing rotting past its sell-by date. He had prepared before taking his vacation.

If only I knew where that vacation was, but search as I did I could find no further clue. However, the highlighted route on the locator maps had begun in New York. And the address on the answering machine had been in New York. Even the skyline in the background of those strange photographs had been Manhattan's. Returning to New York seemed the best bet.

I took two beers from the refrigerator and went back outside.

Valentina was in the lounge chair. Her dress was on the ground beside it.

I gave her one of the beers, sat in the chair, and told her what I'd found, ending with the remark that we should head back to New York, because that's probably where Trainor was.

"Good idea," she said. "In a while."

"A while?"

She lifted her sunglasses and smiled. "Why don't you see if you can find some suntan lotion," she suggested. "The oilier, the better."

ELEVEN

THE following morning, back in New York, I called the offices of a famous fashion magazine from which one of the photographs on the disc had been taken. I claimed that I was a marketing consultant looking for a model to publicize a new client's product, had seen the woman on the cover of their March edition, and had decided that she would be perfect. Now I was trying to locate her.

The operator transferred me to an editor's voice mail. I left the same story on the machine, giving both the suite number and the Plaza's telephone number, hoping that an expensive address while in town might add credibility to what was otherwise a very thin story. I need not have worried. The woman who returned the call a few minutes later was not the editor but someone from the magazine's marketing department, obviously smelling a new account, and eager to be helpful.

The model's name was Celeste Stevens, the woman told me. That accounted for the pink roses. Perhaps the crimson had been for counterpoint. Celeste was represented by General Models in New York, which from her tone I assumed was a well-known agency. That was all I needed but the woman, in the manner of marketing people everywhere, was persistent. I was only able to extricate myself by taking her name and number, and assuring the woman that I would call her personally when the time came for the advertising to be placed.

I called General Models. The receptionist transferred me. I knew there would be no chance of getting Celeste Stevens's address, and so I embellished the previous story. I was now scouting talent for an upcoming campaign, had seen the cover and called the magazine, and so wanted to see the model in the flesh before proceeding.

The woman I spoke to had a Southern accent. She was polite and businesslike, and surprised me by inviting me to meet with her at the agency's offices in half an hour. I had little choice but to agree. I tried to sound enthusiastic.

Thirty minutes later I was at the Soho address. I didn't look very fashionable, and hoped that this would be mistaken for inverted snobbery rather than plain indifference. The receptionist must have been a model herself, perhaps supplementing earnings with part-time work, for she towered over me, and appeared dressed for an avant-garde cocktail party. She looked at me with something between mild curiosity and outright disdain.

Before I could get out a word, she announced, "This is General Models," as if to suggest that I had obviously gotten the wrong address, and that the Army & Navy Surplus was elsewhere.

"I have an appointment with Elizabeth Houston," I said. "My name is Simon Anderson."

I was reluctantly invited to take a seat as she called to announce me. The sofa was comfortable leather. The walls were decorated with large posters of advertising copy, featuring models who were no doubt represented by the agency. There were fashion magazines scattered about, of little interest to me, but I picked one up in order to look the part. Eventually a woman came through from the offices inside. She was tall, too, but unlike the girl behind the desk she had not exaggerated it with enormous heels, and wore simple flat shoes instead. She had red hair, but her skin was smooth and unfreckled. She was very attractive, but looked too intelligent to be a model herself. She quickly fixed me with a critical but amused eye.

"Mr. Anderson," she said. "I'm Elizabeth Houston."

I stood and shook hands.

"Pleased to meet you," I said. "Please call me Simon."

"And I'm Beth." Her eyes were as green as the ocean, and as unforgiving, too. I knew I was in trouble from the start. "Please come with me."

I followed her through a short passageway into a large conference room. There was a long, sleek table surrounded by leather office chairs, fit for a corporate boardroom. A sideboard held mugs and a coffeepot, as well as bottles of mineral water and a bowl of fruit—safe fare for the workers perhaps. At one end of the room was a wide flat-screen monitor, and an array of electronic equipment feeding into it. We sat at the opposite end, where floor-to-ceiling glass windows gave onto Greene Street.

Beth Houston sat back comfortably in her chair, crossed her legs, and entomologically pinned me to the specimen tray with those green eyes. I tried hard to meet her gaze.

"I was very intrigued by your call, Simon."

"Glad to hear it," I said. "First rule of advertising: be intriguing." I thought that sounded like something an old pro might say, but Beth Houston just smiled politely, obviously unimpressed.

"Exactly what is it you're advertising?"

"I'm afraid I'm not at liberty to reveal that."

"Must make advertising a little difficult, when you're not at liberty to reveal the product."

"Well, of course, when the time comes . . ."

"And when will that be?"

"We're not sure yet."

"Not sure?"

"Development is still proceeding," I explained. "All I can say for now is that the product is in the field of cosmetics, and that it's going to blow the rest of the industry away."

Another polite smile.

"And what company are you representing?"

"I can't reveal that either," I said. "They don't have the patents yet, and this thing is too big for them to risk tipping off the competition. Hence they hired me, rather than use their own in-house marketing people, to maintain anonymity."

"And you want to use Celeste Stevens as the face of the product?"

"Yes."

"Why?"

"Why?"

"Yes. Why Celeste in particular?"

I tried desperately to think of some intelligent reply. "Cheekbones," I said eventually. I knew that models had a big thing about cheekbones.

"What about them?" Beth asked.

"She has them."

"As do many of our models," she said. "In fact all of them, as far as I know."

"I mean memorable cheekbones," I said. "My client specifically wants memorable cheekbones."

Beth Houston looked at me as if wondering whether or not I was retarded. The interview was not going well.

"Which advertising agency will be handling the campaign?" she asked. "Or is that a secret, too?"

"We haven't selected the agency yet," I said.

"No agency, but you're already choosing the model?"

"When you see the face, you've got to act right away."

"I see," she said. She picked up a remote control from the table and pointed it at the end of the room. The monitor came alive. The same magazine cover featuring Celeste filled the screen. "And this is the face?"

"Yes," I said, "that's her."

She continued to use the remote, sequencing through a number of shots, perhaps two dozen, all of Celeste Stevens. Some I had already seen on Trainor's disc although, predictably, none were from that last series of mock-wedding photographs. Finally the monitor was turned off.

"Of course, I would need to see her in the flesh before proceeding," I warned.

"Of course. And what sort of campaign are you considering?"

"Big," I said.

Beth Houston gnawed quietly at her lip. I got the impression that she was having difficulty not laughing.

"Actually," she said at last, "I was wondering if it would be print or electronic."

"Print," I said.

"Four-color spreads?"

"Heck," I said, "we'll use all the colors of the rainbow."

This time Beth did laugh. She was still laughing as she stood up, went to the sideboard, and selected an apple from the bowl. She polished it briefly, controlled her laughter sufficiently to take a bite, and leaned back on the sideboard, legs casually crossed at the ankle, and chewed while looking at me with amusement.

"Well," she said at last, "at least you're not creepy." I was glad to hear it. "Some of the people we have coming in here asking for specific models are downright weird." She took another bite of the apple. "They scare me sometimes," she added.

"And I don't?"

"No," she said. "You're just an old possum."

I wondered if this was a Southern term. And why "old"? She wasn't much younger than me. Perhaps she was an admirer of Eliot.

"Maybe I *could* scare you," I said. "Want to see my gun?"

"Then you'd just be an old possum with a firearm."

She continued to chew on the apple. I doubted there was much that scared Beth Houston. Since deception and threats weren't working, I thought I might try honesty.

"I'm in trouble," I said. "Celeste Stevens might know something that can help me get out of it."

"If it involves Celeste, then I have no doubt that it means trouble. But it doesn't matter. I can't help you."

"Don't you want to know why?"

"It wouldn't make any difference. We're a professional agency. We don't reveal personal information about our models, short of a court order."

So much for honesty.

"Perhaps you might change your mind after you've heard the story."

"I won't."

"You haven't heard it yet."

She took her time in answering, finishing the apple before replying. I was starting to think she might help me.

"Believe it or not," she said, "I've kind of enjoyed

meeting you." She threw the apple core into a trash can, fifteen feet away. It didn't even touch the sides. "Please don't spoil it by making me call security."

She stepped into the passageway and stood, arms crossed, waiting for me to follow. The interview was clearly concluded. I would have liked to ask if I could call her, but it's not the sort of thing you do when someone's throwing you out, so I just shut up and left.

What I needed when I hit the sidewalk was a drink, but it was only mid-morning. Late in life Churchill said that when he was a young man he made it a practice never to take a strong drink before lunch, but now it was his practice never to take one before breakfast. I decided on coffee instead. There was a Starbucks I'd passed farther down the street.

I ordered the biggest coffee they had and took a seat at a small table by the window. There were newspapers scattered about. I took one to kill some time, but after a while I realized that I'd been reading the same paragraph over and over.

I wasn't reading anything at all. My mind was still full of Beth Houston.

What is it that attracts a man to a woman? In *Angels and Insects* it had been a wrist, or the way Matty Crompton had held it. It was as if in that one extended contemplation of a single joint, William Adamson had suddenly seen all her strength and courage and compassion. For Nick in *Gatsby,* it had been a chin.

For me, I decided, it was every part of Beth Houston that had been visible in our one short and very unsuccessful encounter: the shape of her nose, the angle of her jaw, even her feet—large, as is often the case with tall, slender women.

But as time passed and memory faded, the one thing I was pretty sure I would never forget was those clear, steady, intelligent green eyes.

As I sat brooding on this, I couldn't help feeling angry with myself. I've never actually had a woman threaten to call security before. And of all women in the world, it had to be this one—a redeeming opportunity, lost and gone forever. I felt like a pauper who's won the lottery, only to realize that he's burned the ticket.

I looked up. An elderly lady came through the door, obviously a tourist, looking overwhelmed with New York and in need of a break. The loudmouth at the counter who'd been yapping on his cell phone while waiting for his coffee was still yapping on it as he left. He wasn't paying attention to where he was walking, and bumped the elderly lady hard on his way out.

He paused from his cell phone conversation long enough to say, "Watch where you're going," before roughly shoving past her and going out the door.

Well now, this guy was just what I needed.

I stood and followed him outside and out of sight of the Starbucks. When I caught up to him, we had a brief conversation about courtesy in general, and the correct way to treat women in particular. He didn't share my views at first, but soon came around to my way of thinking. As a finale we reviewed the etiquette of cell phones, and after explaining that he would have no further use for it, I crushed his own phone to shards beneath the heel of my shoe.

When the discussion was over I returned to the coffee shop. The old lady was toddling the other way down the sidewalk as fast as she could—probably headed for the first bus back to Topeka. I resumed my seat.

I didn't really feel a whole lot better, but I didn't feel a whole lot worse, either. I wrapped a handkerchief around my bleeding knuckles, and tried again with the newspaper.

I thought I'd gotten away without anyone noticing what had happened. But then I realized that someone was leaning on the column by my table.

I looked up. It was Beth Houston. She was smiling faintly.

"What are you doing here?" I said. It came out before I realized how accusatory it sounded.

"The office has lousy coffee," she explained, unperturbed.

"Have you been here long?"

"Long enough."

Beth didn't immediately say anything further, and since anything I tried came out wrong I just shut up. It had been a long time since I'd much cared what anyone thought about me, one way or the other. It was a strange feeling, and I wasn't sure I really liked it. She seemed to be content to remain leaning casually on the column, frankly appraising me.

"You're not married?" she said at last.

"No."

"Ever?"

"No." Close, but no.

"Obviously not gay?"

"No."

"And you look like too healthy an old possum to be diseased."

"Fighting fit."

Silence again. Her eyes didn't leave mine.

"Lucky Strike at ten P.M.," she said at last. "Be on time, and have a Cosmopolitan waiting."

"Are you saying you'll listen to my story then?"

"No, I'll allow you to buy me dinner and amuse me. Afterward, we'll go back to my place. I might let you tell me your story then."

"Okay."

"Bring a condom."

"A condom?"

"Yes, a condom. You know what a condom is, don't you?"

I admitted that I did.

"Good," she said. "Better make it two."

That's New York City for you. In Virginia they expect flowers. She made ready to leave.

"Before you go . . . can I ask why?"

"If you know what a condom is," she replied, "then surely you know what it's used for."

"I meant 'why' in a more general sense."

"Well," she said, crossing her arms and holding a chin in one hand, as if considering the question. "I guess it must be your memorable cheekbones."

She laughed all the way out the front door.

TWELVE

VALENTINA was not in the suite when I returned to the hotel. No note; she was not the sort of woman who leaves notes. I decided to ignore Churchill and mixed a drink, then took a seat. I tried to put Beth Houston out of my mind for a while, and think through what I knew.

Trainor and Martin were into some sort of crooked operation, that much seemed obvious. Whatever it was required a tractor-trailer rig, and a lot of diesel. Obviously the fuel was for the truck, although why it was necessary to purchase so much in advance was unclear. Perhaps they were going someplace with few gas stations, or maybe just somewhere where Yip Yip didn't want to be remembered.

Whatever Yip Yip had been up to, he had expected it to be profitable. Considering the fact of the truck, it would likely involve the transport of contraband. Perhaps he had brought his friend Trainor on board to take turns with the driving. Trainor had taken the opportunity to settle an old score along the way.

None of this explained the presence of an assault team. Who were they? Veterans possibly—since Trainor and Martin were, too—but if so, where did they get the equipment? And why would they take such risks to help Trainor settle what was clearly personal business? I couldn't make sense of it.

And lastly there was Valentina. A woman who just happened to be racing her Porsche past my house that night. A woman who had just happened to be armed. And a woman who just happened to frequent the Factory.

A coincidental woman. The time had come to confront her.

I finished the drink, and was considering a second when my eyes fell on the luggage rack in the corner. It had been full of Bergdorf bags last time I'd noticed. Now it was empty. I stood and went to the closet where Valentina hung her clothes. That was empty, too. I quickly went through the drawers, without result. Then the other closet; finally the bathroom—but everywhere was the same: there was nothing that wasn't mine. Valentina was gone.

There were two possibilities: she'd gone of her own accord, or someone had taken her. But Valentina was not the sort of woman likely to have gotten herself in a position to be taken without a struggle, of which there was no evidence. And an abductor would hardly have given her time to pack.

I went to the phone and called the number for Tate, Tate & Buchanan. A receptionist answered. This time there was no west Texas drawl.

"Valentina Mariposa, please." There was a pause as the operator tapped at a keyboard.

"I'm sorry, sir. Valentina is no longer with the firm."

"She quit?"

"She's no longer with the firm, sir."

"Do you know where I can find her?"

"I'm sorry, we're not allowed to give out personal information, sir."

"Do you know where she works now?"

"All I can tell you is that she is no longer with the firm."

"She's representing me."

"Her caseload is now being handled by Mr. Thompson. I'll be happy to connect you with him."

"No, I need to contact Ms. Mariposa directly."

"I'm sorry, sir, but I really can't help you."

I wasn't going to get anywhere with this. I ended the call.

So Valentina had not only run from me, she had decided to disappear completely, even to the point of quitting her job. Either that or Tate, Tate & Buchanan were in on it—whatever "it" was—but that seemed unlikely. Conspiracies involving entire law firms only happen in the movies.

I tried to think of what I could use to track Valentina down. The only things of her own that she had brought with her when we fled the Preston estate were her underwear and shoes, her gun and her American Express card. And the American Express card wasn't even hers, or so she said. Nevertheless there had to be a billing address.

I looked up the telephone number and called. After passing the account name and number I told the operator that "we" hadn't received the last bill, and I wondered if the address was correct. The operator told me that the last bill had already been paid in full, and suggested that perhaps my wife had already paid it. Has your address changed? she asked. I could think of no way to turn this question around in a way that would get her to reveal the address she currently had, so I just admitted that it hadn't and ended the call.

That credit card had been my one good lead. Now I had nothing.

Not quite nothing, I realized after a while. I had the serial number of Valentina's Beretta. I tried the phone book again, with more hope than expectation, but luck was still on my side: it turned out that there was a Beretta store on Madison Avenue. It must have been the only fashion house on the block that sold guns as well as haute couture.

I called, and asked the person who answered for the number to the headquarters of their North American operations. She gave it to me, and a minute later I was speaking to someone from the firearms guarantee section. I gave him the serial number of the gun, told him I was a police officer from the nineteenth precinct in New York, and that the firearm had been used in an armed holdup. I told him I wanted to see if the original owner had sent in a guarantee card after purchase.

He asked me if I'd sent a copy of the warrant. It took me a moment to realize that he meant a police warrant for the information. I admitted that I hadn't. Just fax it up to me now, he said, reminding me that of course he wasn't allowed to divulge the names and addresses of gun owners without a court-issued warrant. Especially for something as routine as armed holdup. I wished I'd made it a double homicide, with a kidnapping to boot. He gave me his fax number. I hung up.

My second lead, slender though it was, had also drawn a blank.

It was supposed to be the information age—surely there had to be a way to get someone's address more easily than this. I grabbed a beer from the bar refrigerator, sat down, and tried to think of another way.

Eventually I came up with something: maybe Valentina

voted. Voter registration rolls are public information. I had the hotel bring up a laptop, which I plugged into the eighteenth-century high-speed network port.

It turned out that although voter registration rolls are public information, it doesn't mean they make it easy for you. The rolls could only be inspected in person at the Board of Elections offices in D.C. However, the District of Columbia's Recorder of Deeds was much more helpful. After a quick registration using a hastily subscribed e-mail account, I was able to do an on-line database search. There were no deeds under the name Valentina Mariposa. On a hunch I tried Gillian Devereux, but that drew a blank, too. But then, among the Devereux listed, one item stood out: a deed in the name of Valentina Devereux. I clicked on the details. The deed had been filed three years ago. There was a deed number, the seller's name, a legal description of the property, and down in the bottom left-hand corner, the address: 1624 Twenty-eighth Street, Washington N.W., District of Columbia. Valentina lived in Georgetown.

It was still morning, and I had a long time to kill before meeting Beth Houston at ten o'clock that night. I decided that I might as well put the time to good use.

A hour later I was at La Guardia, and twenty minutes after that on board a shuttle flight on the way to what is now called Ronald Reagan Airport, but which in the days when I had to make the occasional journey to the Pentagon, had simply been called National.

On the flight down I had nothing to do but think. But I didn't think about the events of the last few days. Instead, I thought about home.

When I was released from Leavenworth I put every cent I had left in the world into purchasing the vineyard. It was more than a home, more than an investment, too. The first time I stood on the little rise by the house that looks over the vines, deed in hand and hefty mortgage to go with it, I knew that what I'd bought was sanctuary. Here I would stay, for the rest of my life I assumed, secure from the world. I would tend the soil, and it would harbor me.

What of my sanctuary now? The power would still be disconnected. There was the damage from the grenade still unattended to. My bed was full of lead. I wondered what I would find when I got back there. Police tape and blood-stains? And then I realized the obvious: I might well never even see the place again.

What I would like to have done when we arrived in D.C. was to rent a car and drive down to my farm—not neces-sarily to stay, just to see it. But instead I hailed a cab, and give the driver Valentina's address.

Valentina's apartment was in an old redbrick building, something between Federalist and Victorian. Most of the apartments around here were in buildings that had once been town houses, but Valentina's looked as if it had once been a stable, or perhaps a firehouse. There were only two apart-ments, one on the first floor, and Valentina's, which pre-sumably occupied all of the second. The entrance was a door set into two larger wooden doors through which once carriages or fire engines had emerged. There was an inter-com discreetly set into the wall to the side. There were no names by the intercom, just plates engraved with "Apart-ment One" and "Apartment Two." I buzzed the second, not in expectation of a response, but to ensure that the place was empty before breaking in. There was no answer.

A narrow path went between the building and the brick wall separating it from its neighbor, leading to the rear of the property. In back there was a small yard and a large magno-lia tree, a reminder that being below the Mason-Dixon Line meant Washington was technically in the South. A town of

Northern charm and Southern efficiency, Kennedy had once called it. The tree was in bloom and the scent of the flowers filled the air.

A metal fire escape ran down the back, probably added as the building's role had changed late in its life, necessitated by regulations mandating two stair exits in case of fire. This one had no pull-down ladder at the bottom as they do in New York—the stairs went all the way to the ground. The lower apartment must have had very high ceilings; it took three flights to get to a window giving onto Valentina's.

The windows were genuine paned glass, very old—perhaps original. I used the butt of the gun to smash one near the latch, reached inside, and undid the window. I waited a moment for the sound of an alarm, but there was nothing, at least nothing so far. I opened the window and went inside.

I was in a bedroom. The wall that separated it from the remainder of the apartment was made of thick greenish glass tiles—translucent but not transparent. The ceilings were high in this apartment, too, at least twelve feet, and had been finished in pressed tin coffers which must have been original. A firehouse, I decided, not a stable. A stable would not have had coffered ceilings in an area destined to store hay. The firemen would have slept up here when on watch, dormitory style.

They wouldn't have recognized it now, for the apartment was the sort of place that appears in photo layouts in fashionable architectural magazines. There was a king-size bed, minimalist in design, but sleek and well finished. That level of craftsmanship could not have come cheap. I looked closer, trying to get a sense if it had been slept in recently, but the sheets looked to be fresh. I examined a label. Italian, and obviously expensive.

There was a closet whose design matched the bed. I

briefly went through the contents. It was full of the things you would expect to find in a woman's closet, but not as much. At first I thought it must have meant that she had come and gone, packing some things and leaving others. But when I looked more closely there was no evidence of that, no empty coat hangers or obvious spaces where things had been removed. I looked at the labels on some of the dresses. Valentino, Cavalli, Versace. Italian, like the linens. So were the shoes.

It seemed that Valentina simply liked things well made, and was willing to forgo quantity to be able to afford quality. Or maybe she just didn't like clutter.

On the opposite wall was a long, low chest of drawers in blond wood. The first drawer I intended going through contained underwear. I quickly closed it, embarrassed at having opened it. But a moment's reflection made me realize that being embarrassed at going through a woman's underwear when that woman has gone missing after having been involved in multiple killings, and much else besides, was not logical. So I reopened the drawer. But I didn't spend long in there, just the same.

There was nothing of interest in the drawers, just more clothes and more Italian and French labels; even her swimsuits were European. Valentina had come down to domestic brands only for her stockings—perhaps that thigh holster tore through so many of them that they never lasted very long anyway.

There was nothing on top of the chest of drawers. Yes, Valentina was definitely a woman who despised clutter.

I examined the last piece of furniture in the room, a bedside table, again simply but well crafted in blond wood. This at least had something on top of it: a clock. It had a big round analog dial inside a brushed steel case. I looked at the short hand, which showed the alarm time. It was set to five-thirty. I wouldn't have taken Valentina for an early riser. Perhaps it meant P.M.

I opened the top drawer. Tissues—she couldn't even bear to have an exposed tissue box. Nothing else. Below that was a second drawer, in which there were two books. Given what I knew about her, the first one was perhaps predictable bedside reading: de Sade's *Justine*. The second was more of a surprise: *Atlas Shrugged*. It's a very long book, and I imagined Valentina struggling to finish it—perhaps there would be a bookmark, a hastily snatched piece of convenient paper on which there would be some important note scribbled. In fact I did find a note, but not one of Valentina's. It was from the rare book store which had sold it to her, certifying the book as a first edition.

So Valentina read first editions of Ayn Rand—not something I would have guessed. I looked at that famous first line.

"Who is John Galt?"

Who is Valentina Mariposa? I replaced the book, and left the bedroom.

The next room I entered was the main room, very large, occupying the remainder of the second story. The floor was of wood, smooth and well polished. Two items immediately caught my attention. To the right there was a heavy punching bag, hanging on the end of a thick rope running from a hook embedded into the ceiling. I had a closer look. The leather was well worn—it had taken a beating over the years. Lying on the shelf nearby were gloves, not true boxing gloves but sparring gloves, much thinner, designed to prevent bruising of the hands during a heavy workout. They, too, were well worn—the bag wasn't for show.

Alongside the gloves were two small metal weights, each a cylinder a couple of inches long and maybe three-quarters of an inch in diameter. I recognized them as the weights used in ankle weights. In the recon unit we used to work out with ankle weights to simulate the heft of combat boots.

But that's not what these would have been used for. There were just two: Valentina would have practiced on the punching bag with these enclosed in her fist, increasing the weight of her hand and thus the momentum of her punch, the equivalent to holding a roll of quarters in your hand when having a fistfight. In other words, Valentina fought dirty—even practiced it.

I couldn't help smiling to myself. Why would I have thought anything different?

The other object which had immediately caught my eye was a bathtub. It was standing alone in the middle of the floor beyond the punching bag, a big old-fashioned one, white enamel with worn but polished nickel-plated fittings. There was a wooden rail running around its perimeter, like a taffrail on a ship. White bath towels hung from it.

Perhaps Valentina liked to work up a sweat on the heavy bag then flop exhausted into a bubble bath. I continued going through the room.

There was a bookcase, a legal bookcase with a glass front. That at least fitted with the lawyer story, but when I looked at the titles I could find no legal texts. Most were nonfiction, many of them reference works, and there were some volumes of history, among which I recognized Thucydides' *History of the Peloponnesian War*. It was the first adult book I ever read. My father had given it to me when I'd asked about my unusual first name. Reading it had taught me the basic truth of history: civilization is maintained only by uncivilized means. A nation that has lost the will to fight is already beaten.

There was a kitchen area next, big cupboards and a wall

oven on the side, and low counters projecting into the room so as not to break the feel of immense space. I made a cursory glance through it, but there was little in the way of food—Valentina was not the sort of girl about whom friends would exclaim, "And she's such a good cook, too." I suspected that the only thing Valentina did with the stove was to occasionally dust it.

Beyond the kitchen area was a large bureau running along one wall. I recognized it from my marine days. Every bridge on a warship has a chart table. The "table" is really a set of wide, shallow drawers designed to store navigation charts. Whichever chart is currently in use is placed on top, which is set at a comfortable height to be worked over by a man standing—as the officer of the deck is while on watch.

Valentina had obviously located one from somewhere, and this one had either been little used or recently restored, because it was in perfect condition, even down to the shiny brass trim.

I opened the top drawer. She didn't use it for charts.

There was a shotgun, lying flat, and beyond that the case it had come in. Several boxes of 12-gauge were packed on the side. I picked up the weapon, checked the safety, then ran the pump back and forward until all the rounds had been ejected. Then I inspected it more closely.

It was a Benelli—even Valentina's guns were Italian. But this weapon had not been chosen on the basis of design elegance—it was an M3 model, more assault weapon than hunting gun. It had a pistol grip and could be fired in automatic self-loading mode—something useful when you've been clipped in one arm, and have therefore lost the ability to reload using pump action, but need to keep firing the weapon. Not many animals shoot back—you don't need that feature in a hunting weapon.

Valentina must have kept it out of its case and loaded because it was her weapon of choice, should anyone decide to enter her apartment uninvited. I was glad she hadn't been home when I broke that rear windowpane. I reloaded the weapon and wiped it down to remove fingerprints—not in the forensic sense; it was just that Valentina kept this weapon, like her entire apartment, in immaculate condition. It would hurt her feelings to find greasy finger marks on her weapons, which she clearly loved.

And she had many lovers. The next drawer turned out to be the Glock drawer. Not just one—there were three of those famous, ugly, lightweight, heavy-punching and ultra-reliable handguns. Smallest of the three was a subcompact Glock 26. Subcompact it may have been, but whereas other brands' subcompacts fire .22 or .25 ACP, a Glock 26 fires 9mm—big ammunition in any other manufacturer's arsenal. There was a larger weapon fitted for .357—a Glock 32, I read on the slide, a weapon I had never seen before. I ejected the magazine. The gun had been loaded. I took a closer look at the ammunition: Hydro-Shok, a type of hollow-point ammunition designed to flatten and spread on impact, causing the most damage. Biggest of all was a Glock 21 firing everybody's favorite, good old American .45. I picked up the 21—nice balance, but there would be a lot of kickback for all that plastic composite to absorb. I've never been a Glock fan.

I ejected this magazine as well, expecting to find more Hydro-Shok, but not only was this ammunition not hollow-point, it was jacketed. The jacket was not metal. I picked up a box of ammunition next to gun. It turned out to be Teflon-coated. Teflon is slippery, and Teflon-coated ammunition has only one purpose—to penetrate bulletproof vests. Its nickname is cop-killer.

I wasn't liking what I was finding here.

The next drawer had a Heckler & Koch SL8, an assault weapon that fired .223. It was a very modern design, carbon fiber polymer construction, fitted with a three-power scope and electronic red dot that made it look like something from a *Star Wars* movie. The German army used these now. No pretense here: this weapon had no purpose but killing people, lots of them.

In the drawer below that was a USC .45 carbine. As with the H&K, this weapon was fitted to fire in full auto. I wasn't sure, but I thought that these were illegal now.

The next drawer was more familiar territory. The empty case for the little .22 she carried was there. Beretta, as I knew—naturally: Valentina would never wear anything but Italian on her inner thigh. Next to that was a Walther PPK—favorite of James Bond, but whose mid-weight .380 ammunition M had once found so objectionable. As with 007's, Valentina's PPK included a removable silencer.

The second-last drawer didn't have guns; it had electronics. There was a parabolic microphone, designed to pick up sound at a distance by placing the microphone at the precise focus of the parabola, and thus at the focus of sound waves reflected from a single direction. There were recorders, digital and tape. There was night imaging equipment; fiber-optical cable with a handheld monitor; a handful of small speakers like the ones inside telephone handsets. And there was a box of little lightweight cylindrical devices that I guessed were electronic bugs.

The last drawer contained yet another weapon. It was a Ruger M77 target rifle. Unusually long twenty-six-inch barrel. Unusually powerful ten-power scope. Vernier sight windage-and-range correction. Bolt-loaded, one round at a time, intended for long-range precision work.

There's only one type of work that requires a gun like this: sniper. Or two: sniper and assassin. Which was Valentina?

I replaced the weapon in its case, closed the drawer, leaned back on the chart table, and thought about what I had found. Maybe she was just a gun nut: certainly she was the only woman I had ever met who had more firearms than lipsticks.

But I knew it wasn't much of an explanation. Whatever else was unknowable, one thing I knew for sure: Valentina was a woman of purpose. She would not possess weapons she didn't use, or weapons for which she'd have no need. But what possible use could Valentina have for nine firearms, including a sniper's rifle? Perhaps the desk would yield a clue.

The desk was modern and elegant and spare, like most everything that I had seen so far but the bathtub and punching bag. There was a laptop hooked into a VPN connection sitting on top of the desk. But unlike normal laptops this one had a metal casing instead of the usual plastic. There were two locks, which I would happily have broken in order to try to see what was on that computer, but a small stick-on label on the side warned that the barrel locks were connected to the hard disc, and that opening them by force would physically disable the drive.

It may or may not have been true, but I wasn't going to try. Even if I opened it and the thing worked, any computer with that much physical security was sure to come with more than enough software protection to prevent me gaining access. I'd never seen that much physical security on a laptop. I wondered what sort of cases Tate, Tate & Buchanan handled, that they went to so much trouble to protect their files.

I had no similar qualms about the desk locks. I found a screwdriver in a kitchen drawer, and used a heavy cast-iron skillet as a hammer to punch the barrels straight through.

The top drawer held nothing of interest, just pens and pencils, a stapler, blank CD-RWs, a notepad which looked little used, the usual stationery in a desk drawer.

But the second drawer was more interesting. Here I found three passports belonging to three different people. The first was an American passport, Valentina's. She had been born in Los Angeles thirty-two years ago. The second was a Columbian passport, belonging to Consuela Diaz. She had been born in Cartagena twenty-seven years ago. The third was a Swiss passport, belonging to Margot Hauser. She had been born in Basel, thirty years ago.

The photographs in all three passports were Valentina's. They were identical: precisely the same picture, as if she had gone out and gotten all three at once.

At least I knew I had broken into the right apartment now.

Given her unaccented English, I had to assume that the American passport was the genuine one. Perhaps she had grown up in one of those households were the parents are native Spanish speakers, but the children speak English at school, and thus end up fully fluent in both languages, allowing her also to pass for a Latin-American national, hence the Columbian passport. Or perhaps she had dual nationality, both were genuine, but she had changed her name.

But that didn't explain the third passport. Switzerland has four native languages: German, French, Italian, and Romansch. Basel was an interesting choice for a birthplace: the town is right on the borderline of the German- and French-speaking parts of the country—even the passport showed it as "Basel/Basle." A bilingual town. I presumed that Valentina spoke both languages, but she would have an accent that might lead to her identity being challenged. Since she supposedly came from Basel, if challenged by a German speaker she could claim to be a native French speaker, and if challenged by a French speaker she could claim to be a native German speaker.

I put the passports in a pocket, and opened the next drawer. In this one there was cash, lots of it, but none of it was denominated in U.S. dollars. It was packed in five neat stacks, arranged by currency. I picked the first one. They were Mexican pesos. I counted the stack: ten thousand pesos—about a thousand dollars' worth. Next to it were Colombian pesos, and then Swiss francs, matching the passports. Behind these were two currencies that were more difficult to make out. Both had Arabic script, and from the cedar tree on the notes in one lot I guessed that pile was Lebanese currency. The other was a mystery to me: Saudi perhaps, or Iraqi, or Syrian, or maybe even Afghani.

I went through the rest of the desk but found nothing further of interest. Eventually I went and sat on the sofa at the front of the room by the windows giving onto Twenty-eighth Street, and thought about what I'd found.

Multiple passports. Large quantities of foreign currency, much of it Latin-American. Guns. Guns with dumdum rounds, guns with Teflon, guns with sound suppressors. Surveillance electronics. This was no lawyer, at least no lawyer who represented legitimate clients.

Valentina was into something crooked. And since it was a fair guess that Yip Yip and Trainor were, too, there seemed only two possible conclusions: they were in it together, or they were competitors. Either way, it seemed that I was the meat in the middle.

What was also notable was what I hadn't found. There was nothing from Tate, Tate & Buchanan, for example, and

I was starting to wonder if this Valentina Mariposa and their Valentina Mariposa (when they had one) weren't different people after all. But if Valentina worked elsewhere, there was no evidence of that either. Whatever she did, she went to considerable length to keep it a secret. Considering all the passports, perhaps she traded in stolen identities. And perhaps the real Valentina Mariposa was one of the victims, and was an identity that my Valentina had decided to keep for herself. Along with Consuela Diaz and Margot Hauser.

There were other items, too, that were conspicuous by their absence. Apart from those I had found in the passports, there was not a single photograph in the apartment. No letters. No diaries. No mementos. No history. There were no bank statements or brokerage account statements—perhaps Valentina kept all her financial records on her laptop. There hadn't even been any sign of there being anyone else in her life, and none of the paraphernalia of sex, but I knew her too well by now to imagine that she was celibate.

Given so much missing, I had to consider that the place might have been gone though before I got here. It was possible, but there was no evidence of it having been ransacked. No mess. No spaces where things were obviously missing. And if someone had tossed the place, the cash would surely have been taken. The guns, too.

The more I thought about it, the more it seemed to me that this was simply the way Valentina Mariposa lived. A hidden woman. But who lives like this, secretively, almost impersonally? The answer was obvious: only someone with something to hide. Valentina might or might not have been an attorney, or might have been an attorney but one who was on the wrong side of the law. She was into something, that much was certain.

Considering the Colombian passport, it wasn't hard to

guess what that something had to be. There are only two things that come out of Colombia, and Valentina wasn't in the coffee business.

There was only one unexplored lead left. The time had come to call on Tate, Tate & Buchanan.

THIRTEEN

I left the apartment and walked down to the K Street address I had found in the phone book for Tate, Tate & Buchanan. The sidewalks were lively with businesspeople in business suits—K Street is an outpost of private enterprise in a town dominated by government, a reversal of the usual pattern in most American cities. The address was a modern office building several stories high. I went though the revolving doors into the lobby. There was a security desk that I couldn't avoid, so I stepped up to it without prompting and asked the man for the location of Tate, Tate & Buchanan. I feared he would ask me for the name of the person with whom I had an appointment, and then call ahead to check before letting me up, but all he did was tell me they were on the third floor and direct me to the elevators.

The reception area of Tate, Tate & Buchanan was designed to impress. The walls were marble, or perhaps travertine, soft brown and cream. Beige carpeting deadened the sound of clients being fleeced. A wide curving front desk projected from a side wall and ran across almost the entire width of the room, perhaps thirty feet. Behind it sat a single receptionist. She looked like a lone sailor manning a battleship's bridge.

She gave me a hard, brittle smile. "May I help you?"

"I'm here to see Mr. Thompson," I replied. "Or if he's not here, then someone else. It's regarding Valentina Mariposa, and it's quite urgent."

"Do you have an appointment?"

"No."

The brittle smile cracked. "And your name?"

"Jim Bowie."

"And what is this regarding, Mr. Bowie?"

"Passport problems," I said.

The brittle smile completely crumbled now. "We don't handle immigration law, Mr. Bowie."

"The problems aren't mine, they're Valentina's." I took the three passports from my pocket and dropped them onto the desk. "She seems to have an overabundance of them."

The receptionist stared at the passports for a moment in dumb silence, then quietly mumbled, "I'll get someone right away." She scooped up the passports and headed for the door leading into the inner offices. Before pressing the key panel to open it, she glanced over her shoulder at me, perhaps checking that I wasn't following. Her face was a mixture of displeasure at my presence and relief to be escaping my company unharmed. She disappeared inside. I took a magazine from the rack, sat back, and waited.

There was a security camera mounted in a wall bracket above the door through which the receptionist had disappeared. A little red light was blinking. The thing began to move, shifting from a position which had given it wide coverage of the entire room to point directly at me. The lens twisted and lengthened, focusing for a close-up.

I gave them a little wave, and tried to show my good side.

It must not have impressed them very much, because I waited a long time. I glanced at my watch every now and then. When fifteen minutes had passed I again waved at the camera, and pointed at my watch. Still no reaction.

When eventually someone did show up, it wasn't through the interior door, but through the front door.

There were three of them, all big, all black, all wearing some sort of security outfit's uniform. The first held a gun on me while the other two came either side and hauled me to my feet. They roughly patted me down, found nothing, then locked onto an arm either side and hauled me from the room to the elevators.

So maybe that entire law firm conspiracy stuff wasn't confined to the movies after all.

They pressed the *down* button, and an elevator quickly arrived. There was a man and a woman inside, dressed in business clothes, discussing some matter of office politics. They stopped talking when they saw us. My companions made no move to enter the car, and said nothing, just continued to stare straight ahead. The woman looked openmouthed at the immense mounds of flesh that served as pillars either side of me. She avoided looking directly at me. Her companion quickly took it all in, including the gun held on me. His reaction was to bravely reach out and hit the *close door* button. There was an awkward interval of elevator inaction, during which we all continued to look at each other pretending that nothing was amiss, then eventually the doors closed.

When the elevator had disappeared, the one with the gun pressed the *down* button again. We waited.

"How about those Orioles?" I said. No one replied. It seemed that my companions weren't baseball fans.

The same elevator car returned, this time empty. We got in and went down. I had expected that we would go to the basement, or perhaps an underground parking lot where a dark car would be waiting, but instead we went to the first floor. When the doors opened I was swiftly marched through the lobby and past the front desk, which was now empty. The man I had spoken to on the way up must have decided that discretion required a temporary retreat.

Next to the revolving door through which I had entered was a normal plate glass door with a big hip-level automatic button, meant for disabled access. The shooter slapped the button, the door slid open, and the two Corinthians at last let go of my arms in order to thrust me outside onto the sidewalk. They remained inside.

It seemed that I was simply being thrown out. Not a word had been said by any of them the whole time.

I picked myself up. A few pedestrians on the sidewalk stopped to stare, but the three big black faces on the other side of the glass must have intimidated them, and they quickly moved on.

I moved on as well, in case the goons decided that they wanted to consult with me further. I walked a little way down toward the Mall, through the area of George Washington University. It was July, but there was still a scattering of students around, books in hand, summer students trying to make up for too many frat parties during the previous semester. There was a little park. I bought a soda from a street cart, found an empty bench, and sat down to think through what to do next.

The bench faced back the way I'd come. When I turned to sit I noticed a man who had been going in the same way as me suddenly change direction. He went to the same street cart I had gone to, and spent a few minutes trying to figure out what he wanted.

I wouldn't have thought about it any more if he hadn't been wearing a tweed jacket. One of the people who had been on the sidewalk in front of Tate, Tate & Buchanan had been wearing a tweed jacket. I had noticed it because it was so out of place on a hot, humid Washington summer day. The sort of day you'd only wear a jacket if your job required it.

Or if you had to wear it to cover something. Like, say, a gun.

Tweed Jacket continued to suffer from indecision at the street cart. I could see from the proprietor's body language that he was getting impatient. I took my time sipping the soda. Eventually Tweed Jacket bought a hot dog. He was a little overweight, and I could see the hot dog was piled high with sauerkraut and plenty of mustard.

He took a bench at the diagonally opposite corner of the park. As soon as he had the hot dog in his mouth for the first bite, I stood, tossed the half-finished soda into a trash can, and walked swiftly away. I couldn't see behind me but I could hear him, even from thirty yards away, huffing to his feet and coming after me.

So that's why it had taken so long at Tate, Tate & Buchanan. They had had to find someone to follow me.

I tried to keep casual, not walking too fast, looking around as someone from out of town and unfamiliar with the streets would do. There would be a time to let him know that I'd made him, but that time was not now.

I walked down to the Mall and along Constitution Avenue, looking for a good place in which to try to lose him.

What I needed was somewhere big, crowded, and with multiple exits. I soon found a suitable candidate: the National Gallery of Art.

I'd been there before. The National Gallery is two buildings. The west wing is the original, built in that classical style favored for most public buildings, especially in Washington. The east wing is more modern, a trapezoidal structure that is all angles and planes. The two are connected by a tunnel which runs under the street that separates them.

I entered the west wing. There was an information kiosk which had maps of the floor plan. I took one and stood to the side to study it, with my back against the side wall so that the entrance would be in my peripheral vision. Tweed Jacket came inside in a rush, but slowed when he spotted me. He got a floor plan, too.

"Americans Abroad in the Late 1800s" looked to be the best room for me. I went through the central galleries, past sculptures and drawings, to a long room at the northwest corner of the building. There were half a dozen people in the gallery, including a guard.

I began going from picture to picture, spending a moment or two in front of each, glancing at the accompanying card to see who had painted it. Tweed Jacket entered the room. He began going from picture to picture, too. His pace soon matched mine.

I stopped at the last painting, the one nearest the door, and became immensely absorbed in it. I spent a minute in front of it, then another. Actually it wasn't bad, a John Singer Sargent from 1911 called *Nonchaloir (Repose)*. According to the card, which I read through several times in order to waste time, *nonchaloir* meant nonchalance. The painting showed a young woman lying back on a sofa, wrapped in silks and looking more insouciant than nonchalant, but then I have an indelicate soul, so what would I know.

Tweed Jacket had slowed down as well. But he was just three paintings away now, having trouble looking interested, and obviously not wanting to get too close to me. The last of the other people left the gallery, leaving just the two of us and the guard in the room.

I remained fascinated with the Sargent. Finally Tweed Jacket did what I'd hoped he might do: he started over. He began going painting by painting again along the side wall through which we had both first come. Eventually he reached the far wall, perhaps forty feet away, and momentarily had his back to me as he looked at the paintings there. At that moment I bolted from the room.

I raced through the adjoining gallery, pushing past the tourists, and into a small passageway where a set of stairs led up to the next floor. I went through the swing doors and up the stairwell as fast as I could. When I reached the next floor I could hear the steps behind me as Tweed Jacket begun thundering up the steps, all pretense of not following me now gone.

I gave the swing doors on this second floor a good push, but I didn't go through. Instead I quietly continued up the stairs. There were no more floors above; the stairs would have led to the roof, or perhaps some small utility rooms. I hung back in the shadows at the top of the flight as Tweed Jacket came huffing up the stairs below me. He wasn't in very good shape.

The doors were still swinging. He went straight through, not even thinking of going farther up. I knew from the floor plan that there was a maze of galleries on the second level, full of European masters that would likely attract the biggest crowds. It would take him a while to realize that I wasn't there. By that time I hoped to be long gone. I quickly went back downstairs to the first floor, and then along the galleries through which I had first come.

If Tweed Jacket was smart he would go straight to the entrance and wait for me there. But the east wing has its own entrance. Tweed Jacket could only cover one entrance, and my guess was that he wouldn't be smart enough to think of the one across the street, or the tunnel connecting the two buildings.

I walked down the length of the west wing, quickly, but not so fast as to attract undue attention.

At the end I took the steps down to the tunnel and was soon in the east wing. There was a concourse with a cafe and a shop. Eventually I located the way up to ground level. At the top of the stairs was a big open space with people coming and going. The entrance doors were to my far left. And there, standing by the wall with his arms folded and looking straight at me, was Tweed Jacket. I had obviously underestimated the guy.

There was a guard nearby. She was unarmed, but she carried a walkie-talkie. I walked up to her and said, "Excuse me, but I noticed that the guy over there in the tweed jacket is carrying a gun. He's probably wearing the jacket to conceal it. He's muttering to himself—I couldn't understand because it's a foreign language, but it sounded like prayers. I think he's working himself up to start shooting people." She looked at the man, then back at me.

"You sure?"

"About the gun, yes."

She grabbed the walkie-talkie and made a call. A moment later another security guard came racing down the steps, and a cop came out of an administrative office by the entrance.

The cop was armed. The two newcomers eyeballed the original security guard. She nodded at Tweed Jacket, then turned to me.

"Stay right here, okay?"

"Yes, of course," I lied.

All three converged on him. The cop's hand went onto his weapon. Tweed Jacket realized what was happening, and held up his hands. "Hey, no . . ." I heard him say.

But I didn't get the rest—I was already leaving. I turned as I opened the front door, and gave Tweed Jacket a wink. He was looking at me, hands held high now, submitting to the pat down that had already begun.

He nodded his head and smiled. "Okay," he seemed to say, "you got me."

FOURTEEN

AT ten o'clock precisely, Beth Houston strode into Lucky Strike. At least I assumed it was Beth, although the businesslike persona of this afternoon had metamorphosed into a tall sultry woman who radiated sex. The pants and flats were gone, replaced by a cocktail dress, high-heeled shoes, and a lot of leg in between. Her hair was bunched up in the back, but casually, with dissolute strands falling loose. The face that had been devoid of cosmetics earlier was now expertly made-up.

I stood as Beth approached the bar, and kissed her on the cheek in greeting. She kissed back. When I was five years old I'd kissed Gretchen Carter, who was also five. She had immediately burst into tears. It's good that women change when they grow up.

Beth lingered near my ear long enough to whisper, "I'm

not wearing any underwear." As if to emphasize the point she gently rubbed her hip across my trousers. She stopped halfway, and gave me a cheeky grin of surprise.

"Is that a gun in your pocket, or are you just happy to see me?"

"Actually, it *is* a gun in my pocket. But I'm also happy to see you."

Beth sat on the bar stool. Her dress rode up. She was right, she wasn't wearing any underwear.

She picked up the Cosmopolitan, drained the glass in a single gulp, and nodded to the bartender, who, like every other male in the room, had been more or less mesmerized since she had entered. He began to mix another. Well, they were kind of small Cosmopolitans. He looked inquiringly at me, and I nodded for another, too.

Beth fixed me with those green eyes, whose piercing clarity the cocktail had done nothing to dilute.

"Satisfactory?" she asked.

"And then some."

"And you have come equipped?"

"With three."

"Is that boasting, or merely wishful thinking?"

"It's the way they come packaged. But looking at you now, I'm wondering if three will be enough."

She laughed. The fresh drinks arrived. We held our glasses aloft in a silent toast before drinking. This time, she merely swigged it.

"You're an expert flatterer, Simon Anderson."

"My real name's Lysander Dalton," I admitted, "and I've never flattered anyone in my life. Also I can assure you that if I were really looking for a model, you'd be my choice."

"Not Celeste?"

"No, you."

"There now, I gave you an opening to ask about Celeste and you missed it."

I looked at those long legs. Usually a woman's legs disappear under her dress, but in this case the dress disappeared before the legs did.

"I seem to be a little distracted," I said.

She smiled, emptied her glass on the second swallow, and stood.

"I'm going to the bathroom," she announced.

At the rate she'd put away those cocktails, I wasn't surprised.

"Would you like me to get you another while you're gone?" I asked politely.

Beth smiled the smile of a pasha indulging a slightly dull concubine.

"I think you should go to the bathroom, too," she said.

"But I don't need to go."

She laughed and held out her hand.

"Come and fuck me," she explained.

Ah, now I got it. I took her hand and we retired to the back of the restaurant. Fortunately the ladies' room was unoccupied. We careened inside. I had just enough presence of mind to lock the door behind us. As I turned the bolt, Beth was already yanking at my trousers, single-minded, breathing rapidly. I hitched up the dress and hauled her onto the sink.

We didn't waste any time on niceties. I only hoped that Lucky Strike's music covered the noise, although Beth was loud enough to have silenced a rock concert.

By the time we got back outside—having regained breath, regroomed hair, and resumed clothing—our table was ready. I hoped the incident had gone unnoticed, and that the hostess's smile was due to a naturally sunny disposition.

We were left alone, and studied our menus in awkward silence.

"Excuse me," Beth asked after a while, "what did you say your name was again?"

I laughed. "A lesser man might be insulted."

"A lesser man wouldn't have gotten this far," Beth replied. "And besides," she added quietly, "I wasn't paying attention when you told me before." She turned a lovely shade of pink.

"Lysander Dalton," I said.

Beth held out an arm. "Pleased to meet you," she said. We shook hands.

The waiter came, took our order, and brought the wine. Beth resumed the conversation when he was gone.

"So tell me, Lysander Dalton, what do you do when you're not stalking fashion models?"

"I'm a farmer."

"You don't look like the corn-and-hogs type."

"More like cabernet and merlot. I make wine."

"California?"

"Virginia."

"And what brings you to New York?"

"But that means telling the story," I said. "And you said the story had to wait until after dinner."

"Tell me the story now," she instructed. "You're going to be busy after dinner."

I am not usually inclined to talk much about myself, but something about this woman sitting in front of me—a woman I knew so little of that she was still trying to get my name right—made me trust her. So I told her the story, blow by blow from the time I had woken up less than a week ago to go to the bathroom, up until how I had spent the rest of the day since we had met this morning. Beth was equal parts amazed and amused.

The only parts I left out involved Valentina, and didn't matter anyway.

After dinner we walked to her apartment. Beth Houston's place was a pleasant second-floor walkup on Barrow. The apartment was like its owner: casual but stylish, chic but unpretentious. It had once been a cramped one-bedroom, with a living room facing the street and a bedroom giving onto a modest garden in the rear. These two rooms were separated by a small kitchen, bathroom, and narrow hallway in between. But Beth told me she had had the interior walls removed—the entire apartment was a single airy space lit from both ends, hardwood floors brightly polished, and furnished with just a few well-chosen pieces: a beige leather sofa opposite the fireplace; a writing desk by the front window, with computer and telephone; a small Parisian cafe table and chairs by the kitchen; and, under the garden window in the rear, a low Japanese-style bed. The bed was where we went.

It was a very nice bed, low enough not to impose itself on the limited space, but wide enough not to risk falling off. Beth reached behind her, unzipped the dress and let it fall to the floor. In Lucky Strike's bathroom, things had been too urgent for serious contemplation, in fact too urgent for either of us to have removed any more than the minimum clothing necessary. Now there was time.

Eventually we lay back exhausted, sweat-soaked bodies on sweat-soaked sheets. In the candlelight I could see a framed poster on the wall, a woman on a barren red landscape—Arizona or Utah perhaps—wearing jeans and little else, rear end stuck out in an engaging pose, which also just happened to emphasize the maker's name on the label. The woman's red hair went with the landscape. Her eyes were green.

"You?" I asked.

Beth nodded. "I used to model," she said dismissively. "But I never had presence, so I got into management instead. I knew I wasn't going to have a long career on the catwalk, or in front of the camera." She shrugged her shoulders, as if to reject her good looks as unimportant. Perhaps they are, but there is pleasure in beauty and I was grateful that she was who she was nevertheless.

"Well you certainly have presence now," I said.

She shrugged dismissively.

"I'm serious," I insisted, "and I speak on behalf of males everywhere. The temperature in Lucky Strike went up ten degrees the moment you walked in the door."

"I'll take your word for it," she said. "Would you like a drink?"

"Whatever you're having."

She padded away to the kitchen, and soon returned with a liter of San Pellegrino. It was a good choice, as we were in danger of dehydration. She poured two glasses, and we drank in restful silence for a while.

"I haven't had sex since the Clinton administration," she said eventually.

"What did we just do?"

She hit me and said, "I meant before tonight."

"There was a lot of it going on back then."

"Do you know how many decent single men there are in Manhattan that any self-respecting woman would actually *want* to have sex with?"

I admitted that I didn't.

"You're it."

"Gee, maybe I should move here."

She hit me again. I was bathed in sweat, and her little fist squelched on my chest.

"Sorry," she said. "No air-conditioning."

"Good, I don't like it."

"You don't?"

"I took it out of my house when I bought it."

"How come?"

"It's an old house, and it didn't fit in. Besides, I don't mind being hot in summer. And I don't mind being cold in winter either."

"Me, too," she said, delighted that we had found this in common. "In winter I put on my ski underwear, wrap myself in a goose-feather comforter, and read on the sofa in front of the fire."

"What do you do in summer?"

"Take off all my clothes, spray Evian water over myself, and lie here by the open window with the warm breeze."

"It's warm tonight," I said.

"The Evian's on the table."

I found it and began spraying. One thing led to another, and before long the condom supply was exhausted. We must have dozed for a while. Eventually Beth went to the bathroom. She returned with a bucket of ice and a bottle of whiskey, both of which she added to the Pellegrino.

We sipped our nightcaps. I looked at the clock: two in the morning.

"What was prison like?" Beth asked.

"Great."

She laughed. "Sorry, stupid question."

"No, I really did enjoy it, in a way. Truth is, after commanding a marine special operations unit, Leavenworth was basically a six-month vacation. The food was better, there was a real bed every night, and I finally had time to read."

"I'd get claustrophobia."

"Since I was only in for a short time, I was allowed out to work the fields during the day." It was what had made me think to become a farmer. After the rice paddies and jungle, those wide, flat plains looked pretty good to me. The plowed earth was open and dark and fertile—honest soil, not a hiding place for water snakes and land mines.

"I've got some bad news," Beth said after a while.

"What's that?"

"I'm a liar."

"What did you lie about?"

"I let you believe that I might give you Celeste's address or phone number. I'm sorry, but I'm not going to do that."

"You don't buy my story?"

"That's got nothing to do with it," she said. "In fact, I was sympathetic to you before you even told me; God knows Celeste is made for trouble. But we promise confidentiality, and I don't break promises."

"Okay."

"You're not angry?"

"No."

"No?"

"Beth, considering that I'm probably wanted for murder, and that there is some sort of special operations team trying to kill me, the truth is I couldn't be happier."

She smiled, whether from relief or from the implied compliment I couldn't tell.

"I can tell you what's common knowledge," she said, "in the public domain, so to speak. What you do with that is up to you."

"Fine," I said, "just tell me what you feel comfortable telling me."

She took a long sip of whiskey and contemplated the glass for a moment in silence. Then she began the story of Celeste Stevens.

"Celeste was sixteen when she showed up at our agency. She was from the Midwest somewhere—Decatur or Gary, someplace like that; I can't remember exactly. She'd dropped out of high school and run away from home, I think. She didn't talk about it much. I was still modeling then, and occasionally we were together in shows or on sets. Celeste wasn't very smart, but she was cunning, and she knew how to use her natural assets to best advantage. She certainly had presence. Every night I was in bed by nine, trying to be in best shape for work the next day. My only sin was motorbikes."

"Motorbikes are a sin?"

"In the modeling world they are—the professional insurance is voided if a model rides a motorbike. Too dangerous, they say. But I'd been riding them since I had a dirt bike when I was a kid, and I used to still ride one when I was modeling. Eventually I sold it and settled for a car, but it had to be a convertible."

"You like fresh air?"

"And light. Light and air," she replied. "Opposite to Celeste, I guess. Celeste liked the dark. She was a party girl, and would prowl the nightclubs until the early hours. Soon she fell in with the rock star crowd, and soon after that she began taking drugs. But luck was on her side: 'heroin chic' was still the big look. Celeste would turn up for work wasted, hollow-faced with dark circles under her eyes, and the photographers loved it. For a while Celeste Stevens became a twelve-month girl—that's what they call a model who gets bookings a year in advance; it means she's hit the big time.

"Then she started coming in bruised. Not needle tracks; bruises on the wrists and the ankles, bruises in places you wouldn't expect to see bruises. It was never clear what was going on exactly—what was accidental and what was intentional—but it was obvious enough that, whatever it was she was into, it was kinky. After a while it seemed that she had moved on from the rock stars—perhaps even rock stars need sleep, but Celeste never did. There were all sorts of rumors: rumors that she was dealing drugs; rumors that she had a sideline working as a millionaires' call girl; rumors that she had become the plaything of the underground sex clubs. Whatever was going on, one thing was for sure: it was rough. One day she showed up for a session with a cut on her face—that would be enough to kill a shoot normally, but the photographer loved it. It became quite a famous shoot within the industry, like those Benetton ads.

"But for all that, Celeste was no fool, and realized that it couldn't last. She knew well enough that the money would run out when her looks did, and that would mean an end to her high living. I got the feeling that she was always on the lookout for a sugar daddy, and a few months ago she apparently found one: a rich businessman, supposedly connected with the mob, but that wouldn't disturb Celeste."

"What was the mob connection?"

"Business: he's a nightclub impresario. He has legitimate places, but supposedly he also owns a club of the type that Celeste had lately come to frequent—an expensive place where the rich or beautiful can indulge themselves as they choose. Perhaps that's how they met. Anyway, the first I found out about it was when someone at the agency saw a piece in one of the gossip magazines. Apparently the wedding had been a private affair."

"What's the impresario's name?"

Beth sipped her drink and tried to recall it.

"Leonetti," she said eventually, "Tommy Leonetti."

FIFTEEN

THE phone was answered on the first ring.

"Hello?" It was only a single word, but there was no mistaking the accent.

"Miss Honeysuckle," I said, "this is Lysander Dalton." No reply. "I don't know whether you remember me . . ."

"I remember you very well, Mr. Dalton. Tartan boxers—Douglas, I think—and a problem using doors."

"Black Watch," I corrected. "And sorry about the window."

"The police have temporarily closed down the club."

"I'm sorry about that, too."

"Does that mean you were the cause, Mr. Dalton?"

"I'm afraid it's possible that the people who came to your club that night may have been looking for me."

"You do seem to fall in with bad crowds, Mr. Dalton.

A bunch of lunatic gunmen, not to mention that rather poisonous-looking creature you left the club with."

"She's my lawyer," I said.

"May I recommend Ogilvey & Wallace? Their counsel wear suits, and do not usually carry concealed weapons."

"Miss Honeysuckle, I'd like to talk with you if I can."

"Certainly, Mr. Dalton. Tea at four?"

I said that tea at four would be fine. She gave me an address in the Flatiron district, and ended the call.

The cab dropped me at precisely four. The address was a restored cast-iron building. The pediment bore the original owner's name, a dry goods company, and the date 1873. When it was built, this area, Broadway below Madison Square, had been the commercial hub of New York City. The first floor was still occupied by stores: fashionable boutiques too funky for uptown, but insufficiently hip for Soho or the West Village. The rest of the building had been converted to residential use.

I went into the entrance vestibule. There were eight buzzers for apartments on the second and third floors, but only one for the fourth, marked "Penthouse." That was the one I pressed. The red light on the video camera blinked. Eventually I must have passed the inspection, and the door buzzed open.

There was an elevator, industrial size, but I took the stairs. There was only one door giving onto the small landing at the fourth floor. Miss Honeysuckle opened it before I could knock.

"My first name's Laurel," she said by way of introduction. "My parents liked trees."

She turned and walked inside. It seemed that I was supposed to follow, so I did.

It was an impressive apartment, but I took the opportunity

while following her to admire the hostess instead. Laurel
Honeysuckle wore a sweater and cardigan set in pale green
cashmere, and a linen skirt whose length was just a touch
shy of completely respectable. The heels of her expensive
shoes were too low to qualify as seductive, but too high to
qualify as sensible. Her hair was pulled tightly behind her
head, as on the first occasion I had met her, and she was
wearing the same tortoiseshell glasses. Librarian-like she
may have been, but this was a librarian of schoolboy fan-
tasies.

She had a good walk, with the upright carriage of someone who will never be oppressed by life. Her deportment
teacher at Smith would have been proud. We stopped by a
modern sofa and chairs arranged around a coffee table in
the center of the room.

"I'll be right back," she said. La Giaconda would have
envied the smile that accompanied this otherwise innocent
remark. Laurel disappeared through a door. I took a seat. It
occurred to me that I hadn't yet managed to say a single
word. Valentina was right: my interview technique could
use some work.

The room was huge, bigger than Beth Houston's entire
apartment. It was minimally furnished, perhaps to emphasize the vastness of the space. The ceiling must have been at
least fifteen feet high, occasionally supported by columns—
decorative, but no doubt concealing cast-iron structural
beams within. The floor was a warm-colored wood—cherry
perhaps—and finely joined, smooth enough to have played
billiards upon. My father had been a contractor, and he
would have appreciated the level of craftsmanship that had
gone into the making of this floor.

There were two fireplaces, one on either side of the room,
with elegant sandstone mantles, and each with a large canvas
above: horizontal bands of vibrating color whose warmth

matched the floor. Either they were reproductions or, if original Rothkos, they were worth a small fortune. The huge windows gave onto the street. A writing desk by one window and a comfortable reading chair under another were the only furniture besides the little island where I now sat.

Laurel Honeysuckle returned, carrying a tray. She placed it on the coffee table and began unloading. I helped. There was a silver tea service, white damask napkins, and a little plate of finger sandwiches. Real cups and saucers, no mugs. We might have been on the lawn at Buckingham Palace, taking tea with the Queen.

Laurel placed a strainer on the rim of my cup and began to pour.

"I hope Darjeeling is satisfactory." she said.

"Sure." I hate tea.

"Cream and sugar?"

"Yes, thanks." Anything to disguise the flavor. "You have a very nice apartment, Laurel." The comment made her laugh.

"Do you really think executive assistants are paid enough to afford a place like this?"

"It's not yours?"

"I'm house-sitting for Mr. Leonetti. This is his apartment."

"House-sitting? You mean he's away?"

"Since the Factory has been shut down during the police investigation, he decided to take a short vacation," she explained. "He and his wife are in Martinique."

We sipped our tea. I tried a sandwich. It was filled with cucumber, nothing else, just cucumber. No wonder the English lost their empire. Laurel sat primly at the edge of her chair, knees together, one hand on the teacup, the other in her lap, a thoroughly proper hostess.

"There's no bookie, is there, Laurel? Leonetti wanted to find Yip Yip for himself."

She paused with her cup in midair.

"I had so hoped this was a social call," she said.

"And the fifty grand has nothing to do with a sports bet, does it?"

She put down the cup and looked away. Perhaps she was trying to think of an answer, or perhaps she was merely imagining the invisible presence of some overzealous prosecutor's hidden microphone. She sighed and returned her gaze to me.

"You disappoint me. I'm not privy to Mr. Leonetti's personal financial transactions. And were I so, I couldn't possibly in good conscience answer you."

"I'm not after Leonetti, Laurel. In fact I'm trying to help him."

"How's that?"

"I'm after the people who are blackmailing him."

Her face showed genuine surprise for the first time. She replaced the cup in the saucer.

"Blackmail? What are you talking about?"

"Yip Yip Martin was blackmailing Leonetti."

"I find that very hard to believe."

"Nevertheless, that's what seems to have been going on. I don't know how much your boss told you, but I'm pretty sure that fifty grand was blackmail money."

Laurel was silent for a time, composing her reply carefully.

"Firstly, you should understand that Yip Yip Martin was a very low-level employee of Mr. Leonetti's. His potential access to any evidence of a business impropriety that could be used for blackmail—were such improprieties to exist—was extremely limited. He wasn't even allowed into the control room unless accompanied by Mr. Smith or Mr. Jones. Secondly, Yip Yip Martin was not exactly—how shall we put it kindly?—intellectually gifted. What I'm saying is that he couldn't have understood a balance sheet, even if he got his hands on one."

"He didn't need to. He wasn't blackmailing Leonetti over business."

"Then what?"

"His wife."

"Celeste?"

I nodded and sipped the tea. "How well do you know her, Laurel?"

"I know that she was a model; still is, in fact."

"Laurel, Celeste was into kinky sex."

"Kinky sex?" She smiled slightly. "And exactly what is 'kinky sex'?"

"Exhibitionistic sadomasochism," I said, trying to keep the language abstractedly mutlisyllabic, but from the look on Laurel's face I guessed that such things had not been on the curriculum at Smith. "Bondage and discipline," I explained, "with an audience."

"Really?"

"Really."

"And how do you know this?"

"I've seen the photographs."

"You have pictures?"

"That's the problem," I said. "Yip Yip had them, too."

"I see." She took a sip of tea, replaced the cup, and stood. "Would you like to see the rest of the apartment?"

What I wanted was to finish this conversation, but if she wanted to show me the apartment first, then I would see the apartment first. I stood.

Laurel led me down a long hallway, past open doorways,

one of which led to a study, another to a den, three or four
to bedrooms. We arrived in front of a closed double door at
the end of the hallway, which she opened to reveal what
must have been the master bedroom.

It was a large room, furnished with pieces of modern
European design: a king-size bed against the wall, tables on
either side, and matching chests of drawers against the side
walls. There were four gigantic photographic reproductions
mounted on the walls, all of Celeste Stevens, all nudes,
but nothing that, with a little airbrushing or a strategically
placed perfume bottle, could not have made advertising
copy.

Laurel looked at me in silence.

"No," I said, answering her unspoken question. "They
were nothing like these."

Laurel smiled in reply, and led me across the room to a
door on the opposite wall. She opened the door and we
walked through.

At first I thought the room we had entered was a gymna-
sium. One of the walls was mirrored, and there were several
pieces of equipment, chrome metal with padding, which I
took for exercise machines. But then I looked again, and realized they had no weights. The side wall was faced with
stone blocks, like a dungeon, but smoother—sandstone perhaps. Embedded into these at intervals were ring bolts and
chains. A rack nearby held various implements: whips,
blindfolds, paddles, gags, and many others whose purpose
I could not immediately identify.

I recognized the place. The photographs I had found at
Trainor's cottage had been taken in this room.

I looked back at the wall through which we had entered.
It was made up of television monitors, like a smaller version
of the wall at the Factory. Laurel went to a video player in

the corner, and inserted a tape. She picked up a remote control, returned to stand by me, and fast-forwarded through the tape. At some random point she pressed *play*.

The screens came alive, filled with a giant image of Celeste Stevens. She was handcuffed to a padded bench, her head over one end with her hair hanging loose. She was not alone; a man and another woman were also with her. There was no sound apart from the music. The film was frankly pornographic, but the filmmaker must have known his or her business, for the cinematography was of a higher quality than is usually associated with the genre, more art film than X-rated one.

Laurel watched with detached interest.

"The wedding tape," she explained.

"You knew about it?"

"Yes," she replied, with a mischievous smile. "I was a guest."

"You?"

"Who do you think introduced them?"

"You knew Celeste before?"

She shrugged her twin-set shoulders matter-of-factly. "I've probably had sex with Celeste Stevens more often than Mr. Leonetti has."

We were no longer having tea with the Queen.

"Are you telling me you were having an affair with Celeste?"

Laurel burst into laughter. "An affair?" She took off her glasses and looked at me curiously, as if unable to believe the evidence of her own eyes. "How very old-fashioned you are. Perhaps I should explain: the Factory is certainly Mr. Leonetti's primary enterprise, but it's not his only one. Among his other business interests, Mr. Leonetti owns a second nightclub, much smaller, very exclusive, very expensive. This second nightclub caters to people with particular interests, and who are unencumbered by the usual social constraints. Celeste frequented that club; in fact that's where I introduced them. But you mustn't think that their relationship in any way inhibited them sexually. It would not be unusual for Celeste to have sex with a dozen people in a single night. Occasionally I was one of them."

"I see," I said, suddenly feeling very provincial. It seemed that this kind of thing was reaching epidemic proportions. "Well, whatever the case, it seems that somehow Yip Yip Martin got ahold of compromising photographs, and was using them to blackmail Leonetti."

Laurel smiled again. "Do you really think Yip Yip could have blackmailed Mr. Leonetti over this?"

"What makes you think he didn't?"

"After the wedding, every guest received a sterling silver cigar case, from Tiffany's. Inside each was a copy of the tape, a computer disc with high-resolution copies of the best photographs, and a piece of the bride's wedding dress—things to remember the occasion by. Does this seem to you the behavior of a man and woman trying to maintain a secret? They are usually discreet, but I assure you that neither Mr. Leonetti nor Celeste conceal their lifestyles. Now, how Yip Yip got his hands on the photographs I don't know. But the notion that Mr. Leonetti was susceptible to blackmail on the issue is, to put it politely, quaint."

So much for my theory. I looked around the room. "Must have been a hell of a wedding."

"It was," Laurel said, taking the comment at face value. "We had a wonderful time. It was in early May, the first really warm day of spring, absolutely cloudless. We had the ceremony itself on the roof garden. Celeste was beautiful, she wore a fabulous dress—Gaultier, I think. There were flowers everywhere."

"It was a real wedding?"

"Oh, yes. Episcopalian, at least until we got rid of the minister. Pagan from then on." She smiled, enjoying the memory. "After the ceremony itself we had the wedding feast, still on the roof garden. Oysters, caviar, wild salmon that had been smoked for the occasion. Lots and lots of champagne. Then we came downstairs for our own special ceremony. We modeled it on the Elysian ceremonies, but adapted for our own special tastes, of course."

"Of course."

"You disapprove?"

"Does it matter what I think?"

"No," she admitted. "We're beyond caring about such things. Which of course is why Yip Yip Martin could not have been blackmailing Mr. Leonetti."

"Then how did Yip Yip come to owe Leonetti fifty thousand dollars?"

"For the simplest of reasons. Mr. Leonetti lent him the money."

"What for?"

"The truth is I don't know. He asked, Mr. Leonetti gave."

"Why would he do that?"

"Purely business. Yip Yip offered a tempting rate of return."

"How much?"

"One hundred percent," Laurel said. "In a month."

"That must have been a very risky bet."

"There was collateral involved."

"Which was?"

"Yip Yip Martin's life. When Yip Yip asked for the money, Mr. Leonetti agreed to give it to him, but with the condition that he would kill Yip Yip if he didn't pay back both principal and interest within thirty days. No extensions. No exceptions. No excuses. Yip Yip Martin knew

Mr. Leonetti well enough not to doubt the threat. His acceptance of the condition convinced Mr. Leonetti that whatever Yip Yip was up to, he was confident of its success."

The video was still running. The man had disappeared, leaving Celeste alone with the other woman. The latter was wearing nothing but long satin gloves, stockings and shoes, and a corsage on one wrist. She had her legs either side of the bench, astride Celeste. Her back was arched, her arms straight, her hands on Celeste's breasts, and she was slowly rocking back and forth on top of the bride. I recognized the profile. She still had her glasses on.

"You look good with your hair down," I said.

Laurel followed my look to the tape and watched it for a moment in abstracted silence, like an actress watching the rushes, curious to see how well she had played the scene.

"I should have trimmed those roses," she said. "The thorns scratched."

"You were a bridesmaid?"

"Yes, I was." She returned her gaze from the tape to me. "Mr. Leonetti still wants his money back."

"There is no money, Laurel. Leonetti took a bad risk."

"If that's true, then that's fine," she said. "But may I offer you some advice?"

"Go ahead."

"Don't get rich quick, Lysander Dalton."

"Not much chance of that happening."

She looked at me for a long moment, thoughtfully chewing at the end of the glasses held in her hand, with just the hint of a smile in her eyes. Apparently the sound on the film was not completely erased by the overdubbed music. Above it I could faintly hear someone, either Celeste or Laurel, inarticulate but expressive. Laurel heard it, too, and smiled.

"Now," she said, "is there anything else I can do for you?"

Before I'd met Beth, I would have considered this question more closely. But now it was unthinkable. I took a deep breath. "No," I replied. "Thanks for the tea."

The smile disappeared from her eyes, but she had been too indifferent to the outcome of the invitation to be in any other way visibly disappointed. I followed her back through the penthouse to the front door. We stepped onto the landing. Laurel shook my hand in farewell.

"You still have my number," she said.

"Yes, I do."

"Perhaps next time you can bring your lawyer friend."

I couldn't imagine Laurel and Valentina being in the same room without attacking each other. "Not without tying you both down first," I said.

"Yes," Laurel replied, the humor returning to her eyes. "That would be the general idea."

She stepped back inside and closed the door.

SIXTEEN

I returned to the Plaza, mixed a drink, and looked through the Yellow Pages for another hotel. My funds were rapidly dwindling, and the time had come to stay someplace cheaper. The Chelsea had a room available—shared bathroom, but the rate was reasonable. I told them to expect me in an hour.

I called the front desk to prepare the bill, packed my few possessions into the only thing available, a laundry bag, and went downstairs to check out. I looked over the bill before they entered the total onto the credit card imprint taken when we had checked in. Besides the room charge there were amounts for taxes, minibar, and telephone calls. These latter were listed by telephone number. I looked through each of them, recognizing all but one of the entries. It was a local Manhattan number, and the call had been placed while I was meeting Beth Houston the previous morning.

Valentina must have made it shortly before disappearing.

I settled the bill, went to a pay phone in the lobby, and dialed the number. It was answered on the first ring by a male voice.

"The Mark Hotel," he said. I had to ask him to repeat it before I understood that I had dialed a hotel, not someone whose first name was Mark. But it made sense: before disappearing, Valentina had arranged for alternative accommodation.

"Do you have a guest named Valentina Mariposa?" I asked.

"One moment, sir." I could hear a keyboard tapping in the background. He was soon back on the line. "I'm sorry, I have no guest under that name."

"What about Valentina Devereux?"

More tapping. "Yes, sir, Ms. Devereux is currently staying with us. Should I connect you?"

"That's okay, I'm going to meet her. What's the address there?"

"Twenty-five East Seventy-seventh Street," he replied, "between Fifth and Madison."

Less than a mile away. I thanked him and hung up.

Seventy-seventh is a quiet block, lined with trees and stately town houses. Central Park is at one end, and the expensive boutiques of Madison Avenue at the other. There was little traffic, even at the hotel. I had initially gone to wait in the lobby, but the Mark is a discreet European-style establishment with a lobby not much bigger than the reception desk, and I was clearly out of place. I retreated back to the street, installed myself on someone's million-dollar stoop, and kept watch on the hotel's entrance.

What the hotel traffic lacked in quantity it made up for in quality. Limousines were more frequent than cabs, and the guests had that confident air of people who have never had trouble finding the rent money. One car was particularly memorable.

I have a theory that Ferraris—notwithstanding their awkward road manners, huge maintenance bills, and temperamental natures—are the best value-for-money vehicles in the world. How can this be? Simple: Ferraris are the only cars that consistently sell for more used than they originally cost new. Own one for long enough, and the rate of increase in value eventually offsets the costs associated with purchase and maintenance. The trick is to have enough money to buy one to begin with.

Nowhere is this theory better illustrated than with the Ferrari Daytona. Daytonas were built in the early seventies, the last front-engined V-12s Ferrari made for a quarter century, and a car that became the stuff of legend, even as they were rolling out of the factory. New, they cost around $20,000—a large sum at the time, but which now would only get you a Ford Taurus, and then only if you went easy on the options. Today, a Daytona will fetch $150,000 easily. But for one in pristine condition, such as the silver convertible I saw pull up in front of the Mark that evening, you shouldn't expect any change out of a quarter million.

The driver was middle-aged, carrying a little too much weight, wearing an Italian sports coat that went well with the car. He stopped by the awning, emerged awkwardly from the vehicle, and tossed the keys to the valet. The valet smiled: this was the reason he had become a parking valet. He got in and pulled the car forward—very, very carefully. The owner went into the hotel with the careless demeanor of someone who knows that if this car disappears, he can always get another.

He came back a few minutes later, accompanied by a woman in a tight black dress. I immediately recognized the walk, the slightly unsteady gait of someone wearing a thigh holster.

The doorman opened the passenger-side door for Valentina, while the other man tipped the valet. Everyone nearby stopped to admire the pretty girl getting into the pretty car—everyone except me; I was racing down to the corner of Madison, desperate to find a cab.

I got lucky, and the cab turned into Seventy-seventh Street before the Daytona had left the curb.

"Follow that car," I said to the cabdriver. In any other city that line would have been worth at least a laugh, but the only acknowledgment I got was a curry-flavored grunt.

We followed the Ferrari down Fifth Avenue and across Central Park. There was little risk of losing them: they drove slowly, apparently enjoying the cooling dusk and leaf-canopied passage through the park. On the West Side the trees were filled with tiny fairy lights, just becoming effective in the gathering darkness. This turned out to be their destination: Tavern on the Green. These were the same lights we had seen from our suite at the Plaza. I wondered if, while on the balcony there, Valentina had looked out at the distant scene and thought it was a place she'd like to try.

They pulled up in front of the restaurant and went inside. The cab dropped me nearby. I paid the driver, took up a position on a park bench with a good view of the restaurant, and kept an uneventful watch for the next two hours.

When I saw them come out—and had stayed long enough to be sure they were going straight to the car rather than taking an evening stroll beforehand—I raced out onto Central Park West, and hailed another cab.

"There's a silver convertible about to come out of Tavern on the Green," I explained to the driver. "I want you to follow him." This one didn't even grunt.

Soon I was again following the Ferrari through the park,

this time through the West Eighty-first Street entrance, which emerges on the East Side at Seventy-ninth. We ended up where we had begun: in front of the Mark Hotel. But only Valentina got out.

"Where to now?" the cabdriver asked.

It seemed a safe bet that I could find Valentina at the Mark later. Before confronting her, I decided to find out all I could from the other man. "Stay with the convertible," I said.

The Ferrari pulled away. We followed.

At first I thought he must have realized he was being followed, because he made so many turns. But then I figured out that the plethora of one-way streets dictates the occasional complexity in getting around town in New York City. Six left turns after leaving the Mark, we were at the same place where we had emerged from the park: East Seventy-ninth Street. This time the Ferrari pulled into an underground parking lot, between Fifth and Madison.

I paid the cabdriver, and waited on the opposite side of the street. Soon the other man emerged from the parking lot, whistling quietly to himself, tossing and catching his keys as he strolled along the sidewalk. He was in a good mood. I was looking forward to ruining it.

He skipped up some steps and unlocked the front door to a four-story Beaux Arts town house, the sort of residence you might expect of a man who drives a $250,000 car. He disappeared inside, and I crossed the street for a closer inspection.

The door was made of polished walnut, with frosted glass inserts, but protected by a solid steel grating that would be difficult to get through. There was a brass plaque to the side: "The Clifford Ward Gallery," and underneath in smaller letters, "By Appointment Only." It seemed that he was an art dealer. The art dealing business was obviously profitable.

I guessed that the lower part of the town house had been given over to galleries, while the upper floors were the residence. I stepped back and looked up. As if to confirm the theory, a light came on through the second-floor windows.

I pressed the intercom and waited.

"Yes?"

"Your car's on fire," I said.

"What?"

"I'm from the garage," I said. "The Ferrari you brought in caught fire as soon as you left."

It was just the sort of thing that a thirty-year-old Ferrari might do. He said nothing more. The intercom clicked off, and soon I could hear the thump of rapid footsteps from within, crashing down the stairs and across the entrance foyer. There was the sound of keys jangling before the front door opened and the man, coatless and frantic, burst onto the stoop. I shoved the barrel of Trainor's shotgun under his chin.

"Hi, Cliff," I said. "Let's chat."

Close up he looked to be less than the sum of his parts. He was forty or so, but had a face with too much pudge and too little character. It was smooth shaven to the point of glistening, although that may have just been a sudden sheen of sweat from having a shotgun at his throat.

"What do you want?"

"I have a few questions about your date tonight."

"My date?"

"Yes, Cliff—the woman you just dropped off at the Mark."

He relaxed slightly, perhaps relieved that I wasn't here to take his paintings.

"Okay," he said. He glanced up the street. "But we should get back inside before they see us."

"They?"

"Yes, let's go inside, okay?" He was eager to get back into that house.

"How many are there inside, Cliff?"

"How many what?"

"Other people."

"I live alone."

"That's not what I asked."

"There's no one inside."

"One more chance, Cliff. But understand that if it turns out you were lying, I'll pull the trigger on you first."

He swallowed. "There's no one. Now can we please get inside before they see us?"

"Before who sees us, Cliff?"

"The neighbors, of course."

He's being threatened with a 20-gauge tonsillectomy, and all Clifford Ward can think about is his reputation with the people next door.

"Okay," I said. "But keep it slow. Anything sudden, and I pull the trigger."

He nodded in assent. We went inside the town house.

The entrance foyer was simple but elegant. The floor was tiled in marble, and the sole piece of furniture was a small table bearing a silver platter with a dozen or so of the gallery's business cards. A wooden staircase led up. It was lined with an Oriental runner, secured at each step with a polished brass rail. The front rooms leading off either side of the foyer were hung with paintings: galleries, as I had guessed. A hallway led back to what I assumed were more galleries. I closed the door behind us.

There was a coat closet and, opposite that, an alarm panel, switched off. The sound of keys that I had heard had been Clifford Ward deactivating it before opening the front door.

"Which way?" he asked.

"What's upstairs?

"Scotch whiskey," he answered. "I sure could use one."
That settled it. We went upstairs.

Double doors at the first floor landing led to a large sitting room occupying the entire front of the second floor,
with wide windows giving onto Seventy-ninth Street. One
wall had a fireplace, unlit, with a sofa and two comfortable
chairs facing it. There was a writing table by the window,
and a large cabinet built into the wall opposite the fireplace. Curiously there were no paintings, nor the objets
d'art scattered about that you might expect to find in an art
dealer's sitting room. Perhaps he got sick of the stuff.

We went to the cabinet for the liquor. He took out two
double old-fashioned glasses and put in ice cubes, carefully handling the tongs, one cube at a time. He was a fussy
man, the sort of man who never gets dirt under his finger-
nails, the sort of man my father would never have trusted.
He was generous with the Scotch in his own glass, under-
standable enough with a pump action shotgun pressed into
your back. I topped mine with soda from the siphon. He
took his undiluted with anything but ice. We went by the
fireplace and sat, him on the sofa, me in the adjacent chair,
with the shotgun resting on the arm, pointed at my companion. My finger never left the trigger.

"Let's start with some biographical detail," I said.
"Who are you?"

He took a swig of Scotch before answering. "Clifford
Ward, as you guessed. To be precise—and at the risk of
sounding pretentious—Clifford Ward, *the Third*. Andover
and Yale. Art history was one of my majors. Dealer for
many years, here for the last seven. That's about it."

"Who's Valentina Mariposa?"

"A lawyer from Washington."

"How do you know her?"

He paused before answering, forehead beading with sweat, obviously making up a reply. I hoped he was better with his clients when sticky questions about provenance arose. "Valentina went to Yale, too," he said eventually.

"She went to Georgetown, Cliff."

He smiled weakly and said, "A story without inconsistencies is probably a lie?"

I briefly pointed the shotgun at the cabinet we had just left, and pulled the trigger. It made a nice big boom, and there was lots of shattered glassware.

I returned the aim to Clifford Ward.

"Well, that's just wonderful," he said. "Just wonderful." He looked genuinely angry.

"I don't like inconsistencies," I said. "If I hear another one, your knees are next."

"If you want to inflict injuries, then I'll be happy to get you something quieter. But please don't go letting off that blunderbuss again."

"That's entirely up to you. Start talking."

He took another large swig of whiskey, then sat back and sighed. "The truth is that, although I am an art dealer, in a manner of speaking I also work for the federal government," he said.

I glanced around the room. "Gee, they pay better than I would have thought."

"The house isn't mine," he said, ignoring the sarcasm.

"And the car?"

"Loaner from the government."

"Sure, Cliff. Classic Ferraris are just the sort of thing that would get into the federal budget."

"Actually, it didn't cost them a dime," he insisted.

"I see. Someone donated it?"

"You could say that, yes." He smiled for the first time. "I'm led to believe that the DEA confiscated it from a drug dealer in Miami. We're borrowing it, so to speak."

"Who's 'we'?"

The smile disappeared. "I fear that you're not going to believe me." He eyes flickered nervously toward the shotgun.

"Try me."

Clifford Ward took a deep breath. "The CIA," he announced.

"Think of your knees, Cliff."

"It's true," he insisted.

"You're trying to tell me that *you* are a CIA agent?"

"Goodness gracious, no, not me. But Valentina is."

I was considering shooting him when I remembered the phone calls: Tate, Tate & Buchanan's 202 area code being answered by the same voice as the Preston estate's 540 area code. And then there were all those passports and guns I'd found in her apartment.

"Tate, Tate & Buchanan?" I asked.

"A CIA front. It's a genuine law firm, but it was set up specifically to handle CIA business."

"The Preston estate?"

"I'm told that's where they used to debrief defectors in the old days. Now it's mainly used for conferences and meetings. I've been there myself. Charming house— Palladian, you know."

I recalled the bookcase full of foreign language literature. It also explained the picture books of the U.S.: welcome to America, comrade.

"What's the security like there?"

"At Preston? Tight as a miser's purse. They have microscopic fiber-optical cameras embedded in the walls, like surgeons use. Invisible, if you don't know they're there." Which explained why Valentina and I had ended up outside that evening. She had not wanted to be recorded on video-tape.

"And how do you fit into this, Cliff?"

"You mean you haven't figured it out yet?"

"Figured what out?"

"How I fit in."

"No," I admitted. "Why don't you enlighten me?"

"Very well." He stood, more confident now, and gestured toward the bar. "Do you mind?"

"Go ahead."

I kept the shotgun leveled at him as he returned to the bar, stepping gingerly around the shards of broken glass.

"I just hope this still works," he said. He began manipulating part of the fixture. Soon there was an audible click, followed by a section of the cabinet swinging away. Behind it was a large area of bare wall and a series of gray boxes—obviously electronics—with multiple cables coming out. I stood and made my way through the broken glass for a better look.

One of the cables was a power cord, others were coaxial connectors, the remainder went to what looked like large suction cups attached to the wall.

I pointed at one of the gray boxes. "What are these?"

"Digital recorders," he said. "They don't use tape anymore. Too clumsy."

"And these?" I pointed to the suction caps.

"Think of them as electronic versions of a doctor's stethoscope."

CIA associate or not, Clifford Ward III was obviously an eavesdropper who listened in on his neighbors.

"Who's on the other side?" I asked.

He smiled at me, a magician about to reveal a neat trick. "The ambassador's office."

"What ambassador?"

He named the nation—one of those hardscrabble Middle Eastern countries with which we seem to be in permanent conflict over theology or oil, and ruled by misogynistic dictators with a taste for harboring anyone with a pathological dislike of things American.

I put down the shotgun. It seemed that Cliff was working for the CIA after all.

SEVENTEEN

CLIFFORD Ward III called the Mark, and briefly explained the situation to Valentina. To both his relief and mine, the Scotch bottle had not been among the victims in the cabinet. We sat with refreshed glasses, and he began the explanation.

"I understand that originally the CIA were installed in an apartment across the street," he said. "They did that well before my time. Apparently it wasn't a very satisfactory arrangement. They set up video surveillance, and had directional antennae pointed at the windows. Occasionally they picked up something interesting, but for the most part all they got was a record of who came and went through the front door. Eventually this building came onto the market. It was expensive, but not much compared to the cost of all the cruise missiles they were then regularly sending hither and thither. They bought it. Of course they needed someone as a front man. In those days I had a small gallery down on Lexington, not terribly successful I'm afraid to say. One day a lawyer from Tate, Tate & Buchanan called out of the blue, requesting an interview. Of course I asked what it was about, but all he said was that he would prefer to discuss it in person. We met. I was hoping that it might be a bequest from some distant but very rich relative. In a way that's what it turned out to be: a surprise gift from my old Uncle Sam. Eight weeks later I was installed here."

"Lucky you."

"I actually do sell quite a few paintings now—I think the address makes them more appealing. And I have to look as if I belong in a place like this, hence the car. Anyway, that's the arrangement. As far as I can tell the neighbors have no suspicion that I'm here for any other reason than to sell art." He looked sternly at me. "Of course with your antics tonight, that may have changed now." At that moment the doorbell rang. "And either that's them now, dropping by to find out what all the noise is about, or Valentina has arrived." He stood and whispered confidentially. "Between you and me, I'm not sure which I find the more frightening: the neighbors or Ms. Mariposa."

He went to the intercom. It was Valentina. He pressed the buzzer to open the doors below. A moment later Valentina entered the room like a dyspeptic Valkyrie. Clifford Ward and I looked at each other with that silent comradeship of men in a room with a woman they both know to be unmanageable. Valentina put her hands on her hips and looked at the damage to the cabinet before fixing me with a hard eye.

"Temper problems?" she asked.

"Failure to communicate verbally."

"You suffer from immoderation," she said. "I thought

you would have given up after your trip to D.C. was so pointless—except the voyeurism, of course."

"I spent hours examining your underwear," I said.

She looked at the drink Clifford Ward was holding. "The whiskey survived?"

"Yes."

Valentina went to the bar and poured a drink before joining us at the fireplace. She sat in the unoccupied chair and looked at the shotgun I was still holding.

"I should have taken that," she said. "Some people can't be left alone with firearms."

"Thanks for the farewell note."

"What could I have told you?"

"Good-bye?"

"I couldn't risk you not accepting it."

"Don't overestimate yourself."

"I didn't mean personally," she said. "You were a lead that had turned into a dead end. I am a resource that could be better used elsewhere. The time had come to move on. The most effective way to do that unimpeded was for me to simply disappear. When this operation is over I will reappear, and all would have been explained. Except that you seem to have short-circuited the process."

"What is 'this operation'?"

She turned to Clifford Ward. "How much have you told him?"

"Only who I am, and about the setup here."

She turned back to me and took a contemplative sip of whiskey before beginning.

"So you know the reason we're here is to capture intelligence from their United Nations' mission next door?"

"Don't they sweep for bugs?"

"Bug sweeps look for transmitters. That's why we're

right next door. It's all hardwired. There are no transmitters to find."

"Do you get much?"

Clifford Ward leaned forward, interested in the answer himself. They obviously told him very little.

Valentina looked at him, as if uncertain whether to continue, then back to me. "Every pin dropping," she admitted.

"What has any of this got to do with me?"

"One of the pins that dropped had your name on it," she replied. "By the time we got the translation, the operation was already under way. All we knew was that you were the target."

"Of the next-door neighbors?"

"Not the country itself, but some terrorist group with training camps on their soil, and now with people in the United States."

"Why me?"

"Good question. The night they attacked your house I was trying to get to you before they did. But you got to me instead."

"How did you know?"

"From in there." She pointed at the splintered cabinet. "A terrorist cell has entered the United States. We know very little about them, just that these are not the usual wild-eyed religious lunatics with a Koran held in one hand and a detonator trembling in the other. They are highly trained soldiers, as you already know. Perhaps they're not even zealots, just a team of professional mercenaries hired to do a job. How or when they entered the country we have no idea. More importantly, we don't know what their purpose is, although it's obviously not likely to be benign. All we know for sure is that they're here. The first mention we got of them came from the other side of that wall a week ago. That mention included your name and address. I was already at Preston that evening. I received an urgent call to get to you as fast as possible. I was on the way when you suddenly emerged from the undergrowth and pointed a gun at me. The rest I think you know."

"Why didn't you tell me all this then?"

"We had no idea who you were. You could have been one of them, for all we knew. As things worked out, my cover as a lawyer turned out to be an excellent excuse to stay close while I found out all that I could. So I stuck with it."

"Are you a real lawyer?"

"Yes. I'm a member of the D.C. and Virginia bars."

"So what did you find out?"

"Well, as you know, you and I unearthed Yip Yip Martin's involvement, which connected it to Trainor. When we got the connection with Trainor, we suddenly had an explanation of why you had became a target. I know it's your life we're talking about, but in the big picture I'm afraid that you're simply a side issue—just a payback from Trainor. It was clear that you would be of no further use, so I left. End of story."

"And you became involved in this only a week ago?" Leonetti said that he had seen Valentina in his nightclub at least a month before. She looked at me curiously, perhaps sensing that the question was a trap.

"No," she answered carefully. "I said that we only discovered there was this terrorist cell in the country a week ago. The surveillance operation here been going off and on for years."

"When did you personally become involved?"

"About five weeks ago."

"How?"

She looked questioningly at Clifford Ward. He shook his head, as if to say he hadn't revealed anything. Valentina said, "Go ahead, Clifford—this is your moment of glory."

Clifford Ward smiled broadly and took up the story, as eager as a child.

"Well, it seems that the deputy attaché for cultural affairs next door is actually the . . ." He looked questioningly at Valentina, lost for words.

"He's the head of station for military intelligence," she said.

"Yes, that's him," Cliff continued. "Ugly fellow, a real needle-under-the-fingernails type. Now, strictly speaking, my role here is to do nothing but sell paintings—maintaining the facade, so to speak. But one does want to do one's duty and all that, so I took it upon myself to keep an eye on this fellow." He looked sheepishly at Valentina—this had been a subject of discussion before, and she had not approved. He turned back to me. "The only living creature he likes is his dog, a bull terrier, which every morning he takes for a walk in Central Park. I took to going out for a morning walk myself at the same time. After a while I became acquainted with his routine. The pattern is that the dog runs around on the hill, then eventually does his thing, which the deputy attaché cleans up. He then goes to the bathroom outside the boatshed, and flushes it. I always thought that was a little strange: why not just toss it into a trash can? But no, the attaché always walks along the same path, past several trash cans, all the way to the boatshed bathrooms. I assumed it was some sort of Middle Eastern thing—perhaps there are hygienic rules for doggie-doo in the Koran." Valentina rolled her eyes. Clifford pointedly ignored her and continued. "Anyway, one day while on the way to the boatshed, he suddenly stopped. I was behind him, and I stopped, too. For a moment I thought that he'd realized I was following him, and was going to confront me. But it wasn't me he was looking at, it was a *tree*." He placed great emphasis on the last word, as if it was a remarkable thing to find in a park.

"A tree?" I offered, hoping to prompt an explanation.

"Exactly," Cliff confirmed. "He was completely focused on a tree. A particular tree. Now, I thought that was odd—even the most enthusiastic of arborealists is unlikely to pay special attention to a tree when holding a load of hot doggie-doo in his hand. But instead he actually went right up to it and examined it." Clifford paused to allow me to express appreciation of his thought process.

"Yes, you're right," I said, hoping that we might eventually come to a point. Valentina, who had obviously heard it all before, looked ready to explode with impatience.

"Well," Cliff continued, "after a while the fellow eventually moved on and went to the bathroom as usual. After he left the park I went back to the tree and examined it closely, trying to see for myself what had interested him so. And sure enough, I *found* something." Dramatic pause.

"What did you find?"

"A chalk mark," he announced, much as Lewis and Clark may have reported finding the Pacific.

I turned to Valentina. "Huh?"

"It's a classic signal for a dead letter drop," she replied, eager to remove the story from Cliff. "My colleagues had asked Mr. Ward to report anything unusual. When he got back to the gallery he phoned them. That was when I was brought in—until then it had really only been an ongoing administrative operation, with the day-to-day running left in the hands of the translators, and just occasional oversight from a field officer. But it was obvious what had happened: the deputy attaché put the chalk mark on the tree as a signal that he had left a letter in a dead letter drop. That was when I was called in."

"What happened?"

"The first step was to try to spot the pickup. I made some calls and had a man on surveillance within an hour.

I was afraid that we might be too late, but it turned out to be ridiculously easy. The pickup should have been wearing sunglasses, so that no one could follow his eyes, and is supposed to walk casually by the tree without explicitly looking for the signal. But this guy not only looked directly at the tree, he actually went up and examined the chalk mark. Needless to say, our man followed. Can you guess where he went?"

"Bathroom at the boathouse," I said. Valentina smiled.

"Exactly. The pickup went inside, my guy followed. The pickup went into a stall. My guy went to the sink and watched in the mirror. It was comical: the pickup actually got down on his hands and knees, feeling around the back of the toilet until he found the drop. He left without even flushing. My guy stayed with him. Can you guess who the pickup turned out to be?"

"Yip Yip Martin."

"Very good." The teacher was pleased with the pupil. "What happened next?"

"I began investigating Yip Yip."

"At the Factory?"

"Yes, at the Factory." She took a sip of the whiskey, then leaned back in the seat before continuing. "The trick in these things is not to be too curious. First get known, and save the questions for later. I went to the club a few times, letting people get used to me being around. I even danced up on that observation platform outside Leonetti's office, hoping to be seen, maybe even get invited inside."

"You were seen," I said. "And if Laurel Honeysuckle hadn't been there, you probably would have gotten an invitation, too."

She smiled. "So you knew?"

"I knew."

"For how long?"

"Since I talked to Leonetti."

"And you said nothing?"

"No."

Valentina looked a me for a long moment in evaluative silence. "For an immoderate man," she said eventually, "you have unusual patience." She sipped the Scotch and continued the story. "In the end I didn't find out much before Yip Yip suddenly disappeared. It was clear that he'd been planning to do so for a while, and had taken some of Leonetti's money with him. My boss decided to gather the various operational units at Preston on Monday, and try to figure out what was going on. I went down there the weekend before, so it was pure luck that I was nearby when suddenly your name and address were overheard next door."

"Am I really wanted for the two police officers?"

"Yes, that part's true."

"The bodies were at my house?"

"They were."

"And the gun with my fingerprints?"

"That was there, too."

"Do the police know about you?"

"Of course not," she said. "I don't exist."

I was beginning to understand. When Clifford Ward had revealed the listening operation on the embassy, I thought the knowledge had given me the upper hand. Now I realized that Valentina had had me trapped all along. The one witness to my innocence was, as far as the authorities were concerned, fictional.

"And what will it take for Valentina Mariposa to reappear?" I asked.

"Full cooperation."

"Until?"

"We've found out what the terrorists are up to. And stopped them."

"What guarantee do I have that you'll come forward then?"

"None," she replied.

"I might just go to the authorities anyway. I might reveal everything I know, including all about this little setup here."

"You might," Valentina said. She took a sip of whiskey, and nodded toward the writing table. "The telephone's over there. I believe the correct number is 911."

It occurred to me never to get caught in a high-stakes poker game with this woman.

"Okay," I said. "Consider me on board."

"Splendid," Clifford Ward said. "It's so nice to see an ordinary citizen volunteer to serve his country." He managed to say this without the least trace of irony.

"What's the plan from here?" I asked.

"You have to understand that our first priority is to locate that terrorist team," Valentina said.

"Makes sense."

"It's clear that they're being aided by the embassy staff next door. They already made one mistake when they revealed you as a target, and if we'd had more resources available the night they attacked your house, we might have got them there. Perhaps they'll make another mistake, something that will reveal their location to the listening devices we have here."

"Perhaps."

"And the license number of the truck Yip Yip rented has been passed through the FBI to state and local authorities. Of course the usual national terrorist alerts have been activated: greater airport surveillance and baggage checking, tighter border inspections, increased security in federal buildings, that sort of thing."

"Okay."

Valentina moved uncomfortably in her seat, but seemed reluctant to continue.

"Well?" I prompted.

"Well," she said, "there is one other lead we're going to try."

"Yes?"

"You tell me, what were *you* going to do next?"

"There was that message on Trainor's answering machine," I said, "setting up a meeting for tomorrow night. I was going to go and see if he shows up."

Valentina and Clifford looked at each other meaningfully, then returned their eyes to me—two scientists gazing at a rat in a maze.

"Yes," Valentina said, "that's what I thought you'd do."

A predictable rat, apparently.

"So?"

"So, do you recall that there were *two* messages on Trainor's answering machine?"

"Yes," I said, "but the first one was just a hang up."

"Do you know who it was?"

"No. Like I said, it was just a hang up. Do *you* know who it was?"

"Yes," Valentina said. "I do."

"Who?"

"You."

"What?

"It was you. Remember, *you* called Trainor's number. You got the answering machine, and listened to the tape. The voice on that tape confirmed we had the right L. Trainor. But the machine must have started recording before you ended the call. It recorded you, even though you said nothing."

"Okay, so what does that mean?"

"It means that the second message was left *after* you called."

"Yes?"

"But we know that Trainor was already long gone by then. So why would someone leave a message for him?"

"Presumably they didn't know he wasn't there."

"There's a better explanation than that."

"Which is what?"

"Which is that the message was left for *you*."

"What are you talking about?"

"This assault team has tried to take you out twice: once at your house, again at the nightclub. Now, instead of continuing the chase, they've decided to invite you to come to them."

I was starting to figure it out. It occurred to me that Valentina didn't think I was very smart. It further occurred to me that she was probably right. She continued the explanation, apparently in the belief that I would not understand until it was all spelled out.

"Here's what we think happened: they made the hit at the Factory, missed you, and then evacuated the area. Meanwhile, you and I went to Olga's apartment, and you found the photograph. Perhaps it had been left there deliberately. Perhaps they went to Olga's place later, and discovered that we had already been and gone. In either case, they knew that you'd recognize Trainor, and assumed that you would track him down. The rest is simple: they leave a message on the answering machine, knowing that you'll listen to it. Then all they have to do is wait at the appointed time and place. Instead of chasing around after you, they organized it for you to come to them."

Once again I could not help feeling a grudging respect for whoever was leading the team: the plan was admirably simple, but I had never even begun to suspect. "It was a trap," I said.

"You have a gift for stating the obvious," Valentina responded.

"And it was a trap that you were going to let me walk into."

"As I told you, our first priority is to find the terrorists. If we could have identified them before they hit you, we would have moved in."

"And if not?"

"Must I state the obvious, too? It's a risk that we had to take." She was not apologetic. Perhaps she felt no need to be.

"Did you trace the number of that second call?"

"Pay phone on Delancey," Valentina said. "Near the address for the meeting."

"What's at the address?"

"Abandoned warehouse, built under the approaches to the Williamsburg Bridge. Three BMT lines run across the bridge: the J, M, and Z. There's usually one going past every minute or so. Makes a racket as it goes over the warehouse. We figure they would have looked for you coming in, then waited for a passing train to cover the noise of the—"

"Yes," I said. "I think I get the rest of it."

I went to the cabinet and refilled the glass. No club soda this time. I could feel her eyes on my back, watching curiously, wondering which way the rat was going to turn. I tried to think of alternatives, but it was clear that she'd left me only one way out of this particular maze.

I turned to face Valentina.

"Okay," I said, answering the unspoken question. "I'll be your bait." She merely nodded—I was too unsurprising a rat to warrant anything more. "I want body armor," I continued.

"Of course."

"Kevlar."

"Naturally."

"And I want a 5.56 with metal jacket ammo."

"Why not Teflon?" she asked. "Better penetration."

Yes, she was of course acquainted with Teflon ammunition. She was also doing a very good imitation of concern.

"Okay, Teflon," I said. "And stun grenades. And smoke. And hands-off communication."

"No problem. You'll wear a wire and earpiece."

"And a small nine mil., for backup."

"Okay," she said. "Ankle holster?"

"No, that's for the knife."

She nodded like a sommelier approving a customer's choice of wine. "Any particular type?"

"Buck."

"Buck it is."

Valentina went to the desk and returned with a notebook, on which she made a list of my requirements, careful to get the details right. She drew a map of the location, showing the exits from the warehouse and what other features she could recall. Tomorrow morning we could go down at dawn and check it out firsthand, she said. She wanted to get one surveillance pair in early, but putting lots of people in too soon would make them obvious. She would start to trickle in the rest an hour or so before the scheduled meeting time.

We finished the basic plan. I took a spare bedroom on the third floor for the night. We agreed that the next morning, while Valentina and I surveyed the warehouse, Clifford would pick up my stuff from the Plaza's baggage check, then we'd all meet at the Mark for breakfast.

We said good night. Valentina returned to her hotel. I retired to my room. I lay back on the bed, and thought about what I'd been told while waiting for the sounds of Clifford moving about to quiet down.

The more I thought about it, the more convinced I was that they had believed me.

I had no intention of doing what they asked. Valentina would know that acting without probable cause could legally jeopardize everything that came after, and place the burden of proving intent on her own people. But if the assault team gunned me down first, they'd have all the probable cause in the world, and there could be no question as to the intention. And, as an added bonus, a witness to some CIA acts of questionable constitutionality would have been neatly removed. It was too big a temptation for a practical woman like Valentina to ignore. Body armor or not, my intuition was that she would prefer I not come out of that warehouse any way but feet first.

I gave Clifford Ward III an hour to go to sleep before I got out of bed. It had been a struggle to stay awake; I hoped that he had found no difficulty in dozing off. I picked up the shotgun, clicked off the safety, and quietly left the room. I presumed that the motion detectors, if he had any, would be confined to the galleries, and that the alarm system he had reactivated after Valentina's departure was connected to the doors and windows only.

I tiptoed down the stairs to the second floor and into the big sitting room we had occupied earlier that evening. I found the keys where Clifford had left them, in the top left-hand drawer of the desk.

I found something else, too: a handgun. I took it from the drawer and examined it in the streetlight coming through the big front windows. It was a Sig Sauer P232 automatic. These are interesting handguns: they use .380 ammunition—shortened 9mm—as a balance between power and concealability. They have no manual safety, just precision internal mechanisms guaranteed to prevent discharge unless the trigger is pulled, which gives the user that extra split second of speed in getting off the first round. I already knew that this had made them the weapon of choice for the Secret Service; perhaps the CIA had joined with them for the bulk buyer's discount. This particular example was the lightweight version with an aluminum frame, which turned an already fairly small but powerful handgun into something so light as to be barely noticeable. But this gun had something extra that most others don't: a sound suppressor fixed to the end of the barrel. Now I knew what Clifford Ward had meant when having earlier offered to find me something quieter than the "blunderbuss." I ejected the magazine, found it full, and pocketed the weapon. I grabbed two bottles of liquor from the bar, and went downstairs.

In the entrance vestibule I opened the coat closet and removed the fanciest thing I could find, an expensive-looking cashmere overcoat with an astrakhan collar. I put it on, despite the season. The two liquor bottles fit nicely into the exterior pockets, the guns inside. I slid the key into the alarm panel, deactivated the system, and opened the front door. No bells or buzzers went off, and I stepped out into the night.

EIGHTEEN

TOMPKINS Square Park sits in the middle of Alphabet City, close by St. Mark's Place, and a few blocks north of the Delancey Street approach to the Williamsburg Bridge. It is the East Village's traditional haven for the homeless: for Midwestern runaways with dreams gone sour, junkies too strung out to hustle for a hit; for the demented, the freaks, the losers, and the outcasts. That's where I went. It was two in the morning, not a great time to be in Tompkins Square Park.

I could smell the guy before I was able to make him out: a dark bundle of wretched humanity lurking on a bench, reeking of body odor and stale alcohol. The Temperance Fountain was nearby, erected to encourage the quenching of thirst with water, something it had conspicuously failed to do in this case. His face was half-hidden in a woolen cap, perhaps a ski cap, that had been pulled down low over his face. He took some waking.

He had no interest in the overcoat, showed suspicion at the money, but grew wide-eyed at the bottle of bourbon.

"I want your clothes," I repeated.

"All of 'em?" he asked, the first words he had spoken.

"All of them," I confirmed. "You can have mine."

He eyed the bottle wistfully, but shook his head. Stinking rags they might be, but he had grown used to his clothes, and was unwilling to part with them, no matter how good the offer. Or perhaps the one thing he had not lost in this world was his pride.

I pulled out the other liquor bottle, the Scotch we had been drinking earlier that evening. I had been planning to douse myself with it, for added effect, but my friend here was driving a hard bargain. He took the bottle from my hand like a monk handling a cherished relic, and ran his blackened thumb under the name.

"Laphroaig," he said. To my surprise he pronounced it correctly—lahFRARG. In the light from the distant street lamps I saw a tear roll down his dirty face. At first I took it for joy at the sight of the whiskey, but then he spoke.

"I was a man once," he explained, the voice surprisingly clear, "and I used to drink this. Now I'm an animal, and I lap like a dog."

He began to weep quietly. I didn't know what to say. I handed him my handkerchief, which he wordlessly accepted. We must have stayed that way for several minutes, me standing mute, he hunched double, lamenting for a lost life that he had been reminded of by a bottle of good Scotch. Finally he recovered himself, and blew noisily into the handkerchief before silently offering it back to me.

"Keep it," I said. His arm quickly withdrew. He was used

to people declining things he had touched. "Do we have a deal?"

"You want all of them?"

"Yes."

"I don't think you're gonna want the underwear."

"I want everything."

"You haven't seen 'em yet."

He stood and removed his overcoat, an old greasy garment that had once been brown. We apparently had a deal.

His spirits seem to have improved, and he began to chat as he undressed.

"I used to play golf," he said. Perhaps he was imagining himself back in the locker room, changing after a good round. "Do you play?"

"Sometimes," I said. "Not well."

"I had a handicap of six," he continued. "That's pretty good. Once I found a broken umbrella in one of the trash cans here. The handle was made from a pitching wedge. I used a chestnut for a ball, and played an imaginary round. People laughed at me, so I only did it once, but I enjoyed it just the same. I finished two under par."

He removed the last garment, a big pair of boxers, and held them toward me. I gagged.

"Told you so," he said.

"It doesn't matter. I'll take them." I needed all the smell I could get, and his boxers had plenty to spare.

I stripped, gave him my clothes, and began dressing in his. Compared to putting on the underwear, doing battle with a highly trained special operations team would be a breeze.

The final articles we exchanged were the coats. Before giving him mine, I emptied the pockets. His eyes opened wide as I removed a silenced automatic, then again when the sawed-off shotgun came out, but he was used to keeping to himself and said nothing.

I would have given him all the money I had, but I needed to buy some equipment, so I gave him what I could. He accepted it wordlessly.

"Thanks," I said.

He nodded in reply.

I turned and began to leave the park. I had gone twenty yards or so when I stopped. I went back, stood in front of the man, and extended my arm. We silently shook hands.

Delancey splits either side of the Williamsburg Bridge approach at Suffolk, then goes past old rotting brownstones and abandoned storehouses down to the projects that run along the East River. The monotony of the constant overhead bridge traffic is regularly interrupted by the thunderous passage of a subway train. It is not a high-rent district.

I had already rubbed dirt onto any exposed skin, especially my face, and with the woolen cap pulled down and a couple of days' worth of beard I hoped I was not easily recognizable. Nevertheless, it would be best if whoever was there saw a lot of me during the day, and so got used to the homeless man being around. I made my stumbling way along the sidewalk, tried to pick a relatively clean patch of concrete by a boarded-up storefront, and lay down to get some sleep. With the discomfort and smell I would have imagined sleep impossible, but I must have been very tired, for the next time my eyes opened it was bright daylight.

And my eyes opened very wide indeed, for I was awakened by a kick in the stomach. Not a gentle tap, but a barely restrained steel-cap toe right into the solar plexus. It took the wind out of me. I looked up to find the source.

It was a cop, young and thick-necked, one of those types who spend too much time on weight machines to make up for their lack of height, or perhaps for their lack of gray matter between the ears. He was smiling. He was happy in his work. He kicked me in the stomach again, harder this time.

"I told you to get moving," he said. His hand rested on his truncheon, aching for me to give him an excuse to use it.

I spent a moment amusing myself in imagining what I could do to him. A quick grab and lift of that steel-toed shoe would have him on his back. Then a heel into his larynx, softly to disable, or harder if I had chosen to asphyxiate him by crushing it. Better still would be to put the heel into his patella, breaking the knee, and leaving him with a permanent limp which would serve as a daily reminder of the NYPD motto: "Courtesy, Professionalism, Respect."

I smiled at the thought. He didn't like being smiled at, and kicked me again.

"Get moving," he repeated.

I stood weakly and stumbled away. He was pleased, he enjoyed bullying people—it was why he had become a cop in the first place.

What he didn't know was that he had done me a favor. There would have been watchers in place by now. Perhaps some of the special operations people were here, too. In New York, the sight of a homeless man sleeping on a sidewalk was so common as to be almost invisible. But being moved along by a beat cop was too genuine to be scripted—it would have legitimized me to all who saw.

I stumbled away from the area, bought coffee and a bagel from a cart, and ate breakfast while continuing uptown. I tried a few electronics stores around the Union Square area for what I wanted, but I had to wait until one of the sales clerks, holding his nose and trying to be helpful in order to get me out of the store, gave me the address of a place on the West Side that stocked the equipment I was asking for.

By lunchtime I had what I needed: a combination GPS

satellite receiver and cellular telephone. The total unit
wasn't much bigger than a cigarette packet. It came with a
CD-ROM. The unit would receive signals from GPS navigation satellites, which gave its continuous position. To
find out where it was, you simply called it over the cellular
system. Do that via a computer with the software installed
and you would even get a map, pinpointing precisely
where the unit was. It was designed for emergency use to
locate injured hikers or people lost in wilderness areas, but
would work just as well to find anything you attached it to,
as long as the batteries held out, which would be at least
twenty-four hours.

The difficulty would be attaching it to the opposition's
vehicle without getting caught. But a stumbling bum might
get away with it.

I hid the unit inside the overcoat and made my way back
toward the Williamsburg Bridge. I ate a couple of slices of
take-out pizza, guessing that I wouldn't be eating anything
more for a long time, and bought a packet of bubble gum
with which I could attach the unit to the car. I checked the
action and load on both weapons, made sure that they and
the GPS phone were well concealed, then returned to Delancey Street. I took up station on the sidewalk, a dozen
doors down from the address where a lot of people were
hoping to see me expire this evening.

I slept most of the time, like the homeless do. During
the intervals I was awake I surreptitiously searched for any
watchers, but if they were there I never saw them. As the
time ticked closer, there was a small but noticeable increase in foot traffic. A black man went into the nearby
deli, and was taking a long time deciding what he wanted.
A woman pushed a baby carriage along the opposite sidewalk, frequently stopping to coo at the child. It made no
sound in reply that I could hear. A delivery van had driven

past and parked down the street earlier, but no one got out.

I tried to think of what I would have done if I had been running the assault team. I wouldn't bring in the escape vehicles because it would be too easy to trap them, as perhaps that van I had seen earlier was positioned to do. But coming in on foot would make them extremely vulnerable. Then I remembered the guy wire at the Factory, and suddenly realized why they had chosen as a meeting place a location under a bridge.

I looked up. Nothing. Then I checked carefully along the massive span rising across the East River. It took a long time but I found them: four that I could see, minuscule against the industrial mass of the bridge, slowly making their way along the girders and beams under the roadway, perhaps three hundred yards away, and one hundred feet above street level. They were dressed in black, all but invisible if you weren't specifically looking for them. It was a great idea: take me out from the bridge while I'm waiting for Trainor to show up, then extract via a wire before anyone has even figured out where the shot came from. Once again I had to admire the operational mind behind all this. It was just a pity that I was the intended target.

I wondered if Valentina would think of the bridge. She was here somewhere, I was certain of that, but she was a spy, not a special operations officer. My money was on the assault team.

I tried to think where the extraction vehicle would be. The only possibility in the direction from which they were coming seemed to be the FDR Drive, but where could they park on a freeway?

I stood and slowly shuffled down the sidewalk, trying not to look purposeful. The black man came out onto the front step of the deli. He had finally chosen a beer, and was drinking from a can concealed in a brown paper bag. I avoided his eyes, but could tell that he was giving me a long hard look. I gripped the Sig in my pocket and spent a moment thumbing for the safety until I recalled that there wasn't one. I was just past him when I felt a hand on my shoulder.

I turned around.

"Want a beer?" he asked. His mouth smiled, but his eyes were without humor. He offered me his can. The other hand was in the pocket of a jacket. It occurred to me that we were likely holding the same model weapon on each other.

I took the beer and drank some. "Got a cigarette?" I asked.

"Sorry, don't smoke."

I nodded toward the deli counter, just inside the door. "They got some."

He laughed, relaxed now, certain that if I was suspicious I would have been unlikely to extend the interview by trying to cadge cigarettes. "What brand?" he asked.

"Salem," I said. "Menthol freshens the breath."

"Well, you sure could use that." He nodded to the guy behind the counter, who turned around, found a packet of Salem, and tossed them to the black man.

He didn't ask for any money. Now I knew where the watchers were: somewhere in or above this delicatessen.

The black man gave me the cigarettes.

"Thanks," I said. But he was already scanning the area by the warehouse, no longer interested in me. I scrabbled away down toward the East River.

There was plenty of traffic on the FDR, but none of it stationary. A footbridge led across the roadway to a thin strip of park on the other side, lying between the Drive and the East River. I took the footbridge, guessing that I would find the vehicle hidden among the trees on the other side. But I was only halfway across when, above the noise of the FDR traffic, I began to distinguish a deeper engine note than comes from any car. I went into the park and over to the edge of the water.

A boat was tied up fifty yards downriver. It was a Cigarette, one of those oversized speedboats with massive inboard engines, capable of driving the thing at sixty knots. The engines were at idle, ready to move at a moment's notice. There were two men, one at the controls, the other ashore, but only a step from the vessel.

So that was how they were going to avoid being trapped in a vehicle in Manhattan's labyrinth. They weren't using a vehicle. They were going to extract by boat instead.

The East River is not a river but an estuary, connecting New York's harbor to Long Island Sound. It is therefore tidal. I looked at the water below. From the swirls and vortices as it flowed past the embankment it seemed that the river was in ebb. At least that was in my favor: I was on the right side of the Cigarette to be carried down to it by the tide.

I took off the overcoat, rolled the shotgun inside, and wedged it into the fork of a tree. I would have liked some face black, but then I realized that the woolen cap would do just as well. I rolled it down over my face, and poked fingers through the fabric to make two eyeholes. The Sig Sauer would work well enough wet, for a while anyway, but I was less confident about the GPS phone. I wrapped it as tightly as possible in the plastic shopping bag it had come with, and hoped to keep the thing above water most of the time. I performed a last check of the action on the Sig, put a stick of gum in my mouth, stepped over the railing, and quietly slid into the water below.

The current was stronger than I had anticipated, instantly carrying me off the bank and swirling down toward the bridge. I still had boots on, used to doing so when fording streams or crossing paddy fields in my marine days. But marine combat boots are waterproof. These that I now wore had holes in the soles. They quickly filled with water, and were like dead weights on the feet.

I maneuvered as best I could, and was soon washed downstream to the Cigarette. It was secured bow to the current. I caught the stem with my one free hand to take the momentum off, then eased along the outboard side down to the back of the vessel. Above the low growl of the engines I could hear the two men talking above, although I could make out nothing of what they were saying, or even what language they were speaking. I reached the stern. The boat's name was painted across the transom in large black letters: *Annihilation*. Nice and cheerful.

There was a ladder and rail, meant for swimmers boarding the boat. I grabbed the rail to hold against the current. I had no hand free for the gun. If they found me now, I was fit for target practice.

I unwrapped the phone and turned it on.

Modern electronics are wonderful, but there are downsides. One of these is that nowadays you cannot go to a movie, play, concert, recital, or opera without the constant risk of people's watches or pagers or telephones beeping and chirping. That's what the GPS phone did: let out a piercing two-tone chirp to inform the user, and everyone within a five-block radius, that the thing was now *on*.

I thought that I had disabled that particular function. I should have read the instruction booklet more carefully.

The talk above stopped instantly. The Cigarette gently rocked as footsteps moved aft. I heard the twin metallic clicks of a gun action being moved back then sliding forward.

I took a deep breath, and dived.

The first priority was to swim up current. I had to find something on which to take a grip, otherwise I would be dragged away underwater, with no chance of getting back to the boat. I felt around in the murky darkness along the smooth hull, desperate for anything on which to take hold. I found a propeller. It stopped me being dragged away, but if they engaged the shaft now, I would lose a hand.

I held my breath for as long as I could. Unseen things bumped into me—I had no idea what they were, except that anything in the East River was unlikely to be a fish. Soon my lungs were burning, and I could think of nothing but the desperate need to breathe. It felt as if the air inside had somehow expanded, urging the lungs to burst. Then, when I could bear it no longer, I made myself stay for a slow count to ten. You can always go further, they had taught us at special ops school: there's no such thing as complete exhaustion. There is such a thing as unconsciousness, however, and by eight I could feel blackout closing in. I released the propeller, glided aft, and grabbed for the rear rail as I broke the surface.

I looked up, although there could have been a whole army there for all I cared—all I wanted now was to breathe. But there was no one: either the soldier had checked it out and found nothing, or had never made it down aft to begin with. I gulped down lungfuls of air as quietly as I could force myself to do, and checked the GPS phone. The display was still lit: it had survived the immersion.

The gum was gone. I had no idea where, perhaps in the desperation to get air I had swallowed it. I took another piece from my pocket and began to chew—salty tutti-frutti. After a minute it had achieved a suitable consistency, and I soon had the phone fixed in place.

Now at last I had a hand free for the Sig. I held it above water, let go the rail, and was carried down harbor, away from the Cigarette and under the towering bulk of the Williamsburg Bridge overhead. I caught a hold by the bank, and stayed in the water awhile to catch my breath before attempting the awkward climb up the embankment. As it happened, it gave me a great viewing position for what came next.

It was over thirty minutes past the scheduled meeting time by now, and it seemed that the assault team, having found no sign of their target, had decided to pull out.

The arch of the bridge of course rises toward its center, meaning that a guy wire running from the approaches above the warehouse toward the river itself would be running slightly uphill, which is useless. I was looking up when I saw their solution to this. Suddenly a metal-wire pendant dropped from the bridge, ending about fifty feet above the water. The guy wire ran down to it. They must have had the pendant coiled on a girder above until ready for use. Soon the first dark figure was sliding down along the wire.

Usually you wait until the wire is clear before sending the next man, in case someone gets caught up, but a second figure was sliding down before the first had released. They were doing it purely on timing intervals, a sign of a highly trained and very confident squad.

The first man reached the end and immediately released, dropping the fifty feet or so down into the water. The big boat's engines suddenly deepened as it pulled out from the embankment. Soon the second figure followed the first, then the remaining two as the Cigarette approached the drop point to pick them up. I hoped no one would notice the unit gummed to the transom while climbing back onboard.

The recovery was quickly completed and the boat's engines suddenly went from low growl to loud roar. It rose onto the plane, carving the first spray two-thirds down its length as it sped toward the harbor.

There was nothing technically sophisticated in the operation, which made me admire it all the more. It had been simple and precise, with the extraction phase executed as cleanly as any commander could wish for. From commencement to recovery could not have taken more than sixty seconds. These were not the Arab soldiers with which I was familiar, the ones who had surrendered to television crews.

Soon the boat was out of view, with just the dull hum of engines echoing through the canyons of downtown. I was about to start hauling myself up the embankment and out of the water when I heard voices from upriver. A dark cluster of people had gathered at the point where the Cigarette had been tied up. I was too far away to see their features. One held something that might have been a beer can in a paper bag. Another stood slightly apart from the rest, hands on hips, one knee bent and chin held high; a stance I knew well. It was Valentina. I could not make out what they were saying, but voices were raised accusingly, making obvious what I had already guessed: no one had thought of a boat.

NINETEEN

I pressed the buzzer repeatedly until at last there was a sleepy response.

"Hello?"

"Beth, it's me, Lysander Dalton."

"What time is it?"

"Two A.M."

"Go away."

The intercom clicked off. I pressed the buzzer again.

"Beth, I need to use your computer. You can go straight back to sleep, I won't disturb you."

A long pause.

"I don't know whether or not I should be insulted by that."

The front door buzzed open. I went inside and climbed the stairs.

Beth answered the door with dull eyes and mussed hair.

She was wearing a bathrobe whose pocket emblem proclaimed it as the property of the Tides Hotel in Miami Beach. It was several sizes too big, and despite being tied around the waist, part of the top bulged outward, revealing a breast whose nipple was peeking timidly around the fold of the lapel, as if wanting to see for itself who had come a-calling at this late hour. Sleepy and disheveled, I thought Beth was the most beautiful thing I'd ever seen.

Unfortunately, the sentiment was not reciprocated. Beth's first reaction on seeing me, dressed like a bum and dripping East River slop all over the hallway, was to bring a hand to her face. Whether this was from shock, or simply to avoid the smell, I never found out.

"God, but you're gorgeous," I said.

"I can't believe I had sex with you," she replied from behind her hand.

"Three times," I proudly reminded her.

"Even once."

"Beth, I need to use your computer."

"Wait here."

She retreated inside, closing the door behind her. It suddenly occurred to me that she might not be alone, and in the minute or so that she was absent I ran the range of emotions from cold fury to red-hot jealousy, finally settling into a dark melancholic despondency. But when she returned, the reason for her absence became clear: she was holding a big garbage bag, which she offered to me.

"Take off all your clothes and put them in here," she said. "I don't want them touching anything in my home."

"Okay." I took the bag.

"I'll boot up the computer," she said. Once again she retreated inside and closed the door.

I quickly removed all my clothes and put them in the garbage bag. Few things in life have given me as much pleasure as removing those boxers. I put the guns in there, too, so as not to disturb Beth. The only thing I kept out was the CD-ROM, which I was holding in my hand, waiting for Beth to return, when a door down the hall opened.

A sharp-nosed woman emerged, conspicuously holding a small trash bag, as if on the way to the garbage chute. But who empties their trash at two in the morning? She waited until her own door was closed before pretending to suddenly notice me. She stopped dead in her tracks.

"Good evening," I said politely.

Her eyes were as big as saucers. She liked spying on her neighbors, and now she'd hit the jackpot.

"Are you a friend of Beth's?" she asked, trying but failing to look me in the eye.

"No," I said, "I'm just selling CDs door-to-door." She looked for an admission that this was a joke, but I gave her none. "Your place is next," I added.

"Oh, no," she muttered, stepping back. "I don't want any CDs." She retreated to her door. "I don't have a CD player."

"I can sell you one of those, too."

"Oh, no . . . Thanks, but no." She retreated into her apartment, trash still in hand. I heard both locks being turned, and the chain going across for good measure.

Beth returned a moment later.

"What are you smiling at?" she asked.

"Nothing."

"Don't think you can just show up here in the middle of the night and sleep with me."

"The thought never entered my mind."

"Not until you've had a very long shower, anyway." She opened the door with a smile. "Come on in."

While the software was installing, I gave Beth an outline of the night's events. Most people on hearing a tale that involves the CIA and terrorists would have been all questions. But Beth's first reaction when I'd finished was a practical one.

"You haven't had food or drink in twelve hours?"

"No," I admitted.

"I'll fix something." She went back to the kitchen.

The most capable and ruthless woman I had ever met in my life was undoubtedly Valentina Mariposa, but it occurred to me that if I was condemned to be a guerrilla in some mountain retreat or jungle valley, with only one companion, I'd like the odds better with Beth Houston beside me. (Although we'd have to do something about that hair, which was a red beacon inviting exposure.)

The software installed successfully. I opened the program, attached the telephone line to the modem and, with fingers crossed, dialed the GPS phone's number.

A small window appeared containing a pair of icons, one a computer, the other a phone, with a line joining them and a red dot going slowly back and forth. Underneath were the words "Preparing message format . . ." A moment later this changed to "Dialing . . ."; then "Connection achieved . . ."; and finally "Position established . . ." A second window appeared, with a button marked "Show Map." I pressed it.

The screen went blank, and the CD whirred in the drive. A moment later a map appeared, in the center of which was Manhattan, with northern New Jersey to the left, Brooklyn and Queens to the right. A flashing red pulse of light marked the location of the GPS phone. It was in New Jersey, but well inland. Either the unit was malfunctioning, or they had found the telephone and for some reason left it on while taking it with them.

Beth brought what she apparently thought was food. It was an arugula salad, with a little oil and vinegar, some hearts of palm, fresh ground pepper, and a few thin shavings of parmigiano-reggiano on top. This came accompanied by a glass of mineral water.

I revised my previously held high estimation of Beth's value in jungle warfare.

I looked at the plate. She looked at me.

"Sorry," she said. "That's pretty much all I eat at home."

"It's just what I wanted," I lied. "Do you have a map of northern New Jersey?"

She did, a road atlas which she took from a bookshelf. I opened it to a page marked "Metropolitan New York City," and soon realized how the GPS phone had come to be so far inland. They had taken a river.

Several rivers, in fact. After leaving the pickup under the Williamsburg Bridge they must have gone across New York Harbor, along the Kill Van Kull that separates Bayonne from Staten Island, and through to the great container terminals at Newark. From there they would have gone up the Passaic River to where it's joined by the Pompton, then through to the farming territory of the Ramapo Valley, in the distant northwestern corner of Bergen County. I wondered what they were doing up there, that they wanted to be so remote.

I ate the salad in three mouthfuls. I was still hungry. No wonder Beth was so slender.

She sat beside me, looking at the computer screen. The red dot was stationary.

"That's where they are?" she asked.

"That's where the phone is. I won't know if it's where they are until I do some recon. Can I borrow your car, Beth?"

"You're going now?"

"Yes."

"What are you going to wear?"

I hadn't thought of that. The clothes I had come in were no use: they'd smell me before they saw me.

"Can I borrow some clothes, too?"

"Sure," she said. "I've got a floral print dress that you'd look just great in."

"I was thinking more along the lines of jeans and a T-shirt."

"Are you a size two?"

I think I detected a hint of sarcasm in this question.

"We're about the same height," I said defensively.

"How much do you weigh, Lee?"

I told her.

"How much do you think I weigh?" she asked.

I admitted that I had no idea. She told me.

It didn't seem possible that someone so tall could weigh so little, although the gnawing in my stomach after eating what was reportedly her usual nourishment was suggestive. Nevertheless, I must have looked doubtful.

"Don't believe me?" Beth asked. She stood, unbelted the robe, and said, "Why don't see for yourself?" The robe slid from her shoulders and fell to the floor. It seemed that there would be no recon tonight.

The next morning Beth returned to the apartment with coffee and pastries in one hand, and a shopping bag in the other. She had gone out early to find clothes for me. I had asked only that she ensure there were no synthetic fibers. Synthetics catch fire easily and, worse, melt into scalding patches on the skin—we never wear them in the special forces. She returned with a hundred percent pure cotton clothes, but not what I had expected. The trousers were fine—khaki chinos—but then she pulled out a loud Hawaiian shirt, covered in prints of bare-breasted hula girls.

"I got them from the office," Beth explained. "They're from a shoot we did last week—resort wear for the upcoming winter."

The pastries had little Stars and Stripes on toothpicks. I realized that today was the Fourth of July.

I'm not much of a flag waver. Overt displays of patriotism are too often accompanied by loudmouthed assertions of American invincibility for my taste—usually by people who have never served in the armed forces. They might as well be rooting for a football team. But the Fourth of July is an exception. I always unfurl the flag over the front porch, go into town for the parade, and clap as enthusiastically as everyone else. Realizing that the day had snuck up unnoticed made me miss my home all the more, and I couldn't help thinking about it.

It hadn't rained in the last week, and today was hot. The vines would need water, but there was no one there to irrigate them. And all the roses would be dead by now.

"What are you thinking about?" Beth asked.

I told her.

"What made you decide to get a vineyard?"

"I like wine, and I like space. Vines are low, so you can see over them—you're never closed in."

"You must like my apartment," she said. "No walls."

"I do like it, but that's because of the owner."

Beth laughed. "Was there space where you grew up?"

"Yes. I was born and raised in San Francisco. We had a house on a hill out by Lincoln Park, beyond the Presidio. There was a big garden. My mother loved to garden. And we could see out across the Pacific all the way to the horizon—when the fog let us, that is."

"Do you do the farming yourself?"

"Yes, except sometimes at harvest. One year a big thunderstorm threatened hail. The local radio station made an announcement, and all sorts of people turned up: housewives, schoolkids playing hooky, even lawyers and accountants eager for an excuse to leave their offices and get their hands dirty."

And a police officer. I was annoyed that I still hadn't remembered his name.

"Sounds like fun."

"It is, unless it rains."

"I wouldn't mind getting my hands dirty."

"I won't start the harvest without you," I promised. "But right now, I have to go and finish this business."

I dressed, made a last check that the GPS phone's position had remained unchanged, and left.

TWENTY

BETH'S car was a battered Alfa Romeo, a two-seat convertible that had been out of production for a decade and, judging by the continuously flashing warning light on the dashboard, must have been out of oil for almost as long. I took it out of the city, across the George Washington Bridge, and into Bergen County, New Jersey.

I stopped at a gas station with a convenience store. I topped up fuel and oil, then searched the convenience store for supplies. There was a children's driving game where the kids check off things in a picture book that they spot on route. This came with a pair of small plastic binoculars—not perfect, but good enough for my needs on a clear bright day like today. There were barbecue fire starters that would be useful if I needed a diversion. In a rack of maps by the checkout I found a reasonably detailed one covering the Ramapo Valley, including some spot elevations. I also got a folding knife, duct tape meant for on-the-run auto repairs, a handful of nutrition bars, and a couple of bottles of water.

A hour later I was in the Ramapo Valley. I parked a mile or so downriver from the GPS phone's position, and went the rest of the way on foot along the bank. I soon saw the Cigarette, tied up to a small wooden jetty, and as far as I could tell unguarded. I examined it through the binoculars. The GPS phone was still in place on the transom.

I climbed up the bank and to the top of a small hill which gave a broad view of the land below. A natural dip behind a tree root made a good recon position. I used branches to better conceal it, put the water I had bought at the gas station in the shade, then settled down for the long wait until nightfall.

The property I looked down over was a dairy farm, about twenty acres in all, divided by post-and-rail fencing into half a dozen paddocks. Besides the main house—an old clapboard building with wide verandahs at the end of a dirt drive—there was a concrete milking shed and a big red barn, large enough to comfortably shelter a herd during winter. But it was no longer a functioning farm. The cattle were gone, and the fields were mown rather than grazed.

There was a single vehicle in front of the house, a large black SUV with tinted windows. Another sign that this was not a working property: a real farm would have had a pickup truck. The main function of the wooden jetty was not to secure a boat but to support an irrigation pump, suspended over the river from which it drew the water. By the barn was a flatbed trailer stacked with aluminum irrigation pipes. It was attached to a tractor, but from the grass growing around the tractor's wheels it was clear that it hadn't moved in a while. But the farm could not have been out of use for long, for there were still stacks of fertilizer by the shady side of the barn, big plastic sacks whose contents would have been fed into the spreader that was quietly rusting nearby.

Two men came out of the barn and walked to the house. They weren't farmhands. They wore combat clothing and carried automatic weapons slung over their shoulders.

I studied them through the binoculars: one tall and thin, the other with a mustache and a shaved head. I jotted down their features on a notepad, and designated them A and B respectively. By recording each individual, I hoped by the end of the day to have a good idea of how many there were in total.

It took me a while to spot the third man, half a mile away down the dirt road. He was stationed as a sentry, hidden from the main highway, but visible from where I lay. I took note of the time, and wrote down every movement of personnel from then on. I wanted to know their routines as well as possible before making the insertion this evening.

The sentry routine was simple: each man relieved every hour, on the hour. There were no other lookouts that I could see. I presumed there would be a patrol later, probably a last check before dusk, and I would study them closely to get an idea of the perimeter defenses they had in place. Meanwhile I watched the foot traffic between the house and the barn, of which there was plenty throughout the day, although I was unable to get any hint of what was going on inside.

I saw no one big enough to be Luke Trainor.

Around noon a second black SUV turned off the highway and came down the long dirt track. Like the other vehicle the windows of this one were blacked out, and I could make out nothing of who or what was inside. It drove straight into the barn.

* * *

By the time the evening patrol commenced, the nutrition bars were gone and so was most of my water. It had been a long, hot day, unrelieved by cloud or breeze. At least it was good weather for the fireworks.

There were three of them, one taking point while the remaining pair surveyed the defensive perimeter. The set-up looked simple: two wires in arcs either side of the drive, and no munitions in place that I could see. After checking the wires, they made a cursory inspection of the grounds between the house and the river, casual enough for it to be clear that there were no mines or entrapments to worry about. They completed the patrol and returned to the buildings, going to the barn rather than house. Most of the other soldiers were there, too. The only one of the ten I had identified during the day that was not in the barn was on sentry duty.

I surveyed the house through the binoculars. There were no air-conditioning units visible, and the window facing the water that had been opened at around noon remained that way now, presumably in the hope of catching any breeze from the river.

It was not yet dark, but with that window still temptingly open, the house temporarily unoccupied, and the turnaround time for the sentry still well away, now was the time to move. I crawled back down the blind side of the hill, checked the load and action on both the shotgun and the Sig, then moved along below the ridge toward the area between river and house, which the patrol had made clear was undefended.

Undefended or not, I wasn't going to take unnecessary risks. I crept along the riverbank as far as the jetty, so as to have the shortest possible distance of exposed approach to the house. I took the opportunity to check out the boat.

I removed the GPS phone from the stern, but the battery was dead, so it was useless now.

I took a last look through the binoculars over the rise of the bank. The window was still open. There was no movement that I could see. I actioned the Sig to get a round into the breech, took a deep breath, and began the dash for the house.

I made it without incident and crouched back to the wall, below the window, regaining my breath, and listening for any noise from within. There was nothing.

Now came the bit I didn't like. I looked up through the window. The room was empty. I grabbed the sill and pulled myself through.

The room was a bedroom, minimally furnished with two camp beds, both with sleeping bags as the only bedding. There was shaving gear and a hairbrush on top of a chest of drawers. The single wardrobe contained a few coat hangers with uniforms, and there was minimal clothing in the drawers. All the gear was military.

One of the shirts bore sergeant's stripes. I checked the name tape. It read "Trainor."

Then I heard music, loud music. It had just been turned on, which meant that someone else was in the house. And then, feeling the hairs stand up on the back of my neck, I recognized the song.

Every company commander in a marine recon group has an individual call sign, selected at random. Mine was Black Tiger. Inevitably the company itself comes to be known by their commander's call sign, and my troops had taken a fondness to being known as the Black Tigers. They had, without any authorization from me, gone out and gotten themselves uniform patches bearing the words, and featuring a snarling tiger. The first I knew of this was when it was wordlessly presented to me as a fait accompli one morning on the parade ground, every man in the troop suddenly with this insignia sewn onto his uniform—even the lieutenants, who should have known better.

Worse, they had acquired a real cat as a mascot. It was a stray kitten, the only survivor of a firefight on our previous mission, found shivering under a strip of galvanized tin which a minute before had been part of the roof of a building that we demolished with RPGs. One of the troops had rescued it, and had apparently nurtured it back to health while hiding it tucked into the warmth of his flak jacket. The cat was inconveniently gray instead of black, but that didn't bother my troops—it was on parade with everyone else, and spent more time yawning than snarling. I was told that its care had been entrusted to the youngest soldier in the company.

It certainly wasn't by the book, but books are for the guidance of wise men and the adherence of fools. I let them keep the patches, and the cat.

There is an old Led Zeppelin track called "Black Dog." Dogs aren't cats—or tigers—but it was close enough for my troops, who were more interested in loud music than semantic accuracy: it became the company tune. At the coming home party after every operation the troops would drink themselves into a relieved and forgetful oblivion to that song, played over and over, as loud as the available equipment would allow.

And now that same song had begun echoing through the house just as I had entered it. It had to be a coincidence that Trainor had picked now of all times to play that music, but it was unnerving just the same.

There was nothing more to be found in the bedroom. The wise thing would have been to pull back, now that the house was clearly occupied. But I told myself that the loud music was a good cover, and that I should take advantage of it to move through the place without the worry of making noise. And the weapon I was carrying had a suppressor, meaning that any opposition could be quietly neutralized without giving me away. But in truth I just wanted to find out where that music was coming from. I opened the bedroom door.

It gave onto a hallway, running transverse. There were three other doors on the river-facing western side, presumably all leading into bedrooms like the one I had just come through. The opposite side was bisected by the main hallway, running perpendicular to this one and, although I could not see around the corner, presumably going all the way to the front door. At one end of the other side was an open door leading to a bathroom—considering the age of the house, probably *the* bathroom. The other was lined with closets.

The music was echoing down the main hallway, coming from the front of the house.

Basic military theory says that you secure your flanks before advancing, but I ignored the other rooms, and went straight to the corner where the two hallways intersected. It was as if I had been hypnotized by the song, and could do nothing else until I'd followed the sound of that music to its source.

I held the automatic in the ready position, and looked around the corner. The hallway ran to the front door, as I had assumed. Four doors led off it, two either side. I could see that the first of these on the left led to a kitchen. That would make the adjoining one the dining room. Both north-facing, deliberately located so that the summer sun would not unduly add heat to that from the stove, and so that dining could be done in the coolest part of the house.

The music came from one of the two rooms on the other side. I advanced up the hallway.

The song ended. I stopped dead still. A brief pause, then the sound of a turntable needle scratching. A little analog static, then the same song began again.

Someone was taking a trip down memory lane. I tried to remember if there had been a turntable in Trainor's place. There was none that I could recall; perhaps he had taken it with him. But there had been no records, either.

I was far enough advanced now to tell that the music was coming from the farthest room. I paused at the room before it, and glanced inside. It was a study, with maps and drawings lying scattered over the desk and pinned to the wall. Apparently the planning had been done in here. This was where I would return to discover what this business was about, but first I had to go to that front room.

A last visual check of the automatic, then I advanced to the corner of the door. My back was against the wall, and the music was loud enough to make it vibrate. I took a deep breath, and swung around, rapidly opening the field of fire.

The room was still, apart from the gentle undulation of the record on the turntable by a chair—apparently the vinyl was not quite flat after all these years. The room must have had the same furniture as when occupied by the farm family: old cloth-covered sofa and chairs, worn and dull except where antimacassars had once lain. There was a television on a little table, so old that it had a rotary channel changer. Rabbit ears antennae sat on top of the set. The floor was wooden planks, with a threadbare piece of rug in the middle. A fireplace which must have once warmed winter nights was fitted with a gas heater around a fake log.

Alone in the room, sitting in the chair next to the record player, feet up, back to me, beer in hand and apparently unaware of anything but the music, was a man who ten years ago had been one of my sergeants.

But it wasn't Luke Trainor.

TWENTY-ONE

I stepped quietly behind the chair, put the gun to his head, and turned down the volume. I pulled the hammer to the rear so that the metallic click would leave him in no doubt as to what was being held there. He moved enough for me to know that he felt it, but otherwise didn't react.

"Hello, Easy," I said.

I felt the smile rather than saw it.

"Hello, sir," Easy Black said. "Long time, huh?"

"Yeah, it's been a while."

"Grab a beer," he said, as if I was some old marine buddy who'd just dropped by. "Take a seat."

"I'll stay right here, Easy, in case one of your friends comes over from the barn."

"Don't worry about the towel heads," he said, waving his beer bottle to dismiss the problem. "I told them not to disturb us."

"Nice try, Easy. I don't buy it."

"Let me guess, sir. You were up on that little knoll just to the south, right? And you came in via the river side—I told my guys to tramp around there like a bunch of lost cows, so you'd know that was the easy way in. We left the back window open to make it real simple. There's a motion sensor on top of the wardrobe, by the way. That's how I knew when to put the music on."

Outdone by one of my own sergeants. I was a fool.

"Guess I'll have that beer after all," I said.

I took one from the cooler and sat in a chair facing his, ten feet distant. But I kept the gun on him. He'd aged, but not ten years' worth. Same old smile—easy by name and easy by nature.

"Nice shirt," Easy said.

"Thanks."

"You get the GPS unit back, sir?"

"Grabbed it on the way in, Sergeant."

"Good," he said, "those things are expensive."

He took a swig of beer, completely at ease.

It reminded me of the photograph that had been on Trainor's mantelpiece—Easy and Trainor sitting back sharing a beer and a joke after a big parade. I suddenly realized what it was that had bothered me about it.

Both of them had been wearing dress uniform—"Dress Blue A's" as we call it in the service, although the blue is so dark as to be virtually black. Their jackets, which hold the medals and rank insignia, had been discarded, leaving them in trousers and T-shirts. But then I recalled that Easy had been wearing something else as well: a sword belt. A black polished leather sword belt—the one that goes with the so-called Marmeluke sword. Only officers wear the Marmeluke sword. That's what was wrong with the picture: it had been taken *after* Easy Black had become an officer.

And therefore after I had left the service. After Trainor had raped and beaten a twelve-year-old girl.

So Easy Black had stayed friendly enough with Trainor to share a joke and a beer with him. I was pretty sure there was no one else in my company who would have done that. Remembering that one picture told me more about Easy Black than any amount of questioning would. More than everything I'd learned about him in the two years he was a sergeant in my unit, for that matter. Easy Black had a serious character flaw: he didn't know right from wrong.

"You used to be smart," I said. "Too smart to be suckered into something like this by Trainor."

"Actually, I suckered him."

"Where is he?"

"Twenty fathoms down, somewhere offshore."

"He's dead?"

"Unless he's grown gills." He smiled and took a long pull from the bottle. "So, sir, what have you been up to these last ten years?" For a man with a gun on him, he was very relaxed.

"I bought a vineyard after getting out of Leavenworth. But I think you've seen it, haven't you?"

"Only by night," he said, the smile ever wider.

"What about you, Easy? What's happened to you these last ten years?"

"Went to officer school after you . . . left. Came back with lieutenant's bars. Did a few ops, but decided to quit and go into business for myself."

"Doing what?"

"Consulting."

"What sort of consulting?"

He grinned. "International security."

"You're a mercenary?"

"Not exactly. It's more of a skills-for-hire thing. Some

Third World idiot's got soldiers can't shoot straight, they pay me to teach 'em how to aim."

I nodded toward the barn. "You did a good job with this lot."

"Took me six months to get them like this." He shrugged his shoulders. "They're okay."

"For terrorists."

He paused with the beer bottle in midair. For the first time he was something other than completely at ease.

"So you figured it out?"

"Yes, Sergeant, I figured it out."

"Doesn't matter," he said, the smile returning. "You're not going to tell anybody."

"You're a traitor," I said.

He nodded. "Guess I am."

"That doesn't bother you?"

He shook his head. "You ever stop to think that wherever we went, we ended up fighting people using our own weapons against us? Claymores in Asia, Stingers in the Middle East. How come no one ever accuses General Dynamics or the Raytheon Corporation of disloyalty?" He took a long swig of beer. "Hell," he added, "I'm Little League compared to them."

"How did you get involved with these people?"

"I'm a businessman now, sir. I supply where there's a demand."

"And who supplies the demand?"

"Just another guy with pocketfuls of petrodollars. Funding terrorists is a hobby for him, like model trains or collecting stamps. He greases a few government palms, gets a little help in return."

"Which government?"

"Let's just say I started in Jordan, and crossed several frontiers without the benefit of a passport."

"And what happened?"

"There was this training camp out in the wasteland. It was a joke—all posturing and no discipline. When I got there the latrines were cleaner than their weapons. I got rid of the wannabes, turned the rest into soldiers. A unit was formed, under my command. These are the best of them. They're okay now."

I could tell that he had bonded with them. It occurred to me that, apart from the question of national loyalty, Easy Black had made an excellent unit commander.

"They speak English?"

"Most do a little. All the NCOs do. But they've got accents, so I don't let them talk to anyone."

I recalled the second police officer in Little Washington. He had let the sergeant—Yip Yip—do all the talking. Now I knew why.

"Why are they here, Easy?"

He looked genuinely surprised. "You mean you haven't figured out that part yet?"

"No."

He laughed out loud. "Why do you think we had to take you out?"

"Payback from Trainor?"

"I killed Trainor before we hit your place."

"Then I don't know, Sergeant. Why?"

"Sir, you recommended me for officer school."

"I know."

"And the only reason I got accepted was because you trained me."

"Maybe."

"Not maybe. I had the physical skills. But you taught me how to think operationally."

"Okay."

"Remember how you trained us?"

"Sure."

I used to spring tests on the lieutenants. Without warning I'd present them with an operational situation, start a stopwatch, and give them a limited time to develop a tactical plan. When I recommended Sergeant Black for officer school, I began including him in the exercises.

Easy continued to look expectantly at me.

"You got it yet?"

"No," I admitted.

"Think about it, sir. When you and I were fighting the Iraqis back in '91, who were we working for then?"

"Uncle Sam."

"Not exactly."

"Okay, technically we were part of a United Nations force."

"Right," Easy said forcefully. "Now do you get it?"

And in fact I was starting to.

When New York's World Trade Center was attacked the first time, back in '93, the task I had set the lieutenants, and Sergeant Black, was to develop a plan for how they would have carried out the attack. Not surprisingly all four had better ideas than the terrorists did, but Easy had come up with the most audacious plan of all.

He had skipped the World Trade Center completely. Instead, he had suggested, why not take out the United Nations? And his plan was beautifully simple: just drive an explosive-laden truck along the FDR Drive, which runs *under* the UN, and simply stop. Set a three-minute fuse, then escape by boat along the East River. Nothing could be easier, he had said at the time.

Now I knew what the Cigarette was for. And I also knew why Yip Yip Martin had rented a big tractor trailer.

"The UN," I said.

"Exactly."

"You gave them the plan?"

"Approved by the man himself. In fact he improved upon it."

"How?"

"With timing. They tell me that every Fourth of July the American ambassador to the United Nations hosts a party on the UN grounds. Only friends of America get invitations, of course. It's a big event: all the allied ambassadors and their families attend. There's a barbecue, and then afterward they all stay to watch the fireworks, which are let off over the East River. It's a prime viewing spot, and they all crowd to the edge, right over the FDR Drive, as it happens. The man I work for decided that that would be the time to do it. He arranged for the people at their UN mission find out the details and pass them to us."

And undoubtedly that was what Yip Yip Martin had picked up at the dead letter drop.

"This year," Easy continued, "the fireworks are going to go off with a very big bang." He glanced at his watch. "The truck's in the barn now. It'll be leaving soon."

"What exactly do these people expect to achieve?"

"Isolation of America," Easy said.

"Then your man's an idiot. They'll be bombed into the Stone Age for this."

"Maybe," he replied. "Maybe not."

I couldn't see how it would be anything else, but I didn't press it. "What type of explosive you using?"

"Ammonium nitrate and diesel fuel."

Now at last I knew why Yip Yip had bought all the fuel. And those bags of fertilizer I had seen by the side of the barn were explained: the source of the ammonium nitrate.

"How much?" I asked.

"A whole container full, around thirty tons in total. Ten times as big as Oklahoma City. And I had my people cut weak points into the containers."

The effective destructive power of a given amount of explosive can be increased by giving an escape route to the blast, so that most of it will be directed at the target. That's what the weak points would be for.

"Way we figure it," Easy continued, "it should completely demolish both the General Assembly and the Secretariat Building." He finished the beer. "Of course, there'll be considerable collateral damage," he added.

Of course. Thirty tons would level a city block.

"So now you see why I had to take you out," Easy said. "I figured you'd remember those exercises, all those years ago, and realize it was me." He was right, I would have remembered. "By the way, that night at your place, how did you know we were coming in?"

"I didn't. I just got up to go to the bathroom."

"No kidding?"

"No kidding."

He laughed and shrugged his shoulders. "Some things you can't plan for." He opened another beer. "Caused me a lot of trouble though."

"Your troubles aren't over," I said. "You're a dead man talking, Easy."

"Maybe," he said. "But maybe not."

"You think I won't kill you?"

"No, I don't think you will."

"Then you're stupider than I thought, Sergeant."

But the comment just made him smile. "That's because you haven't seen what's in the drawer yet." He nodded to the drawer under the table on which the stereo rested. "Go ahead," he urged. "Take a look."

I put down my untouched beer, and approached the

table. Given that he was sitting so close, a booby trap seemed unlikely, but I wasn't taking any chances. I stood to the side, hooked the end of the flashlight into the handle, and carefully opened the drawer.

There was only one thing inside. Easy was right: I wasn't going to kill him.

I didn't move for a long time. Neither did Easy, except to quietly sip at his beer, letting me absorb the implication for myself.

The thing in the drawer was a long hank of hair. Red hair.

I returned to my chair. This time I drank the beer.

"It was simple," Easy said softly, almost apologetically. "They found the GPS phone last night, when they were tying up the boat. I attached a caller-ID unit. You checked the position this morning, and that gave me her number. I used a reverse directory on the Internet to get the address. The rest was easy."

"Where is she?"

"You know I can't tell you that."

"In the barn?"

"Would I be that stupid?"

No, he wouldn't.

"She's already dead, isn't she?"

"That would be stupid, too."

"Prove it."

He pointed at a shirt pocket. "May I?"

I nodded. He pulled out a small cellular phone, opened the mouthpiece, and dialed. I counted the digits. There were eleven: one for long distance, three for the area code, and seven for the number. Not a local call, which meant Beth wasn't nearby. Someone answered the phone.

"This is Black Tiger," Easy said. He covered the mouthpiece with a hand and winked at me. "Call myself that for old times' sake," he explained before resuming the telephone conversation. "Put the girl on."

There was a short delay, during which Easy pressed the keypad. "Erasing the list of previously called numbers," he explained, "just in case you decide to waste me and use the redial."

I hadn't even thought of it. I had to admit that the student had surpassed the teacher.

"Hello, Ms. Houston? I'm sitting here with Captain Dalton. He wants very much for you to survive this little ordeal, which will happen only if he cooperates with us. Before doing so, he asks for proof that you are safe. He's going to ask you a question, through me, to which only you will know the answer. In order for you to give me that answer, the guard will temporarily remove your gag. If you yell or scream, he will hurt you. Do you understand? . . . I'll take that as a yes." He looked at me. "Well?"

"What were in the pastries we had for breakfast this morning?"

Easy spoke into the phone. "What were in the pastries that you and he had for breakfast this morning?" He listened for longer than the answer would have required, and frowned, apparently not liking what he was hearing. Eventually he put his hand over the mouthpiece.

"She says that she's not going to answer, and that I can go jump in the lake." He shrugged his shoulders, at a loss what to do. Eventually he held out the phone. "You want to hear her voice?"

"No," I said. "That reply sounds about right."

He spoke briefly to the guard, ended the call, and put down the phone with a smile.

"You sure can pick 'em," he said. He looked at his watch. It was getting pretty dark now. "There's something else."

"What?"

"Maybe you better hear it from the man himself."

"What man?"

"*The* man."

"You mean he's here?"

"Yep. Came in country to see the fireworks for himself. Wanted to give the boys a little pep talk before the big event. Wants to give you one, too."

I took a swig on the beer. They'd been confident. "How's it work?"

"Two long flashes on a flashlight," Easy said. "He comes in here. He says his bit. He leaves."

"And the other signal?"

Easy smiled. "Five times," he said. "I made a big difference so they wouldn't waste us on account of poor arithmetic."

It's a standard protocol for signaling—either visually or by radio—when doing a covert insertion. One signal means "All clear." The variation means "I am or am about to be captured." The rule in special operations is that you don't leave your guys behind. So there can be two responses to the "I am or am about to be captured" signal: you either go in and get your guy or, if that's not possible, you make sure he's not left to the opposition's mercy. And every special ops soldier knows what comes next in the second case: a hail of RPGs; or a Hellfire antitank missile if the fortification is too solid for RPGs; or a satellite-guided five-hundred-pound glide bomb if there's close air support nearby—an F-18 doing lazy eights at thirty thousand, hoping for a call so that he can put the ordnance to good use rather than drop it in the ocean prior to returning to the carrier.

Whatever form it took, the response to the "I am or am about to be captured" signal would be enough to ensure that there would be no interrogations.

"He'll be alone?" I asked.

"Yep."

"Go ahead, Easy."

He stood and went to the window, made the signal, then returned and resumed his beer.

We waited.

"If this goes wrong," I said after a while, "I'm killing you first."

"Never doubted it, sir."

TWENTY-TWO

A few minutes after Easy Black made the signal there were footsteps on the porch, followed by the screech of an old fly screen being opened, then the front door. It closed, and the footsteps coming down the front hall sounded confident. They ceased to be confident when he walked into the room and saw my gun.

"I thought you said the situation would be resolved," he said sharply to Easy.

"Relax, Mr. Rahmani, he's just keeping his options open, that's all." Easy performed introductions, "Mr. Rahmani, Captain Dalton."

I couldn't see the man who stood before me very clearly. The light had faded while Easy and I talked, and the room was so dark now that I couldn't make out much more than outlines. Rahmani was wearing sunglasses, perhaps having forgotten to remove them from earlier in the day, but more likely they were intended to further disguise his features from me. He was of middle height, perhaps fifty years old, and had dark hair that I thought might have been flecked with gray. He was dressed in a business suit, navy blue, with a white shirt and a tie in a somber and restrained pattern. His shoes were well-polished black oxfords. He was clean-shaven, and I would not have taken him for an Arab—from what I could make out of his face his skin seemed light, almost pasty. And the accent came as a surprise.

"You're English?"

"No, not at all," he said. He went to the other armchair, sat back comfortably, and crossed his legs before continuing. "When I was a child many Arabs—wealthy Arabs, that is—still sent their children to English public schools. A last remnant of empire, I expect." He smiled. "Myself, I was a victim of Winchester—an utterly dreadful place. My own children, I am pleased to say, have not suffered the same fate."

I had expected a robed lunatic, an Osama bin Laden type, the sort of rabid animal with which nothing could be done except putting a round through its head. But this man actually seemed to be a human being.

"*You* are blowing up the United Nations?"

"No, Mr. Black is taking care of that," he replied carefully. "But, yes, I am paying for it." A stickler for semantics. His English master at Winchester would have been proud. "I take it that you have accepted our offer."

"What offer?"

"I didn't tell him that part yet," Easy explained. "All he knows about is the girl."

This obviously didn't please Rahmani—it wasn't what he and Easy had agreed to when they were setting this up.

"Very well," he said. "I needn't say that you have

caused us a great deal of inconvenience, Mr. Dalton, but I recognize that we of course have done the same to you."

"That's one way of putting it."

"I understand that you make wine?"

"Yes."

"And you sell it to a distributor?"

"Yes."

"Which distributor?"

"It varies. Generally to whoever's willing to pay the most for the vintage."

"Do you enter into long-term contracts with these distributors?"

"No, long-term contracts are only offered to established makers. I go year by year."

"Mr. Dalton, what we propose is that next year a distributor will offer you a long-term contract. The price per bottle will be double whatever it was this year. I hope that you will view this as adequate compensation for the inconvenience we have caused you."

There were many things that I would have liked to say in response to this "offer," but Beth's life depended on me getting this right, and I wasn't going to do anything to jeopardize that. I waited awhile, trying to think of what the best answer was before replying.

"Triple," I said eventually.

Rahmani nodded his head slightly—it had been the right response. "I'm in a difficult situation," he said, "but I'm still a businessman. Two and a half."

"Triple," I repeated. "You are, as you say, in a difficult position."

Rahmani shrugged his shoulders. "You would do well in the souk negotiating for a carpet, Mr. Dalton. Triple it is."

"And the girl released unharmed," I added.

"As you wish," Rahmani said. "But you understand that

our offer is terminated should she, or anyone else for that matter, publicly connect the incident with us."

"Most terrorists can't wait to take credit for what they've done."

"Most terrorists are fools and barbarians," Rahmani replied. "I am neither."

"You'd have a lot of difficulty persuading anyone that bombing the United Nations is anything other than barbaric."

He paused for a moment. He wasn't used to people who'd accepted his bribes questioning his motives. "A barbarian is a man who commits senseless violence, Mr. Dalton. That is, violence which does not have a specific intended consequence, violence that is committed for the sake of violence itself. Thus the World Trade Center was a barbaric act, because it had no specific intended consequence. What did it achieve for the Arab cause? Nothing. In fact it led directly to the invasion of Afghanistan, a disaster for the Arab world. Or take the bombing of the United Nations in Baghdad. Until then the U.S. and UN had been at odds. All that bombing achieved was to drive the Security Council sentiments into the arms of the Americans, and persuade them to give the Iraq invasion a UN blessing that had until then been conspicuously absent. It was worse than barbaric, Mr. Dalton, it was stupid."

"And tonight isn't?"

"In fact it *will* be barbaric. Horrendously so."

"Am I missing something here?"

"Undoubtedly. Tell me, when the dust settles—figuratively and literally—what will happen next?"

"They'll investigate."

"Starting with?"

"Physical evidence."

"Which is?"

I shrugged my shoulders. "The truck, I guess."

"And the truck was rented by whom?"

"Yip Yip Martin."

"Correct. And the explosive?"

"Diesel fuel and ammonium nitrate."

"Bought by whom?"

"Yip Yip Martin."

"The fuel only. In fact it was Sergeant Trainor who purchased the ammonium nitrate." He smiled at me. "Then the authorities will seek to discover where the bomb was made, will they not?"

"Yes."

"Which will eventually lead them to this farm. A farm whose lease was signed by Luke Trainor. I assume you're starting to understand now."

I recalled finding Trainor's uniform shirt on the way in. And the shaving gear and hairbrush—that would be there to provide the investigators with some DNA samples.

"Yes," I admitted. "I think I am."

"In Oklahoma City," Rahmani continued, "two disaffected ex-military men made a truck bomb with a mixture of ammonium nitrate and diesel fuel. They exploded it outside a federal building to express a generalized disaffection with government. This time, two disaffected ex-military men will have made a truck bomb—considerably larger this time—from a mixture of ammonium nitrate and diesel fuel. There will be a clear paper trail from both the truck and the bomb leading back to them. Once they investigate the men themselves they will find two unsavory characters: a former Hell's Angel who perhaps murdered his prostitute girlfriend, and a marine sergeant with a history of violence, at whose residence they will find enough evidence of anti-UN xenophobic bigotry to more than convince them."

I remembered the stuff I'd found up there. Rahmani was

right: once the investigators found that, they'd be certain that they had the right people.

"The next thing they'll do is try to discover who, if anyone, Martin and Trainor were connected with. The financing will lead them to a shady nightclub owner for whom Yip Yip Martin occasionally worked. But otherwise the two of them were loners, as people of their type tend to be, the sort who end up in some isolated Idaho outpost taking potshots at postal workers because they deliver IRS notices. But the one thing I have been very careful to ensure, Mr. Dalton, is that among all the evidence, they will find absolutely no link to us whatsoever."

Now I understood why they had decided to pay me off instead of killing me. It would have been okay to kill me earlier—Trainor had motive and opportunity—but it wouldn't make sense now, when Trainor was supposedly blowing up the UN, or on the run after having done so. Rahmani thought things through. It occurred to me that this man was more dangerous than a dozen Osama bin Ladens.

"When the investigation issues its initial findings," Rahmani continued, "it will confirm what by then every paper in the world will be reporting: the bombing was perpetrated by two American citizens who simply didn't like the UN. And it will be thought of, as you say, as an appallingly barbaric act. Except this time the barbarians will be Americans."

I couldn't help nodding; he'd thought through everything. "And it will be all the more believable because it's happened before," he added quietly. I remembered my own reaction after Oklahoma City. My gut had churned when I learned they'd been ex-soldiers.

"The world will be horrified, Mr. Dalton. And the victims? Not just random UN workers—the victims will be the diplomats of America's closest allies. And their families. And their children."

He let that sink in awhile. The children would be the icing on the cake; there could be nothing but revulsion for the killers of children.

"France and Germany both opposed the Iraq invasion," Rahmani continued. "How much more steadfast will they be in opposition to American policy after this? That is the difference between what I am doing and what has gone before. Khobar Towers? Those two African embassies? The World Trade Center? What did they achieve? The loss of Afghanistan and Iraq. That is barbarism, Mr. Dalton: violence which has no purpose. What I am doing is something quite different."

"Not really," I said. "You put a good spin on it, though."

"Not everyone's idea of civilization is *The X Files* and Big Macs." He looked at his watch. "Ah, but we've spent far too much time here talking." He stood.

"Guess you're going to see the fireworks," I said.

"A good carpenter wants to see the results of his craft."

"Sit close," I said.

He didn't like that much. "Remember our arrangement, Mr. Dalton." He nodded to Easy, then walked to the door. But before leaving he turned back to me. I thought he was going to add a few more threats, but instead he did something he hadn't done during the entire interview. He smiled.

"By the way," he said. "This one's just the beginning, Mr. Dalton. There'll be more."

TWENTY-THREE

EASY Black and I were left alone. We didn't speak for a while. Easy got up and turned a light on. The record had finished long ago, and the house was almost peacefully quiet. But then the silence suddenly ended, broken by the deep sound of a big diesel engine starting up. The convoy was leaving. The barn doors must have opened, and I could see the flash of headlights as the rig pulled out. The engine note was deep, the sound a diesel makes under a heavy load. Then the two light trucks started up, too. They would probably drive ahead of the big rig, acting as scouts. Soon the whole convoy disappeared down the dirt track and onto the highway beyond.

"Just you and me now," Easy said.

"When do the fireworks start?" I asked.

"Ten."

I looked at my watch.

"You're giving them a lot of time."

"They'll go slow. I don't want them getting pulled over by a cop. And with all that Jersey shore traffic, getting though the toll gates at the GWB will take thirty minutes alone."

"You're taking the boat?"

"Yes. It'll be much faster. We'll wait awhile yet." He finished his beer. "You didn't fool me with that 'triple' business, by the way."

"What do you mean?"

"You won't take it. Soon as we release the girl you'll go straight to the police. I told Rahmani that, but he's spent so long bribing everyone that he doesn't realize there are some people just don't get bought."

"So how do you see this going down, Easy?"

"I keep the girl until the job's completed, and the rest of the money's wired into my account. You keep quiet until I release her."

"Why would you release her?"

"Because I'm retiring. I'll be a rich man once this is done, and you can tell the world what happened for all I care—I'll be long gone. Truth is I wouldn't be unhappy for them to go after Rahmani, just in case he's got ideas about coming after me. And I'd kind of get a kick out of it—sitting back with a new face and a beer, reading about myself in the papers. But with a record like yours, and that setup with the dead cops, my recommendation would be Mexico."

So Easy Black's loyalty to his new boss lasted until the check cleared. I wondered how I had missed it all those years ago. I thought about him as I finished my beer. Try as I might, I could not remember for sure if he was left- or right-handed.

"Can you pass me another beer?" I asked. He took a

bottle from the cooler and lobbed it to me. He was right-handed. "Thanks," I said. I shot him in the right shoulder.

He seemed too surprised to be in pain, but when I put the second round into his right thigh he felt that pain well enough. It was good that there were no neighbors.

I stood, walked over to the chair, grabbed him by the hair, and threw him onto the floor. He screamed again, and I soon found the reason for all the noise: the second round had shattered the femur, and either the bullet or a bone fragment had severed the femoral artery. Blood was spurting out like a percolator with the lid off. I didn't have much time.

"Where is she?"

"You just killed her," he gasped.

"No, Easy. It was a mistake telling me you knew I wouldn't accept the bribe. If that's true, then there would have been no reason for you to let the girl live. You should think things through, like your pal Rahmani."

He made to grab at the injured leg with his good arm, but I already knew it was a feint. If Easy was a creature of habit, then he still carried a knife on the ankle. I intended to put a round into his left shoulder, but missed and shattered the elbow instead. My aim wasn't so good today.

With Easy now safely disabled, I pulled up his right pant leg. The knife was there, a large jagged-edged diving knife, more flashy than useful.

I pulled it out. "This is a stupid knife," I said. I threw it, point down, into the floor. "Let me show you mine."

I pulled out and opened my own much narrower-bladed weapon, let him have a good look, then drove it under the left kneecap, just like he did to Yip Yip's landlord.

Easy Black might or might not tell me where Beth was, but I was determined that if not, it wouldn't be for lack of pain.

He screamed as loudly as it's possible for a man to

scream. The blood gushed from his other leg with the muscular contraction. When he relaxed, it wasn't spurting anymore.

"Where is she?" I repeated.

But he was already slipping into that far-eyed shaking that men fall into as they bleed to death. He shook his head, but whether it was involuntary or meant to say no I couldn't tell. I flicked the blade under the kneecap, but he barely reacted.

He was right: I had killed Beth the moment I cut that femoral artery.

I tried the knife one more time. No reaction now, although he was still conscious. Trying anything further would be a waste of precious time. I put a round through his head.

The cellular phone was on the side table. I picked it up and checked the previously dialed number function. As Easy had told me, it was blank.

I kept the phone and went back to the study.

I tried the desk first. There was a computer, a laptop which I opened and turned on. While it was booting up I went through the other things lying on the desktop. Largest of these by far was a huge folio volume entitled *Architecturally Significant Buildings of New York*. The fold of the dust jacket was inserted as a bookmark. I opened it to the page.

Predictably, it opened at the United Nations. The entry was mostly photographs, although there was a short article that noted it had been designed by the Swiss architect Le Corbusier, and which enthusiastically praised the building's "sculptural purity" and "refined elegance." The entry included blueprints. One showed a side elevation, with the FDR Drive (then apparently still called the East River Drive) conspicuously running underneath. I closed the book.

There was a newspaper clipping. I read it eagerly, hoping for a clue as to where Beth might be, but it was only an article from *The New York Times* giving details of the July Fourth celebrations, including the fact that the fireworks would begin at ten o'clock. There was a sidebar on traffic restrictions. A part of the FDR would be closed, but that section was downtown from the UN, and so would not affect the insertion route. Not that it would have mattered: nothing was going to stop that big eighteen-wheeler.

There were two maps taped to the wall. The first covered northern New Jersey; the second was a street map of Manhattan. Routes were outlined in black marker, presumably the route that the convoy would take. They were using the freeways to cross New Jersey, coming into New York on the Major Deegan Expressway, crossing the Harlem River at the Willis Avenue Bridge, then down Second Avenue to the FDR at Sixty-second Street, the last on-ramp before the United Nations.

There were various operational notes. "Radio Silence" was scrawled across New Jersey; apparently Easy had not wanted to risk any ham operators monitoring the airwaves, and perhaps remembering some peculiar transmissions in Arab accents that night. An arrow marking the end of the GWB said "Break Radio Silence"—the electromagnetic cacophony of New York City would presumably be protection enough from there. An arrow a little lower down was marked "Go/No Go #1." This is usual in special ops, the preplanning of decision points for aborts. There were a thousand possible reasons to abort a mission: sometimes the weather kills the operation; sometimes you find that the bridge marked on a map no longer exists; sometimes the target itself has moved on. Once we were making a night insertion by Zodiac onto a beach when suddenly my radio operator collapsed with abdominal pain. I aborted. It turned out to be a burst appendix. Apparently he had been in intense agony for the last twelve hours, but not wanting to let the team down, he hadn't told anyone.

There were two similar abort points farther down the map. "Go/No Go #2" was in Harlem, "Go/No Go #3" was just before the FDR on-ramp. From that point there would be no going back. "Scout Drop" was at Seventy-ninth Street; presumably the light trucks would be abandoned there. The tractor-trailer would be on its own from then on.

Like a good commander, Easy had dotted in a secondary insertion route, in case of something unexpected interrupting the primary. I could imagine him sitting in this room with the navigators, making them endlessly repeat the details, drilling it into them as I had once drilled insertion routes into him.

There was no extraction route. Apparently it was the boat or nothing. Now it would be nothing.

I continued to study the maps. Search as I did, I could not find what I was looking for: there was no indication of where Beth might be.

The computer was booted up. I opened the icon for the C-drive, and studied the file names. "Supplies" was prosaic, basically shopping lists of food. The first requirement of any commander is to feed his troops; men don't fight well on empty stomachs. Another file contained the duty routines in the camp: sentry rosters, duty cooks, cleaning details.

"Communications" was more interesting. It contained primary and alternate marine VHF frequencies, along with call signs. I presumed the Cigarette was fitted with a radio. They must be intending to rendezvous offshore after the operation. There was probably an Arab freighter out there now, just beyond the twelve-mile territorial limit, monitoring the airwaves and waiting to hear their call sign.

I went into the Internet downloads.

The first folder of downloads contained material I had seen before: the anti–"New World Order" diatribes that had been at Luke Trainor's place. Easy must have downloaded them here, then gone up to Rhode Island after dispatching Trainor and left a copy of the disc there for the authorities to find. The second file contained a number of downloads from various real estate brokers' websites. I glanced through them, and came across what I had expected to find: an advertisement for the farm. "Rural Haven" it had been titled. The description said that it was "the perfect retreat for those who value their privacy."

The last folder contained downloads of tidal and astronomical data for New York on the Fourth of July. The tide was in flood, presumably going against the extraction route, but there was nothing they could do about that. The moon was more cooperative: it was new, meaning a maximum of darkness. Good for the fireworks. Good for escape, too.

The top drawer of the desk contained a set of keys with a tag marked "Cigarette": obviously the boat keys. The remaining drawers were, apart from an occasional pen or paper clip, empty. I had gone through everything. There was nothing that helped me locate Beth.

I slumped back in the chair. I couldn't help thinking that if I hadn't cut that femoral artery, I would have known where Beth was by now.

Never look back, they'd taught us. Reflection is the refuge of those who've lost the will to act. The only thing that matters is what comes next. And what came next now was the issue of whether Beth Houston would live or die.

There had been a time before when I'd let emotions get the better of me, and it had resulted in the end of my service career and a rapist walking away free. Now was not the time for regret. Now was the time to do what I was trained to do—take a bad situation and resolve it.

I sat up straight and gave that map another try. And then, as if in answer to an unuttered prayer, I noticed something. Something that didn't make sense.

Easy had taken the scouts out at Seventy-ninth Street. But the third "Go/No Go" was down at Sixty-second Street. Who would the truck be talking to then, to know whether or not to abort? The scouts were gone. And the Cigarette couldn't help: there was nothing a boat at water level would see. There was only one other option: there was someone else, someone in a position to tell the trucks what was ahead.

I scrambled back onto the computer, and reopened the folder that had contained the real estate broker downloads.

It took me just a minute to find.

PROSPECT TOWERS BEAUTY

Charming one-bedroom in white-glove doorman building. Hardwood floors and wood-burning fireplace. New kitchen. High floor. Sweeping views over the East River and United Nations. Available for short-term lease.

Now I knew where they were holding Beth. There was no apartment number, but there was a photograph of the building with a circle around the windows of the apartment. It was on the floor second from the top, the third and fourth windows in from the side.

I should have guessed that Easy would have a spotter in place, what we call a forward controller. Forward controllers are normally inserted for an artillery barrage. The guns themselves open up from many miles away, sometimes from ships offshore, in either case from well over the horizon and out of visual range. The forward controller is the only person who actually sees where the rounds land; he radios back corrections for azimuth and range, the gunners adjust, and the target is quickly and accurately destroyed, with only one person ever having gotten within close range.

In this case the forward controller would be directing not gunfire but the truck. From a vantage point high over the UN he would check traffic conditions on the primary and secondary routes, locate the police patrols, advise the optimum final approach, and, most importantly, visually confirm that the scheduled U.S. ambassador's party was going ahead as planned.

He would extract after the truck cleared the final abort point. His last act before leaving the apartment would be to kill Beth.

Then I realized the worst thing of all: he would also extract if the mission aborted. And if the ambassador's party evacuated, the mission would abort. That meant I couldn't call the authorities to evacuate the United Nations. If the forward controller saw an evacuation, he would call an abort, and then immediately extract. He would kill Beth on the way out the door.

The one thing I'd never been and never wanted to be in life was dependent on someone else. But I realized now that it had happened, although not in the way I'd thought it would. I had imagined dependency involved something tangible. But it turned out that I was not dependent upon Beth for what she offered, but simply for the fact of who she was.

Could I get Beth out, then initiate an evacuation at the UN? I did some quick calculations. How long would an emergency evacuation take? Fifteen minutes? But these things always take longer than you expect, and I was betting on being able to quickly convince the on-scene people to believe me when the time came. Call it half an hour. Nearby buildings could be done at the same time.

I knew how far I'd driven this morning, so I used that as a basis for a quick speed/time calculation for the Cigarette, assuming I could maintain a steady thirty knots. A Cigarette was capable of twice that, but the river would be narrow, and there could be boat traffic.

Say another ten minutes to get from the boat into the building.

I added it all up, and then looked at my watch. It left me just ten minutes to neutralize the forward controller from the moment I entered Prospect Towers. There was no fat on the sandwich.

"Too easy," I said out loud. I used to say the same thing to my guys. We all knew that it really meant: "This one's going to be a little hairy."

I grabbed the keys to the boat, and raced outside.

TWENTY-FOUR

THE Cigarette's instrument panel was at first sight large and forbidding, but most of the instruments were just standard engine monitors—water temperature, oil pressure, and the like—mounted in pairs, one for each motor. All I needed to use was the helm and the twin throttles mounted beside it.

The engines started on first try. I untied from the small jetty and kept the berthing lines, knowing that I would need them later. I touched ahead on the outboard throttle, and astern on the inboard. The enormous engines leapt into life, quickly twisting the boat stern out. I went slow astern on both engines, backed out into the river, turned the Cigarette downstream, and put the engines ahead.

Normally I would have prudently begun on low throttle and gotten a feel for the boat's handling characteristics before opening it up wider. The time for prudence was past.

I rammed both throttles fully open, and was rewarded by being all but knocked off my feet as the Cigarette surged up onto the plane. It responded well to the rudder, but the boat's enormous forward momentum, coupled with the little amount of hull in the water, meant that it skidded in a turn, and I was lucky not to inadvertently drive it ashore before getting used to it.

There was a VHF radio mounted on the console. I turned it on and tuned to the primary frequency in the communications plan I had read on Easy's computer. There was nothing but static; they were still in New Jersey, maintaining radio silence. I kept the volume on high.

Occasional boaters waved at me as I raced past, usually with a closed fist or some other digital expression of disapproval, for I was traveling well beyond the posted speed limit, and the Cigarette's wake threatened to swamp anything that was not large enough to be oceangoing.

It took fifteen minutes to find open water, which seemed forever to me, but was probably a speed record for the Passaic River. There was still nothing on the radio. The truck had at least a twenty-minute head start on me, but with a trafficless waterway I must have long overtaken it by now.

The boat shot out of the river into the big Elizabeth terminal. For the first time I met something waterborne that didn't race to get out of the way: a huge container ship with a bevy of little tugs in attendance. I swerved around and continued full throttle past Bayonne and into New York Harbor itself.

It wasn't until a police boat picked me up going past the Statue of Liberty that I realized that on this evening of all evenings—with barges full of fireworks and sightseers on the water—of course the water police would be out in force. I had at least twenty knots on the police boat, and left it behind bouncing in the froth of the Cigarette's wake.

But he would have a radio. If there was a second boat already in the East River I would be in trouble for a lot more than reckless boating.

I went under the Brooklyn and Manhattan Bridges in quick succession, then the Williamsburg. The wire pendant was still hanging there from the previous evening.

A blue light began flashing ahead of me. It was a second police boat, coming down from the Hell Gate, still several miles away. They had me trapped now, a boat at either end of the East River. But it would take them ten minutes to get to me, and I was already at the United Nations.

I came alongside the embankment by the FDR. I presumed the forward controller had noted the boat's approach but now, with the view from nearby buildings obscured by the UN itself, he would assume I was just idling offshore, waiting for the team to appear. I used one line to secure the Cigarette, and kept the other for myself.

I heard voices overhead. It suddenly occurred to me that maybe the police boat had somehow guessed my destination, and that an NYPD welcoming party had arrived. I looked up.

They weren't police. There were four or five laughing people, holding champagne glasses and dressed for a party, leaning on a rail high above both me and the FDR Drive in between. I realized that they must be guests from the U.S. ambassador's party. They were looking down, apparently having come over to see the Cigarette. One of the young women waved and said something in greeting, which I couldn't catch. I waved back, and tried to smile.

I went aft, opened the engine compartment, ripped out the electrical lines leading to the spark plugs, and threw both them and the keys overboard. If the truck did make it through, then their drivers would suddenly discover, too late, that the boat had been disabled. With the fuses already set, they would be meeting Allah sooner than anticipated.

I left the boat, climbed ashore over the rail, and completed the most dangerous part of the journey: safely crossing the FDR Drive on foot, despite a nearly continuous stream of traffic hurtling by. On the other side I walked up the Forty-ninth Street ramp, and as the roar of the traffic behind me deadened I heard the voices and laughter of the ambassador's party. Soon I could see it for myself. There were hundreds of guests spread over the lawn. American barbecue it might have been, but the guests were dressed as if the event were being thrown by Gatsby himself. A large tent had long tables laden with food, and awnings had been erected to provide shelter if the unthinkable happened, and it rained. But there was no chance of that tonight, and the tables had been set up under the open sky. There was a huge champagne fountain, already poured, with a waiter on a ladder taking glasses from the top for guests. Many people were wandering to the edge by the water, eager to get a good position for the fireworks that would be starting soon. Some were admiring the Cigarette. A small orchestra in white dinner jackets played Cole Porter tunes. A children's play area had been set off with a white picket fence, away from the party. Kids of every color were running and screaming. The favored activity seemed to be climbing over the giant statue of St. George killing the dragon. The dragon had been sculpted from ballistic missiles, scrapped under the INF treaty.

I knew what Beth would have wanted me to do here—stop, get someone's attention, tell them what's happening, get the evacuation going, and let her take her chances with the forward controller. I had no intention of doing that. I knew I could get her out and initiate an evacuation in time.

I had a plan, and I had the training to execute it. All that was required from me now was a few minutes of machine-like precision. No second guessing, no what-ifs.

I looked away from the party and went to the corner of First Avenue, where I stood and surveyed the buildings across the street. Prospect Towers wasn't difficult to find, a neo-Gothic edifice standing out among its more modern International-style neighbors. I crossed First Avenue and found the entrance foyer, located on the other side of the building, where it gave onto Tudor City Place. There was a small park across the street. I took a seat and tried to wait patiently for the person I expected to appear. In the big apartment buildings of New York there is a constant stream of delivery people coming and going. It seemed to me to take forever, but it was probably only a minute before I saw a delivery boy scurrying down the sidewalk, take-out bag in hand. There were no further apartment buildings down here: he could only be delivering to Prospect Towers. I intercepted him.

"Which apartment?" I asked.

He looked at the receipt stapled to the bag. "20K."

"I'll take it," I said, not inviting discussion. "How much do I owe you?"

He looked at me with undisguised suspicion, but he wasn't paid well enough to question customers. He gave me the total, and I gave him a good tip.

I waited until he had walked away before coiling the rope into the bag, then going back down the sidewalk and into the entrance foyer.

The doorman was sitting behind the desk, absorbed in the sports pages of the *New York Post*.

"Delivery for 20K," I said.

He picked up the phone, disengaging his eyes from the paper only long enough to dial. I could hear the intercom ringing. He returned to the article while waiting for an answer. The Yankees had been no-hit by the Red Sox the previous evening. The doorman unconsciously shook his head in disbelief. The intercom was eventually answered.

"Delivery, Mrs. Bludget."

He waited a moment for the reply, replaced the receiver, then jerked a thumb toward the elevators. I went back, pressed the *up* button, and waited for a car to arrive. The doorman had not looked at me once the entire time.

The woman who answered the door at 20K, presumably Mrs. Bludget, was a pinch-faced creature who, without a word, snatched the bag from my hand and went through the contents. Apparently they were satisfactory. She put a couple of bills in my hand and slammed the door shut without having said a word.

I heard several locks being turned. The tip came to sixty-nine cents. Mrs. Bludget was not a generous woman.

I went back up the hall, picked up the rope from where I'd left it, and took the stairs to the roof. I had hoped the door at the top would not have an alarm. It didn't, but when I stepped outside I discovered why: the roof was occupied.

I should have thought of this. On the Fourth of July every roof deck in New York with a view over the East River would be occupied. A few heads turned in my direction, most were looking southeast, occasionally checking watches, eager for the fireworks to begin. I walked around casually, trying to look as if I belonged there.

I went to the railing and looked over the side. The windows that had been circled in the real estate ad were dark. I had guessed that they would be, giving the forward controller a better view out, but I had secretly nursed the hope that he might turn a light on, which would have given me an easy shot through the window. Not much had been easy about the week since I had unsuspectingly arisen in the middle of the night to go to the bathroom; there was no reason to have expected the Fates to smile upon me now.

In New York City, the water main pressure is only sufficient to reach the bottom several floors. As a consequence, every apartment building of any size is topped by a water tank, occasionally bare wood, more often enclosed in a structure.

The enclosure surrounding the water tank here was basically a brick box. On the far side there was an iron ladder embedded into the masonry, for service access to the top of the water tank. The water tank was on the northeastern corner of the building. Since the fireworks would be let off over the harbor, to the southeast, it had the positive attribute of being out of direct view of the roof party. I climbed the ladder.

At the top I crawled along the narrow wall to the eastern side, above the apartment I needed to get into. The sliver of roof between the side of the building and the tank's enclosure was occupied by a ventilation fan, not part of the roof deck, and therefore unoccupied. I would be briefly exposed climbing down, but in the dark of evening and with all eyes toward the East River in anticipation of the show, the risk was minimal.

The rope wasn't long enough to loop for a proper descent; I would just have to secure one end to the building, the other to myself, and do the best I could. I tied a turn and hitch around the top of the iron ladder, then ran the bight of the rope across the water tank, making sure it swung free below so there would be no unintended knots. I tied a running bowline around my chest, and eased over the edge.

I went quickly down past the level of the roof deck and out of sight. I kept between the second and third windows, and continued down past the top floor. Now I was on the same level as the apartment. My arms were already tiring.

I hadn't done this sort of thing in a while and, properly equipped, it's your legs that do most of the work anyway.

The window nearest me was open, although from the angle I had I could have seen nothing inside, even if the lights were on. I didn't have time to waste. I took a deep breath, and swung in front of the window.

I was immediately face to face with the forward controller. He had been leaning on the wall by the window, casually looking out the window, and his head was no more than a foot from mine. I don't know who was the more surprised, him or me. For a split second the pair of us remained frozen. Then it became clear that whoever got to their hardware first was going to win.

I went to one-handed hold on the rope and reached for the pistol in my waistband. He stumbled back into the room with a limp that I remembered. Apparently Easy had assigned his least mobile man to the job that required the minimum of travel. Fortunately he had not brought his weapon with him to the window. Had he done so, it would already have all been over.

I fumbled the pistol. It fell from my hand and disappeared into the darkness below.

That pretty much settled things, I thought, but then the other man suddenly fell. I saw why: Beth, bound hand and foot on the floor, had struggled to get in his way. With no light, and in a rush to get his weapon, he had tripped over her.

I took the rope in both hands, forced myself off the wall with all the strength I could muster in my legs, then swung back in a big arc toward the open window. The other man had resumed his feet, but I raised my legs, let go at the opportune moment, and went sailing through the window. I crashed right into him. He toppled like a tenpin. Tarzan would have been impressed.

It was simple work from here. Easy had obviously not trained his people for hand-to-hand combat, presumably not expecting that they would need it. The other man was stronger, and quickly locked me around the throat. But I was still wearing the ankle sheath. I soon had the blade in hand. I drove it into his back at about the kidneys, gave it a twist to open the wound, then pulled it hard across, tearing through the viscera.

A lot of stuff came out, same as gutting deer.

When I was sure he was dead, I wiped the blade on his flak jacket, then used it to cut through the knot binding Beth's hands behind her. She immediately used her newly freed hands to tear the duct tape from her mouth.

"Lee Dalton," she said. "I am very glad to see you."

"Not as glad as I am to see you, Beth Houston." There wasn't really enough time for kissing, but I kissed her anyway. Then I said, "Can you undo your legs while I make a call?"

She nodded and began untying. I used Easy Black's cell phone to call 911. When the operator answered, I didn't waste time with explanations.

"There is a very large bomb at the United Nations. You have thirty minutes to evacuate it and the nearby buildings." I hung up, then dialed operator assistance.

"What listing, please?"

"CIA in Virginia. It's very urgent." She put me through. I bet she was listening in on this one. The phone was answered by another woman.

"Central Intelligence Agency," she chirped.

"Are you recording this?" I asked.

"From time to time calls are recorded to monitor—"

"I get it," I interrupted. "Please make sure this one is, okay?"

"How can I help you, sir?"

"My name is Lysander Dalton. There is a woman I know as Valentina Mariposa, who until three days ago was a lawyer at Tate, Tate & Buchanan, but who now no longer officially works there. You need to get this message to her, or to someone who supervises her."

"Sir, this is the CIA," she interrupted. "You may have heard of us. We're *not* a law firm."

"Lady, I don't have time to be polite. Please just shut up and listen."

She shut up and listened.

"Good," I said, "I think you've got it now. Valentina Mariposa is a CIA officer. She is investigating a terrorist threat. I've found the terrorists, and I know what they're doing. They're going to bomb the United Nations in New York tonight, during the fireworks. There's a large tractor-trailer on its way there now, carrying the explosive in a shipping container. The explosive is a mixture of ammonium nitrate and diesel fuel. I don't know what detonators they're using, but these people will almost certainly have the detonator set and ready to go. The tractor is a Mack CH602. It's a rental from Jim's Truck Rentals in Lodi, New Jersey—perhaps it'll have that name on it. There are also two black Ford Explorers acting as point. To intercept the truck, they'll have to let the point vehicles get by unmolested. This is the route." I gave her the route details for both the primary and secondary, and told her what time the trucks had left. "You getting all this?"

"Yes, sir," she said.

"I just called 911 here in New York, and told them that the United Nations was going to be bombed. I didn't tell them about the truck, because if a patrol cop tries to pull it over, they'll just detonate the explosives then and there. They'll have to take out the people in the truck first."

"I see."

"Are you going to get in contact with someone in authority?"

"Yes, sir, I am."

"I'm not doing any backup," I emphasized. "You're it."

Her voice softened. "I'll make sure it gets acted on."

I hung up and breathed a sigh of relief. It was done.

I went to the window. The party at the United Nations was still in full swing. I used the forward controller's binoculars to scan the scene, hoping to see some sign of an evacuation in progress, but it hadn't begun yet.

Then suddenly the dead man crackled to life. It was his radio. I went closer. It was the static of someone on the same frequency, hitting a transmit key. Then there was a transmission in a heavily accented voice:

"Sierra Team, this is Tango One. Report."

Tango One had to be the truck, as it would be first to break radio silence. But that wasn't supposed to happen until they had crossed the GWB, which they couldn't have done yet.

"Tango One, this is Sierra One. I have you clear primary."

"Tango One, this is Sierra Two. I have you clear secondary."

"Tango One, roger."

The Sierras must be the scouts, which had split—one taking the primary insertion route, the other the secondary. But that didn't happen until Manhattan. Either I had miscalculated, or they were simply early. I checked my watch—it was ticking, but for all I knew the time was simply wrong. Perhaps my old friend had finally slowed down, as would happen to me one day.

"Foxtrot Charlie, this is Tango One. Report, over."

Foxtrot Charlie: forward controller—the man I had just killed. Easy had kept the call signs simple, perhaps in deference to his team's limited English. None of the documents I'd seen on Easy's laptop had included the radio net protocols. I didn't know what to say.

"Foxtrot Charlie, this is Tango One. Report, over." More emphatic this time.

I took the radio from the dead man's belt. The same voice repeated the call, more urgent now.

"Foxtrot Charlie, this is Tango One. Report, over."

I had to respond or they'd know something was wrong. The rule of any voice net is to keep the transmissions short and simple. I put my fingers over the mouthpiece to muffle the sound, then depressed the transmit key.

"This is Foxtrot Charlie. Target is clear, over."

A short silence followed. My voice sounded strange to them, but all voices sound strange over a radio net. If he doubted my authenticity, the next transmission would be ordering a frequency change. I waited, and could practically feel him wondering whether or not to do so. Eventually the voice came back, more relieved now.

"Tango One, roger. Out."

I put down the radio.

"Beth?"

"Yes?" She was working on the last of the ropes, the one around her ankles.

"There's an eighteen-wheeler on its way down here, loaded with explosives."

"What's an eighteen-wheeler?"

"A truck," I explained. "A big one. It's going to destroy the United Nations, and everything else within several blocks, too."

"How far away is it?"

"A few miles."

Beth finished undoing the rope, and joined me by the

window. She looked out over the party below us. We could see the children scrambling about, and the sound of their noisy playmaking floated up through the night.

She rubbed her wrists, still looking out over the view below. "When will it get here?"

"Soon," I said. "Too soon for an evacuation," I added, answering her unspoken question. "I'll try to take them out before they actually explode the bomb, but it's a long shot. You have to clear out of here, Beth."

She said nothing for a long time, or perhaps it only seemed a long time. I was anxious to get moving, but Beth remained leaning against the window frame, still looking out over the view, almost as if in a daydream. I wondered if it had been chemically induced.

"Did they drug you?" I asked.

She didn't answer immediately, but instead turned to face me directly, and those big green eyes went right through me. There were no drugs in those eyes.

"I knew you were going to come through that window," she said quietly. "Or through the door. Or through something else. I wasn't sure how, but I knew you'd come. I knew that you'd find me somehow. I've been planning for it, spending hours thinking what it was I should do when you showed up, trying to figure out what it was that you would want me to do."

"Beth, we need to get moving now," I prompted.

I made a small step for the door, urging her to come with me. But she made no move to leave, instead leaning back on the window frame, hugging herself while gazing out the window again.

"I knew you were going to come and get me before I was even kidnapped," she said. "I knew when you told me your name was Simon and that you had a thing about cheek-bones."

She smiled, still amused by my idiot answer that day, but she was crying, too—I could see the tears glistening in her eyes.

"Will you leave now, Beth?"

"No,' she said matter-of-factly. "I'm going to go down there to those police officers at the UN front gate, and tell them what I know."

"I've already called 911 and the CIA. There's nothing more you can do."

"I can try to hurry them up."

"It won't be in time," I said.

"Yes," she agreed. "That's why you're going to have to stop the truck."

As she finished the sentence, the first of the fireworks exploded in the sky outside.

TWENTY-FIVE

I could have explained to Beth Houston that I'd go after the truck much happier if she cleared the area. I could also have explained that there simply wasn't time for the evacuation now, and that all she'd be doing is adding herself as a victim should the truck get past me, but that would have invited an argument. Alternatively, I could have simply cut the argument short by slugging her, slinging her over my shoulder, and carting her downstairs and out of harm's way.

But since the Stone Age, slugging women has become unfashionable as a basis for long-term relationships, so that really wasn't an option. I was tempted, though.

Instead I just grabbed the freshly filleted Gimpy's AR-15, and bolted from the apartment. Downstairs, the doorman was still engrossed in the results of the ball game, and glanced neither at me nor the automatic rifle I was carrying. I raced down to First Avenue.

Traffic had thickened. Much of it was caused by drivers who had slowed down and stuck their heads out their windows, apparently in the belief that gazing at fireworks and being in control of a moving automobile were not mutually exclusive activities. It was good in that it slowed down the truck, but how could I get to it through all this traffic? I had to get to that truck fast, but short of growing wings I couldn't see how it could be done.

Then I saw the answer. There was a Vespa—one of those little Italian motor scooters—parked on the sidewalk. Vespas can maneuver through any traffic. This one was silver, with a little plastic pannier the same color stuck on the back. It was parked out front of a restaurant. Those Vespas can be left just about anywhere, and so if it was parked out front of a restaurant, it was a fair guess that whoever owned it was inside.

I went into the restaurant. There was a hostess stand. Behind the stand was a hostess. She was leggy and vacant, and would have been more at home in L.A., where the hostess is essentially part of the decoration, than in New York, where all the shapeliness in the world won't save a restaurant that doesn't serve good food. She was dressed in something that used little fabric but would have cost a lot of money. Her job was to be cool and sleek, but the demeanor became uncertain when she saw my bloodstained Hawaiian shirt, and positively ungracious when she noticed the rifle.

"We're fully booked," she declared, before I could get a word out.

"There's a bike outside," I said. "I need to find out who owns it."

"I do," she answered, before she'd really thought about the wisdom of doing so. Then her look changed: she'd realized that it might not have been a good idea to admit ownership to something that a man with a loaded firearm had just inquired about. I was grateful for the look—at least she wasn't going to be trouble.

I held out my hand. "Give me the keys."

She opened the top of the stand, which lifted like an old-fashioned school desk, and retrieved her keys. But then she hesitated.

"I promise to bring it back," I said.

"Yeah, sure." She gave me the keys.

I stepped out onto the sidewalk and raced to the little Vespa, not wanting to waste any more time. I didn't know much about motorbikes, but I figured that something like a Vespa couldn't be too hard. I knew enough to realize that it takes two hands—one for the throttle, the other for the clutch—which meant that I couldn't hold on to the rifle. The weapon was too long for the pannier, so I lay it on the running board and put a foot on top. Not very secure, but it would have to do. Then I put the key in the ignition, or at least tried to. It didn't fit.

At first I thought the hostess, who had no doubt disappeared by now out of the back of the restaurant, had simply fooled me by giving me the wrong key. Then I examined it more closely. It said "Ducati." Ducatis are racing superbikes, the other end of the biking spectrum from the thing I was sitting on.

I got off the Vespa, retreated to the sidewalk, and looked around. Then I saw it.

Twenty feet away, parked between a car and the large SUV which had shielded it from my view, was another motorbike. But this was no Vespa. It was a real motorbike, and it was a big one. I stepped up to it.

The thing was a dark metallic gray mass of metal, except for the wheels, which were cast alloy rather than spokes and, curiously, were the only sign of color on the whole thing: they were red. The brake discs attached to them looked large enough to have stopped a truck. There were racing fairings and a small windshield sweeping back from twin headlights. The gas tank was a large faceted brushed metal affair, unadorned with anything, even with the maker's name. But dominating the whole thing was the engine, a complex metallic brute mass which seemed far too large for any motorbike. Drop this on its side and you would need three strong men to lift it back upright. It looked more like a convertible spaceship than a motorbike.

Beth came racing down from Prospect Towers.

"Good luck," she said on her way past. She went out onto the avenue, waiting for a break in the traffic before crossing to the UN.

I looked at the big Ducati. There were no panniers, and of course no running board. And the AR-15 had no sling. I doubted I could control this thing on first try, and even if I could, where would I stow the rifle?

I called to Beth. She stepped back away from the traffic.

"Beth, can you ride this?" She looked nervously at the great machine, and nodded reluctantly. "There's no place to stow the rifle," I explained. "And without the rifle, I can't stop the truck."

She looked back over her shoulder across the street to where the kids, ignoring the fireworks, were still running and jumping about. "It's their best chance," I said quietly. "Their only chance, really."

She turned back to face me, and nodded.

"Give me the keys," she said decisively. I handed them over.

She mounted the bike, inserted the key, and fired up the engine. It was loud, but not that raspy thudding that you associate with the sort of bikes ridden by the Hells Angels.

Instead the Ducati sounded smooth and even and free-revving, as if there would be no red line—you could just hit the throttle and it would spool up forever, as long as there was enough straight asphalt on which to do it.

"Where to?" she yelled over the roar of the engine.

I hopped on behind.

"Uptown."

"First Avenue?"

"Second."

"Against the traffic?"

"The tractor-trailer's coming down Second Avenue."

She made a quick nod of comprehension, opened the throttle and dropped the clutch. The Ducati burst from the parking spot and into the traffic with a loud squeal from the back tire. I hadn't taken a grip, and was lucky not to have been left behind, rear end on the curb. I put my left arm around Beth's waist and kept the other firmly on the assault rifle.

Beth must have done a lot of motorcycle riding when she was younger, for she took no time at all to fully master the big machine. She traveled at least twice the speed of the traffic, weaving in and out of the gaps, and if the gap was closing she hit the throttle, not the brakes. At Forty-seventh street she turned left through a red light to cross over to Second. The cross street was empty. It wasn't very long, but it was long enough.

Beth hit the throttle hard, sending the bike up onto its back wheel. For two hundred terrifying yards we became a unicycle of ever increasing velocity. We weren't wearing helmets, of course. Any accident at this speed would have been fatal. She relented only as we approached Second Avenue. When the front wheel finally hit the asphalt again, I was able to open my eyes and risk a glance at the speedometer. In the instant before she hit brakes that felt like the hand of God, the needle had been pointing to 120 miles per hour.

There was a red light here, too, and a pair of yellow cabs waiting for the green. There was space between them, not really enough, but the bike had two enormous steel rollover bars protruding from either side, designed to protect the engine, and the rider's legs, in the event of a fall. Beth used them as bumpers, bashing away down the sides of the two cabs like an atomic pinball, sparks flying and metal tearing. We emerged in an eruption of honking from the cabs, but given the reckless abuse they inflict on their victims in New York, who could have any sympathy for them? One of the astonished pedestrians actually cheered.

Now came the hard part: going uptown against traffic. I had thought the rush of oncoming headlights might unnerve Beth, but in fact what mostly happened was that the rush of oncoming Beth unnerved the traffic.

I had once been told there is a rule to living in New York City: one in every ten people you see walking down the sidewalk is insane. This is the secret to that quality in New Yorkers much admired by outsiders: taking everything in stride. In fact they take everything in stride because they expect lunacy. They are always prepared, so to speak. Someone thundering the wrong way up an avenue was simply today's manifestation of the lunacy. So as Beth cut up the middle of the avenue between the two inner lanes, the oncoming traffic simply swerved, both lanes giving a little so that there was enough room. There was a lot of honking and yelling, but we made good progress.

The red lights were more of a problem, but the slightest gap in the crossing traffic was enough to send Beth thundering across the intersection in a tire-smoking flash. But all good things must end, and they finally did when a combination of vehicles was just too knotted to undo quickly

enough to allow our passage. Yet Beth seemed not to notice.
I was about to observe that the combined mass of the oncoming group, being several hundred times our own, meant
that now was a time to slow down and get out of the way.

She did get out of the way, but she didn't slow down.
Instead she took the sidewalk. We burst past pedestrians jumping for their lives, fruit stalls and groups of
Africans selling fake handbags and watches, past sidewalk
cafes where the tables were suddenly and urgently vacated
at our approach.

I risked a glance at Beth, hoping that she wasn't losing it.
Not only was she not losing it, she was actually grinning.

During the journey I had kept an eye out for the scouts,
but we live in an age in which the SUV has replaced the big
sedan as the standard American car. Every second vehicle
was an SUV—or an imitation—and picking out a black
Ford Explorer with tinted windows at night was simply not
possible.

The trucks were easier. We had passed several big
trucks, but they had been hauling freight trailers or tankers
or flatbeds with machinery and so on. None of them
had been carrying containers—Manhattan doesn't take
container ships, and most containers are opened at the
big transshipment warehouses that freight corporations
maintain in the countryside, where land is cheap. By the
time things come into Manhattan they have usually already
been unloaded from the containers they were shipped in.

As we crossed Ninety-sixth Street I saw another truck
coming down. Somehow even before I could see the cargo
clearly, I knew this was the one—the advance was steady
and purposeful, the driving of someone with a mission, not
the hurried rush of a trucker wanting to make his delivery
and get on home in the quickest possible time.

"Stop here," I yelled into Beth's ear. I pointed at the approaching vehicle. "I think that's it."

Beth slowed the big bike, pulled off the sidewalk, and stopped by the curb. A few of the nearby pedestrians came to offer some advice about Beth's riding, but then they saw the assault weapon I was carrying, and changed their minds.

"Turn off the headlights."

Beth cut the headlights. The big truck came slowly rumbling past. The engine was straining, just as I'd heard at the farm. It was hauling a container, a big one. And, in a last confirmation, I could even make out the scarred bare metal where Easy Black had had his people cut the weak points into the container.

There were four men in the cab, all sitting abreast. Taking them out would be the easy part. Taking them out without giving them the opportunity to trip the detonator would be another matter altogether.

"Follow them."

Beth put the headlights back on and pulled out onto the avenue. Progress was much simpler this time, now that we were headed the same way as the rest of the traffic. If there was any difficulty, it was going slow enough. It wasn't the traffic that made the truck's progress so slow, it was the enormous weight in that container.

I'd seen what ordinary size explosives could do: a single Mark 82—the standard five-hundred-pound aerial-dropped ordnance—could wreak damage across a wide area, and completely level a major structure like a concrete-encased chemical plant, or a Baath Party meeting hall. I couldn't imagine what the thirty tons in that container would do. But as Easy Black had said, it would make Oklahoma City look minor by comparison.

I hoped the people in that cab hadn't noticed the

motorbike hanging back, obviously trailing behind them.

"At the next red light I'll get off," I told Beth. "I'm going to try to get on behind the cab."

"Okay."

"I'll need a distraction so they don't notice me in their mirrors. Can you do something to keep their attention for a minute?"

"I was a model," she said. "Of course I can keep their attention."

We didn't have to wait long for the next red light, hitting one at Eighty-seventh Street. The traffic ahead raced across on the amber, but the truck rumbled to a halt on the red. Beth pulled up and I dismounted. Then she continued around in front of the truck, and I heard her stopping the bike somewhere just ahead of it. I gave her a few moments to do whatever she was going to do, and performed a last check of the weapon. Full clip. Action to the rear. Safety off. Gimpy had had it set to single shot, the semiautomatic mode in which only one round is fired for every pull of the trigger. There was no point in conserving ammunition now. I set the lever to full auto. Now it would keep firing until I released the trigger, or the magazine was empty. I wouldn't be releasing the trigger.

It was now or never. I moved around from behind the trailer and walked down the passenger side toward the cab. I passed the rear wheels of the tractor and got to the space between the container and the cab. There was a big round diesel fuel tank which would be hard to get over, but then I noticed small metal stepping points welded into the side, perhaps to allow easy access when connecting up a load. I climbed on board and waited a moment. There was no noticeable movement from inside the cab. I looked around in back of it.

There were the connections that you would expect: a

thick black electrical line coming back from the tractor, with a socket plugged into an outlet on the trailer, intended to power the taillights, plus anything electrical in the trailer like a refrigeration unit. Beside this was a thicker coiled yellow line. This was pneumatic, designed to carry the compressed air to the brakes on the rear wheels.

Then I found the third connection. This, too, was electrical, but just ordinary thin twin flex, not part of the normal rig. It came through a small opening in the sheet metal at the rear of the cab that looked as if it had been simply punched through with a hammer and nail. It entered not the trailer but instead the container sitting on top of it, through a small opening that had obviously been made recently with an oxyacetylene torch.

It had to be the wire to an electrical detonator.

I unsheathed my knife, still discolored with some of the forward controller's blood, and cut the wire. I hoped they didn't have a secondary, a radio-activated backup for example. We'd soon all find out.

I brought the automatic to the firing position and took aim at the back of the driver's head, intending to begin with a left to right sweep.

In the service they teach you to fire automatic weapons in short bursts. It not only helps conserve ammunition, but it also helps conserve the gun. Spraying continuous high-velocity rounds doesn't give the barrel a chance to cool down. In darkness you can even see a momentary redness in the barrel after a long burst.

I pulled the trigger, and saw the driver's head blow apart. Then I began sweeping, and between the mess and the muzzle flash I didn't see much else.

I held the trigger down until the magazine was empty, sweeping back and forth across the cab, slightly lowering the level with each sweep, expending all fifty rounds of jacketed high-velocity ammunition in one big roll of the dice. The noise was astounding, reverberating inside that narrow metallic space between cab and trailer. I couldn't see anything through the rear window—it cracked and shattered, but even if it hadn't, the inside of the cab had quickly filled with a cloud of particulate matter.

At last the action remained locked in the rear position—the weapon was empty. What I saw now was a barrel that did not just have a hint of red, it was actually glowing. I silently thanked the Colt Manufacturing Company of Hartford, Connecticut, for having gone to the trouble to make the barrel extra heavy—an ordinary barrel would have given up by now, and I'd have been holding a jammed weapon, a sitting duck for anyone left alive inside that cab.

But there was no one left alive in there, not even close. When I opened the passenger side door, there wasn't much left of anything above the body armor. Because the four of them had been jammed shoulder to shoulder across the seat, there hadn't been room to bob or duck, and that rain of 5.56mm had more or less decapitated them. The windshield had remained solidly in place, despite dozens of bullet holes, a testament to the wisdom of laminated glass in vehicles. The inside was caked with blood, brain matter, bone fragments, bits of fabric. Some neck vertebrae were jammed in between the visor and the roof. One of the driver's hands was still on the wheel, but had been sheared off from the forearm.

But it was the hands of the man sitting next to him that mattered. In them he still held the small piezoelectric generator I had expected to find. It works just like in the Road Runner cartoons—you lift the handle to set it, then thrust down to create the electrical charge which trips the detonator.

The handle was down—he had tried to explode the

bomb. He must have been holding the device at the ready since they left the farm in New Jersey.

I climbed down out of the cab. I could vaguely hear sirens in the distance, but my hearing was too gone to pick up anything else. I went to the curb and threw up. It was okay, there were no troops around to disappoint now. It's the bit they never show in the movies.

Beth came and sat down beside me. She said something but I was still too deafened to understand. I pointed to my ear and shook my head. She leaned closer and yelled.

"Is it over now?"

I nodded and said yes. I don't know whether any sound came out. She handed me a cloth which I used to wipe my face. I sat, breathing deeply, and gradually my hearing returned—I could hear voices as well as the sirens now.

"You sure know how to show a girl a good time," Beth said after a while.

"How did you distract them?" I asked.

"I did the Greta Garbo."

"Greta Garbo?"

"You know, one of those pouty insolent poses that says 'Leave me alone.'"

I couldn't help smiling. "And that distracted them?"

"Held them spellbound," she said.

"You're the queen of the catwalk," I said.

"I did do it topless," Beth added. I looked at her more closely. Yes, she was indeed topless—in all the excitement I hadn't quite taken it in. I looked at the cloth in my hand— it was the blouse she had been wearing earlier.

I suddenly felt much better.

TWENTY-SIX

NOT only had the vines survived during my absence, they had thrived. My feelings were not unmixed on returning home and discovering this. No farmer likes to find that his crop can get on just fine without him, let alone do better. Now, in late September, the grapes were physiologically ripe, hanging in plump dark bunches sagging on the vines, aching to become wine. When testing for sugar content that morning I had gotten the highest reading the instrument had ever registered. Whatever else was unknowable, one thing about this vintage was certain: it would be high in alcohol. Tomorrow we would begin the harvest. A week from now the last bunch would have gone into the crusher, and the new American oak casks I had bought would be filled with fresh grape juice. There isn't much to do after that; nature does the rest.

I had sent out the usual invitations, but had received

some unsolicited replies. I could hear the first of these coming along the drive now.

I put down the Americano highball—my good luck drink now that it had preserved my life—and took a last look in solitude over the vineyards, golden yellow in the light of the lowering sun. I walked around to the front of the house.

Dust rose from the approaching car. The sycamores and maples that line the road were already turning, but the oaks maintained a persistent green, as if unwilling to let go of the season. Who could blame them?

The singing gear changes told me who it was long before the Porsche skidded to a stop in front of my house. Valentina got out. She made no effort to park the vehicle, apparently the concept was alien to her. She merely drove a car to where she was going, then stopped and got out when she arrived.

I had been surprised when Valentina called and asked if she could come and help pick grapes; she was not a roll-up-your-sleeves-and-get-into-it kind of girl. Now I was even more surprised. She emerged from the car wearing an elegant cocktail dress, more at home in midtown Manhattan than rural Virginia. Her shoes and handbag were made of matching lizard skin. I wondered what she thought a harvest involved. Perhaps she imagined that we sat on the terrace, drinking mint juleps while watching the peasants work.

We kissed cheeks in greeting. Apart from her recent phone call, we had neither seen nor spoken to each other since the Fourth of July. She stood back and looked at me appraisingly.

"Just get off the tractor?"

My working clothes had not passed the test.

"As a matter of fact, yes," I said. "I'll get your luggage."

She popped the hood. The luggage was matching Vuitton, of course. Two suitcases and a garment bag—if this was a weekend's worth, I wondered how much she'd need for an extended journey. I left them on the front porch for now.

"Fast trip from D.C.," I said. I hadn't been expecting her for a couple of hours yet.

"I came from Preston," Valentina said. "We had a meeting there."

"More terrorists?"

"No, I'm on another assignment now." I knew better than to ask more. "Show me your place," she commanded.

We walked around the grounds, taking advantage of the remaining light to see the outside first. We stood on a knoll and surveyed the vines. I pointed out which varietals were planted where, and which vineyards we would be starting on first thing tomorrow morning, as soon as the sun had burned off any overnight dew.

Valentina was more interested in the garden. "Is this where you landed?" She was looking at the rose bed. It wasn't the sort of question you'd ask unless you knew the answer.

"Yes."

She looked up at the house.

"And that's the window you dived through?"

"That's the one."

"I thought that stuff only happened in the movies."

"In the movies they don't end up with six-inch scars afterward."

"Every man should have a least one good scar," she said.

"And every woman should have at least one good tattoo."

Valentina laughed. "I guess we've both got permanent souvenirs. Let's go inside."

On the porch I showed her my recently installed new lock.

"Chubbs," I explained. "I've got them on all the doors now."

"And I've got barred grates on all my windows now,"

she countered with a smile. I'd already apologized for breaking into her apartment.

"You need them, with all those weapons you keep in there. Why so many?"

"I'm a noc," she said. She pronounced the last word "knock."

"What's a noc?"

"Non-official cover," she explained. "It means that when I'm operating outside the U.S., I don't have diplomatic protection." From those piles of cash, I knew she must operate outside the U.S. often enough.

"What's that got to do with having guns?"

"Being a noc is the most dangerous of the operational jobs. It means that if you get caught, they can do whatever they want with you—the U.S. government doesn't have the power to intervene. So for nocs they do everything they can to protect their cover, including minimizing unnecessary contact with Langley. So we keep all the equipment we may need."

That explained the armory I had found in her apartment that day.

I took her around the first floor. She liked the study, recently finished after having been remodeled by the hand grenade. I grabbed the luggage off the porch, and took her upstairs to her room.

I gave her the end room, decorated with a four-poster and other antiques, the sort of bedroom people want to have in rural Virginia. But Valentina was more interested in the details of the attack on the house.

"Show me where it began," she said.

We went down the hallway and stopped at the door to my room. I stood where the gunman must have stood that night, spraying the bed with automatic gunfire. I had a new mattress now.

"And the bathroom's in there?" She pointed to the door.
"Yes."

"You left the water running," Valentina said.

She was right, the shower was on. But before I could reply, the water was turned off.

I had been trying to think of a casual way to explain ever since Valentina called, but smoothness of speech has always eluded me. I could never be in a sales job. I was still fumbling to begin an explanation when the bathroom door opened.

Beth stepped out, toweling her hair dry. Before either of us could retreat, she looked up and smiled.

"You must be Valentina," she said. She took the towel from her head and held it one-handed across her chest, but more out of politeness than embarrassment. Years of photo shoots all but naked amid a bunch of strangers had left Beth immune to unease with no clothes on.

"My name's Beth Houston." She stepped forward with her arm held out. "I'm the cook," she explained. "Hope you like arugula."

Valentina and I retreated to the terrace downstairs while Beth dressed. I mixed a couple of drinks.

"How's your life been since it all happened?" Valentina asked.

"Good," I said. "Thanks to you."

It was true—that night Valentina had worked some minor miracles. The first pair of cops had arrived not long after I finished throwing up: a black woman with a lot of badges and a young guy in a plain uniform, a rookie still trying to get the swagger right. I had expected trouble, but the woman was quick and intelligent. "The truck's got a bomb inside," I quietly explained. "First priority is to keep people away. Call the bomb squad. Whatever you do don't allow anyone to touch the truck—it's almost certainly booby-trapped." She immediately turned to the rookie and said, "Do it." He jumped to like a trained seal for a fish. Then she nodded at the blood-splattered windows of the cab. "I'm supposed to check a scene to see if anyone's still alive," she said. I told her there was no need. She looked again at the grisly mess, and took my word for it. Then she asked who I was.

"I'm sorry but I can't tell you that," I explained. "This is going to sound corny, but it's a matter of national security. Please get Valentina Mariposa from the CIA to come here and explain. And please do it by landline—this shouldn't go over police radio."

To my surprise she did exactly as asked, although she never let me out of her sight while doing so. Soon the place became a maze of fire trucks and police cruisers and EMT vans. After a while a detective arrived and took over. He was less understanding with my refusal to give him a name. Beth was given a blanket, briefly questioned, and then escorted from the scene. Eventually Valentina showed up. She shook her head on seeing me, as if to say it was all my fault, then conferred with the detective. Apparently there is a procedure for things of this kind, and from that point no police officer showed any further interest in me.

I was never mentioned by name. When referred to at all I was, in a phrase which stretched the truth to the breaking point, an "unidentified government agent," and my role was minimized as far as circumstances would allow. It was just what I wanted, and as a consequence my life had remained livable.

The sun was almost down now. It was a warm evening, and I had set the outside table. It was set for four.

"When will he be here?" I asked.

I had been surprised on the phone when Valentina asked if she could bring someone, and doubly surprised when she said that someone was her boss. I had not asked anything more, and wondered if this meant one or two bedrooms. I had prepared two, thinking that if they only needed one, then they could organize it themselves.

"Seven o'clock," she said.

I looked at my watch. "It's five of seven now."

"Then he'll be here in five minutes," she said. "He's never late. And he's never early either."

But he was early tonight, for right then I heard a vehicle approaching the house. We went around to the front. I pulled Valentina's Porsche out of the way as the other car came leisurely along the drive. It was a black limousine, and as it got nearer I could see a uniformed driver in front, but just shadows in the rear. The car pulled up. The driver got out, walked around to the rear door, and opened it.

The man who got out was around sixty years old, and must have spent most of them eating, for he must have weighed at least three hundred pounds. Getting out of the vehicle was not an operation accomplished without difficulty. I thanked the gods that I had prepared two bedrooms.

When he finally emerged, he spent a moment or two disdainfully looking about before finally settling his cold gray eyes on me. He had a Vandyke beard, which helped give him the demeanor of an overweight Cardinal Richelieu, as if wondering whether or not to behead me. The ecclesiastical allusion was not accidental, for he wore a suit of expensive Italian priest-cloth, so well cut that it not only fitted him well, it actually looked good. I'd like to meet his tailor.

His shoes were highly polished, and he carried an ebony walking stick with a silver ferrule. Whatever he was here for, it wasn't to pick grapes.

He huffed over to us, nodded in greeting to Valentina, and held out his arm to me.

"Dortmund," he said. No first name, I wondered if he had one. Perhaps he was like Cher. We shook hands. A soft grip, unused to manual labor.

"Lysander Dalton," I said.

"I don't like bullshit, Mr. Dalton."

The comment was so odd that it took me a second to compose a reply.

"Good," I said at last, "then you won't be tempted to try any on me." There was a trace of movement at the corner of his mouth, which later I came to recognize was his version of a smile. They say Richelieu wasn't given to grinning much, either.

"Can I get your luggage?"

"I regret that urgent business in Washington demands my return this evening," he said "My apologies for having inconvenienced you. My driver will wait here while we dine."

The three of us walked around the house to the terrace. Most people, especially city people (as he clearly was), enjoy this first view over the rolling vineyards, but Dortmund expressed not the least interest, cursorily glancing up as I pointed out this and that, but otherwise looking down, as if lost in thought. Which he probably was, for I was eventually to learn that Dortmund was concerned with only one thing in life: power—how to get it, how to hold it, and how to manipulate it to get more. He had little interest in anything else, rarely ventured outside his office or club in D.C., and more or less despised nature, excepting as it could be used to achieve a particular end. My first impression had thus been unusually accurate, and I would forever thereafter think of him as the Iron Cardinal.

We sat on the terrace, Dortmund with obvious gratitude

for the fact of the chair, but with concern for its small dimensions.

"Would you like a drink, Mr. Dortmund? We're having Americano highballs."

"I never drink liquor, Mr. Dalton, except for the occasional medicinal purpose. However, I make an exception for sherry."

"Amontillado or Oloroso?"

"Amontillado before dinner, I think." I got up to fetch the drink. "A large one," he added.

I went through the French doors into the house. I had a half-empty bottle of Amontillado in the sideboard, but finos are supposed to be drunk chilled within days of opening, and despite the nonsense about not drinking, I was prepared to bet that Dortmund could tell the difference. I took a fresh bottle from the wine refrigerator, rinsed a port glass that I hoped would do, and poured a generous measure.

I could hear Valentina talking outside. I couldn't make out the words, but recognized the orderly cadence of sounds. It was the tone that a subordinate uses when succinctly briefing a commander, just before the guns start going off. She stopped as I returned to the terrace.

I gave Dortmund the glass and resumed my seat.

"Good health," he said. We drank.

Beth came onto the terrace. She was shoeless, wearing only shorts and a T-shirt, as if declaring her refusal to participate in a battle of dress-up. But I saw that the makeup had been applied with all the precise care of her profession.

Dortmund stood, playing the courtly old man. I introduced them.

"Miss Houston," he said, taking her offered hand but just holding it rather than actually shaking it, "I have lived all my life among the treacherous. Seeing you makes me remember that there are still human beings in this world."

He was an expert flatterer, apparently having instantly divined that the last thing someone like Beth wanted to hear was the usual comment that she was beautiful. She knew that already, and didn't think much of those who put value on it. Perhaps that was what Valentina had been briefing him about.

But Beth wasn't fooled. "It seems that you've learned their skills, Mr. Dortmund. A girl could easily believe a compliment like that." She was smiling frankly.

"Nevertheless, I assure you that it's true," he insisted. "There's a Donatello relief in Florence, in the Santa Croce. An *Annunciation* . . . Do you know it?"

Beth shook her head, speechless now.

"No matter," he said, waving the thought away—as if comparing a woman to a Donatello Virgin was a trifle. The old devil; I felt like asking how they fitted him in a plane that he could have gotten to Florence in the first place. I wondered why he was here, and why he was trying so hard to win Beth.

We made an odd foursome, me dressed for work, Beth for the beach, Valentina for trouble, and Dortmund for a cabinet meeting with Teddy Roosevelt. Beth excused herself to check on things in the kitchen. Perhaps she wanted to go in there to laugh.

"I expect you're wondering why I'm here," Dortmund said after Beth had left us. He had read my mind. "Now that everything has settled down, so to speak, it occurs to me that you must have many questions about what happened."

"One or two," I admitted.

"I am here to answer them," he said.

"You came all this way just to satisfy my curiosity?"

"Frankly, we would prefer you didn't get any urges to poke around on your own behalf, something which you are obviously adept at doing. It seems the best way to prevent that happening is to simply tell you the truth. Feel free to ask me anything you like. If I can answer, I will."

"You ordered all the scouts killed, didn't you?"

He immediately looked uncomfortable; this was not the sort of question he had expected to be asked.

Every member of the assault team had been killed that evening. The authorities had taken out the scouts when they'd parked down on Seventy-ninth Street near the FDR, sitting there waiting for the Cigarette to show. The newspapers said that the SWAT commander had not wanted to chance a confrontation, in case one of terrorists had a remote detonator. But amid all the rousing self-congratulation during the following days, there had been one discordant note: a single eyewitness who claimed that three of the scouts had been gunned down while trying to surrender. No one paid much attention.

Dortmund shifted awkwardly in his seat before giving a carefully worded reply.

"When terrorists undergo long trials in United States courts, it tends to encourage further acts of terrorism from those who in desperation think that they can influence the outcome. So much less of a motivation when there is no outcome to influence, don't you agree?"

Now I understood. Up until now I had wondered why they hadn't wanted some of them alive to point the finger.

"How did Easy Black get involved with these people?"

"He had a reputation. He'd done some work in Saharan Africa that we think may have attracted Rahmani's attention. The specifics of how they got together we don't know, probably never will."

"What happened to him? How did he turn from a marine officer into a mercenary?"

"It seems he wasn't very successful as an officer. There were problems—disciplinary problems and financial problems. It appears he had a gambling habit, hence the need for a more lucrative career. Apparently he decided to make money with the only skill he possessed."

"Did Trainor ever know what was going on?"

"We'll never know for sure," Dortmund said, happier now that the questions were more predictable. "Trainor trusted Easy Black, and Yip Yip trusted Trainor. Black apparently recruited them with a promise of fast money and, in Luke Trainor's case, the added incentive of squaring accounts with you. Obviously the real purpose was to set them up to take the blame for the attack, and then kill them so that they could never talk. But exactly how he recruited them, or what they really knew, is still anybody's guess."

"Have you figured out who Rahmani is yet?" In the days after the incident I'd looked at hundreds of photographs for them, even listened to some voice tapes, but I'd seen too little of Rahmani in the dark room that night to be able to positively identify him, and all English accents sound the same to me. I'd narrowed it down to a score or so possibles from the photographs they'd shown me.

"No," Dortmund said. "We've got some candidates, of course, and we're monitoring them as best we can. One day he'll make a mistake, and we'll get him."

I wondered. Rahmani had seemed like a careful man to me. Careful and patient.

"Rahmani wasn't his name?"

"No," Dortmund said. "In fact it means 'merciful.' Which tells us, if nothing else, that he has a morbid sense of humor."

"And Winchester?"

"There is such a school, and as Rahmani told you it was the custom for wealthy Arab boys of his generation to be sent to English public schools. We don't think he was lying—the accent has to be explained somehow—but we think he may have been using poetic license with the actual school name, just in case you decided not to honor his arrangement. We've done cross-checks between our candidate list and the enrollments at all the major English public schools: Harrow, Rugby, Eton, and so."

I could sense they were uncomfortable with this. They knew more than they were telling me. There didn't seem any point in pursuing it further.

I turned to Valentina.

"Were you going to let them take me out at the Williamsburg Bridge?"

She shrugged her shoulders. "Sometimes you sacrifice the one to save the many," she said.

At least she had the virtue of honesty.

"Did that woman at the Hell's Angels' clubhouse really give you Yip Yip's name?"

"No," she said. "I made that up to save us time."

"You took a risk at the police station in Little Washington. Yip Yip might have recognized you from the Factory. Why didn't you kill him right away?"

"You left my gun in the car," she said. Of course, I had forgotten that. "When I saw Yip Yip come through that door," she continued, "I realized that we needed to get one of their guns. Then the kid came around the counter. I tried annoying Yip Yip to distract him."

"It worked."

"Sure did."

"You're good under pressure."

"So are you."

"What if I hadn't seen the tattoo?"

"I would have thought of something." I didn't doubt it.

"Did Leonetti really give Yip Yip the loan?"

"He did."

"Did he know anything else about it?"

"He says not. We have no evidence to the contrary, and it's not the sort of thing that Leonetti was likely to have become involved with if he knew what was going on."

"Did you know his secretary before?"

A pause this time, but whatever the answer might have been was cut short by the return of Beth. She set down bowls and plates, and told us to help ourselves.

Dortmund and I looked for the meat. We couldn't find any.

I shrugged and poured the wine.

I thought we had finished the serious conversation. I brought back coffee and liqueurs after clearing the table. If I'd known what was coming I would have drunk nothing but water that night. Dortmund began obliquely.

"How long does it take to pick the grapes?" he asked.

"A few days."

"And then?"

"Basically I crush them and transfer the fluid to casks."

"How long does that take?"

"It's done at the same time."

"And for the rest of fall, and the winter?"

"There's not much to do then. Service equipment, make repairs, sort accounts, that kind of thing."

"Good," he said. "Then you'll have plenty of free time."

I didn't like the sound of this. "Free time for what, Mr. Dortmund?"

"I didn't come here for the country air, Mr. Dalton."

Beth rose. "Excuse me," she said. "I'm going to go and clean up."

I'd already done that, but I said nothing. She padded away off the terrace.

"I want you to do a job for us," Dortmund said.

"The answer's no," I replied.

"You haven't heard what it is yet."

"It doesn't matter. The answer's still no."

"Perhaps after you've heard the details—"

"Mr. Dortmund," I interrupted, "the details won't make any difference. I like it just fine here. I like growing grapes and I like making wine. But most of all, what I really like is working for myself."

Dortmund made a sound, which might have been laughter. "Is that what you think, Mr. Dalton, that you work for yourself?"

"It's true."

"No, it's not," he said. "This is whom you work for."

He reached into his jacket, which had not been removed throughout dinner, despite the warmth of the evening and his own abundant natural insulation. He withdrew a piece of paper, which he handed to me.

It was a photocopy of my mortgage statement. The outstanding principal was in bold, as it was each month, an enormous sum which made me wince every time I saw it. Dortmund pointed at the paper.

"You work for a bank, Mr. Dalton. You might not have realized it, but *that* is whom you work for."

I passed the paper back. "Everyone has a mortgage."

"Not that big." I shrugged my shoulders. Dortmund withdrew a second piece of paper, which again he passed to me. "Especially not that big in comparison to income."

I looked at this second sheet. It was a copy of my 1040.

"How the hell do you have a copy of my tax return?"

"We *are* the CIA, Mr. Dalton."

"Isn't that illegal?"

"I imagine so," Dortmund said dismissively. Distinctions between legality and illegality were of little interest to him. "The point, as you and I both know well, is that you barely made your payments last year."

"Perhaps," I said, passing back the paper. "But make them I did."

"And what happens when you have a bad year?"

He was an expert at finding a person's pressure points. It was every farmer's worst nightmare: a sickly season and an intolerant bank.

"Still beats working for you."

"Ah, but you wouldn't be working for me," he said, refusing to be insulted. "I am proposing merely that you join us for a limited time as an independent contractor. How you fulfill your contract is entirely up to you, although I am confident that you could do it in a matter of weeks. Feel free to complete your harvest duties here before starting."

"The answer's no."

"I thought you wanted to work for yourself?"

"You can pretend I'd be a contractor, if you like. It makes no difference to me, the answer's still no."

"You mistake my meaning, Mr. Dalton. When you have *finished* as a contractor, then you can work for yourself."

"What are you saying?"

"What I'm saying is this: we'll pay off your mortgage."

"What?"

"You do this job for us, we'll pay off your mortgage. All of it. You'll come back to your farm fully in possession of it, Mr. Dalton, free and clear. You say you wish to work for yourself—very well, I am the means by which you can achieve that. In just weeks. Maybe just days."

I was silent for a while.

"That's a hell of a lot of money for a few weeks' work."

"Yes, it is."

"It doesn't make sense. Whatever it is that you want me to do, you have plenty of people better qualified than me."

"Don't underestimate your own talents, Mr. Dalton. We often recruit from the special operations forces for—how shall we put it?—like-minded work within the agency."

"I'm ten years out-of-date."

"You didn't seem too rusty in July."

I sat back and waited a moment before replying. "You told me that you didn't like bullshit, Mr. Dortmund. Right now, I'm hearing nothing but."

This time Dortmund did smile. "Yes," he said, "Valentina warned me that this approach wouldn't work." He sighed. "I do so hate giving things away without getting something firm in return, particularly when it involves revealing a weakness. Nevertheless, you leave me with no other choice. Mr. Dalton, the reason I want you is because I can't use anyone in the agency. Why? For the simplest of reasons: in a sense you will be investigating us. Without giving away too much, I can tell you that this particular operation has already had several CIA assets assigned to it, without resolution. There can be only one reason for this failure of resolution: something is rotten inside Langley. Who, I have no idea. I know it's not me. I know it's not Valentina. Beyond that, as yet I know nothing. Whoever it is, I will find them eventually. But that will take time, maybe years. Meanwhile, we have an operation that is . . . time-sensitive. I need an unknown, Mr. Dalton. Not a CIA officer, who as you correctly surmise would be my first choice. Nor an ex–CIA officer, who would be my second. It has to be someone completely unknown to anyone at Langley. To be frank, the sole reason I'm here is that you're the only game in town. And even so, after having read your service record I am still extremely reluctant to use you. You lack prudence, Mr. Dalton. Nevertheless, at least you have the training, and I don't have the time to search for someone else. If I did, I certainly wouldn't have come all this way." He lowered his voice. "Especially if I'd known what was on the menu."

Well, at least the flattery had stopped.

Beth came back onto the terrace, carrying a coffeepot, from which she topped up the cups. I wondered if she had heard anything. Our eyes met, and I could see from her look that she had heard enough. She was willing me to refuse.

James Joyce once said that the only weapons he possessed were silence, exile, and cunning. In my own case I wasn't sure about the cunning part, but for ten years I, too, had defended myself with self-imposed silence and exile. Then I'd been compelled to temporarily reenter the world, and it had brought me what I had feared the most: entanglement. But the entanglement was Beth Houston, and only a fool would fear that.

Perhaps the time had now come for a moratorium on silence and exile. I had seen the world for the first time in ten years, and was not averse to seeing some more of it. And if it didn't work out, then at least my exile would be secure in the future.

I said, "Go on, Mr. Dortmund."

"Then you accept?"

"No. I'm willing to listen, that's all."

But he couldn't keep that twitching smile from the corners of his mouth. The old devil knew he had me.

Lady's Choice

The sergeant completed the form, then spun it around and put the pen next to it on the counter. "Sign here," he said.

"My client hasn't made a statement yet," Valentina objected.

"Lady, save the defense lawyer stuff for the judge," the sergeant said irritably. Valentina calmly picked up the pen, dropped it on the floor, and crushed it with her sole.

"As a matter of fact," Valentina told the sergeant, entirely unruffled, "I practice testamentary law, not criminal law."

"Testicle law, huh?" the sergeant said. "Well, I guess that's something you'd be pretty good at, since you obviously got quite a pair of your own." He snickered.

Valentina pivoted on one of her high heels and delivered the other in a swift leg extension to the groin. Even I flinched. He doubled over, eyes watering. Valentina grabbed the .38 Police Special from his holster, opened the cylinder as casually as a Sunday shooter, checked the load, and closed it with a flick of the wrist.

She put the gun to his temple, and calmly said, "Don't move." But he made a grab for her gun arm. Valentina pulled the trigger without hesitation. The back of his head blossomed into a spray behind him. I looked at her in amazement as the gunshot echoed.

"Counselor," I said admiringly, "you're quite an advocate."

"Now you know why you're paying me $300 an hour."

"Enthusiasm's good," I said. "But I think that a successful career in jurisprudence will require a better relationship with the police, don't you?"

"They're not police," she said.

"Not anymore," I agreed.

"Not before, either." She walked into the adjoining room, where there were two bodies on the floor—the real police officers—dressed in their underwear.